"Is it wise ... in the hands of novices?"

Anne looked at the papers her stepfather had handed her. "At least hold back your savings."

The old man sighed. "You and Will are my only heirs. If you run the place into the ground, then you get less when I die. If you decide to sell it off while I'm away, then I won't have nothin' to worry about when I get back."

"Don't worry, Gramps, we won't let the place fall apart." Will reached across the space between their chairs to take the papers from Anne's numb fingers. "The Silver Rose will be here when you return."

Anne wished she shared her new partner's confidence. She could hire staff, revamp the Web page, update the reservation system and handle the guests once they started arriving. But could she manage all that plus keep her daughter safe, hold on to her real job and prevent her head from exploding?

Possibly, but what was she going to do about the crush she still had on Will Cavanaugh?

Dear Reader,

I love books about second chances. The choices we make when we graduate from high school often take us down roads we might not have chosen given the corrective lenses of hindsight and age. Reunions make for wonderful catalysts. There's a class reunion in this book, but the real magnet drawing my hero and heroine home is honor and obligation. My hero's grandfather has a journey to make and he can't do that without help. My heroine needs to heal, too, and the best way is by reconnecting with her mother...and her first love.

I hope you'll enjoy this story about life, love, bull riders and tomato worms. It takes place on an imaginary guest ranch in western Nevada—right down the road from a real place, The Reindeer Lodge, where host Gary Schmidt had many a story to tell about life on Mount Rose Highway. Thanks, Gary. I'd also like to thank Everett Erickson for walking me through the ups and downs of professional bull riding. No pun intended. (Well, maybe a small one.) Ev, you've got heart. It's always a joy seeing someone living his dream. Thanks, too, to his mother, Mary Jane, for helping me understand the complex schedules and amazing dedication these young athletes give to their sport. During the course of my research, I came to admire both the riders and the bulls in this extreme test of strength, timing and balance.

For teaching me what it's like to live with asthma, I want to extend a special thanks to Erin Bass and her mother, Mary— two extremely cool ladies.

To find out "What's Cookin' at the Silver Rose," visit my Web site at www.debrasalonen.com for recipes mentioned in this book, or write to me at P.O. Box 322, Cathey's Valley, CA 95306, to have one mailed to you. Thanks to all my readers for your valued support and kind letters and e-mails.

Happy reading,

Debra Salonen

A Cowboy Summer
Debra Salonen

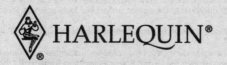

HARLEQUIN®

TORONTO • NEW YORK • LONDON
AMSTERDAM • PARIS • SYDNEY • HAMBURG
STOCKHOLM • ATHENS • TOKYO • MILAN • MADRID
PRAGUE • WARSAW • BUDAPEST • AUCKLAND

ISBN 0-373-71196-4

A COWBOY SUMMER

Copyright © 2004 by Debra K. Salonen.

To Mae and Malte Mae—the cycle of life goes on

CHAPTER ONE

THE ONE-PIECE? Or the bikini?

Anne Fraser knelt before the bottom drawer of her dresser like a novitiate at prayer. Her hand wavered between two disparate clumps of fabric. One sober, practical—useful for the occasional on-site inspection of a World Hospitality Corporation hotel pool. The other a sexy scrap of bright colors purchased at a time when tempting the man in her life took precedence over checking the chlorine levels of a WHC property.

She snatched the black one-piece suit from its spot and tossed it over her shoulder, hoping it would land near the open suitcase on the bed. "I don't even know if the Silver Rose has a pool," she muttered, opening a second drawer. "It didn't when I lived there."

But a lot could change in fourteen years. Lord knows she had.

She stared, unseeing, at the neatly folded summer clothes. Three months in Nevada. Was she out of her mind?

Her boss, Roger McFinney, had asked the same thing less than an hour earlier when he'd accosted Anne in her office. Even though her request for family leave had been approved by the head of personnel, Roger hadn't been pleased. "Am I expected to hold this door open for you for three months while you trot off to the wilds of Nevada to fulfill some tenuous stepdaughter obligation?"

In his early sixties, Roger looked fifteen years younger.

Some in the office attributed this to his vampire heritage. But he'd been Anne's mentor for five years and was the reason she had a shot at an executive-level job.

"Anne," he'd said, softening as much as Roger ever softened, "your mother is dead. Surely whatever guilt you feel for not spending more time with her at the end isn't worth the job of a lifetime."

Anne's mother, Esther, had passed away in February, and not a night went by that Anne didn't think about her with regret. So when A. J. Cavanaugh, Anne's stepfather, called to ask for her help this summer, Anne couldn't say no—especially when Zoey added a little emotional arm-twisting. "Please, Mommy," her eight-year-old daughter had begged. "Grandpa needs us. And you promised I'd get to visit the ranch when I was older. I'll be nine in July, you know."

Anne knew. And Esther's death had driven home one immutable fact: life was fleeting. Zoey was growing up too fast, and Anne was missing out. Maybe that was the true reason she'd agreed to this trip. All Anne knew for certain was that her motivation didn't stem from any love for Nevada. The eighteen months she'd spent there in high school had been eighteen too many in her book. Esther had come to love the sage scrub and fir-covered landscape of the high desert, but Anne didn't share those feelings.

Anne quickly selected an assortment of shorts, jeans and tops then turned her attention to her lingerie drawer. *Two sports bras. Three regular. Maybe the push-up…* Her hand hovered over the satin fabric. Why bother taking it? She didn't have an answer but added it to the pile. A 34–B didn't take up much space.

She chose two sets of pajamas. One summer-weight cotton, one flannel. Late May on the eastern slope of the Sierra Nevada mountain range offered variable weather as she recalled. The snow had probably been gone for a month, but mornings could be chilly.

The historic Silver Rose Guest Ranch was a unique anachronism—a working ranch existing within a stone's throw of a burgeoning population. Thirty minutes from Reno, the Silver Rose was a juicy prospect for developers. Given the economic realities of ranching, A.J. had been forced to sell off several parcels close to the highway in the mid-1970s. He might have sold out completely if he hadn't met Esther. She'd talked him into opening the ranch to guests not long after Anne moved out.

Anne's brief sojourn at the Silver Rose had ended with her graduation from high school. She'd returned several times over the years, but never for a prolonged stay. The Silver Rose was her mother's domain—a shadowy memory that still had the power to haunt Anne's dreams and fill her with a sense of failure.

She let out a sigh and turned on one heel, her bare foot making a squeaky sound on the gleaming hardwood floor. Wood provided a fiber-free surface that was easier to keep clean. Dust, pollen, pet hair, smoke and mold were her daughter's enemies. Once Zoey stepped outside, her fragile lungs and easily compromised bronchia were subject to forces beyond Anne's control. But behind the door of their apartment, Anne was as vigilant as possible. "A clean-freak," Anne once heard Maria, her housekeeper/nanny, tell someone on the phone.

Anne didn't care what the woman thought as long as she followed Anne's rules: no smelly cleaning products, aerosol cans, perfumes or scented lotions. Maria also had to pass an emergency-response course and learn CPR before entering Anne's employ.

How Anne would create an asthma-friendly environment in an eighty-year-old ranch house with barns, a riding arena and a forest just beyond the main compound was anybody's guess. But she was hoping the altitude and clean air would offset any indoor hazards. She'd already shipped their spare ozone purifier for Zoey's room. At worst, the little girl would be housebound, but Anne prayed it wouldn't come to that. Zoey had her heart set on learning how to ride a horse this summer. A prospect that didn't thrill Anne in the least.

Anne had consulted all three of Zoey's doctors, and each was optimistic about the positive benefits of the move. One had even gone so far as to suggest that simply having Anne around more would lessen Zoey's stress level and reduce the frequency of her attacks.

Just what I need, Anne had thought at the time, another helping of guilt. No single mother who worked for a living needed to be told that her absence was stressful to her child—especially an asthmatic child.

And the past six months had been more chaotic than usual—for both Anne and Zoey. Just before Christmas, an opening in the top tier of WHC management had been announced. Roger had assured Anne the job was hers if she wanted it. The position represented the brass ring Anne had been striving for for years. When she called her mother with the good news, Anne learned that Esther was at the clinic in Reno for some "stomach trouble." Three weeks later, A.J. called to say the problem had been diagnosed as pancreatic cancer and the prognosis was bad.

Anne had immediately headed west. Alone. The winter months had already taken a toll on Zoey, who seemed to catch every germ in public school. To everyone's regret, the little girl wasn't well enough to accompany Anne on either of her two trips to Nevada—one to visit her mother in the hospital and the other to say goodbye just hours before Esther passed away.

Now, Anne was going back again. With Zoey. For the entire summer.

Three thousand miles from our respiratory profession-als, Anne thought, a germ of fear replicating with abandon in her belly.

As she folded the clothing with practiced ease, she re-called the conversation that had produced this unwelcome bit of penance. When A.J. had called three weeks earlier, Anne had been touched that he'd turned to her. "I need you, Annie girl." He was the only person in the world who called her Annie.

At the time, she'd been prepared to drop everything and fly to Nevada for a few days to help him over this hurdle of grief. She was still hurting, too. The speed of Esther's demise hadn't given anyone time to prepare.

But A.J.'s call wasn't about solace. He wanted—no, he demanded—three months of her life. "I promised your mother I'd take her home when the time came," he'd ex-plained. "I need you to hold down the fort while I'm gone. Some of our guests have been coming for ten years or better. This isn't going to be easy for them."

Them? Anne had wanted to cry. *What about me? There's no way in the world I can fill Mom's shoes.*

Rather than admit that the thought of trying to take her mother's place terrified her, Anne argued that it was un-feasible to expect a person to request a three-month leave of absence from her job. Her life.

"I heard about something called 'family leave,'" A.J. had said. "An employer can't deny it, if the employee has time coming. You've been with that company since col-lege, Annie. Who's more deserving than you?"

"But…"

Whatever argument she'd planned to use disappeared when he said, "I'm just asking you to handle the guest part of the operation. Will's coming home to take care of the ranch."

When she failed to comment on that astonishing revelation, he added, "For more years than I care to admit, I promised Esther a leisurely trip to the East Coast." His voice took on a gruff edge. "Stop and go when we wanted. See the sights. Visit old friends."

Anne vaguely remembered hearing her mother talk about such a trip.

"Esther made a list of people and places she wanted to see. Mapped the whole route. I kept putting her off." He swallowed the quaver in his voice. "Can't put it off no more, Annie. It's time for reckoning."

After a tiny pause, he added, "I helped you out when you wanted to go to that fancy college. And later on, too—after you and the mister broke up. Now, I need your help."

What could she say? He was right. A.J. and her mother had been there for her anytime she asked. And how had she repaid their kindness? By keeping too busy to visit regularly. By sending e-mails instead of making phone calls.

But his timing couldn't have been worse. "Is there any chance you could make it later in the summer?" she asked, thinking that maybe once she had her promotion in the bag she could swing some time off.

"No, dang it," he barked with unusual volume. A.J. was by nature a quiet, soft-spoken man with a gentle but resolute style. Her mother had often said that once A. J. Cavanaugh made up his mind, it would take an act of Congress to change it. "This is how Esther wanted it. Can I count on you?"

Anne's answer had been the only one possible. "Of course, A.J. I will be happy to help out." Her mother would have seen right through her fake cheer. A.J. probably did, too, but he graciously offered to meet her plane as soon as she let him know the time of arrival.

"Mommy, can I take my PlayStation?"

Anne looked over her left shoulder. Zoey stood in the

doorway. Three foot eight inches tall, ethereally thin, with wispy, blond hair and emerald eyes that looked huge given the pale aubergine hollows under them and regal cheekbones. Zoey Elizabeth Fraser was an enchanting mix of princess, tomboy and scholar. Anne could no more pigeonhole her daughter's character than she could harness a butterfly. Despite being hampered by a fragile bronchial system that betrayed her when her emotions were running high, Zoey was bold and adventurous.

"Yes, love, you may bring anything and everything that will help you feel at home. Books. Puzzles. Videos. Grandpa assured me they have two computers, so put in your favorite games. I can't guarantee how speedy his are, but I'll have my laptop in case they're dinosaurs."

Zoey made a face. "You're not going to work for *him* while we're there, are you?"

Him. Roger had become Zoey's bogeyman—the person responsible for every ruined dinner, missed bath and too-short bedtime story.

"Not unless it means losing my job."

"You mean your pr'motion?"

Anne ignored the contentious tone. "Yes."

Zoey's forehead wrinkled in a way that reminded Anne of A.J.—although biologically that was impossible, since Anne and A.J. were related by marriage, not blood. "If you get it, would we have to move? Again?"

The tone applied to the last word said it all. Since they'd already covered this territory more than once, Anne walked to her closet without replying.

She opened the mirrored doors. Ninety percent of her wardrobe was business suits. "Let's see," she said. "What do I need? Jacket? Yes. Cardigan? Absolutely. Raincoat? I can't remember if it rains there in the summer." In truth, Anne didn't recall much about her Nevada experience. She'd spent most of the time indoors behind a book.

She'd moved to the Silver Rose during Christmas vacation of her junior year of high school—a tough time to expect to fit in, even for someone outgoing. Her natural shyness and Maine accent had labeled her "different." She made a few acquaintances, but no close friends.

In addition to the unhappy school experience, Anne's home life was difficult. She felt left out of her mother and A.J.'s newly wedded bliss and slightly resentful for her father's sake, even though he'd been dead for five years. Then, to make matters worse, she'd developed a ridiculous crush on Will, her stepfather's grandson.

Will Cavanaugh. Rodeo darling. Sexy cowboy sought after by every cool girl in school. And while he bore absolutely no biological connection to her whatsoever, Anne couldn't shake the idea that their being together would seem slightly incestuous.

She made every effort to hide her feelings, but apparently Will guessed that she was attracted to him—or perhaps he just assumed she was, since every other girl in school adored him. A few weeks before his graduation ceremony, they'd bumped into each other on the front porch. Where he'd been headed, she could only guess, but he seemed in no hurry to leave. They shared a soda and a few laughs. Then, to her surprise, they talked.

Hungry for closeness, needing a friend, she opened her heart to him. And he opened his to her. A friendly hug led to a kiss. Her first.

A kiss that ignited a fire deep in her soul. But it was the last they ever shared. His momentary look of wonder changed to one of mortification. A moment later, he mumbled something about needing to pick up Judy—the girl he'd supposedly broken up with a few days earlier.

Anne accepted his excuse at face value. He kissed her and then ran back to his buxom blond cheerleader. Anne was crushed but not completely surprised. Men left. She'd learned that lesson when her father died.

"Mo-o-om."

Uh-oh, the three-syllable version of the word. Anne looked over her shoulder. "Pardon? Oh, you asked about a move. Yes, hon, if I get the job, I'm sure there'll be a transfer involved. Possibly to the Pacific Northwest." Mold capital of the world no doubt, she thought, trying not to frown.

"I don't want to move anymore, Mommy. Couldn't we just stay in Nevada? Please, Mommy." Her daughter's tone was so plaintive it almost broke Anne's heart. For someone so sick, Zoey hardly ever whined. But this particular broken-record complaint about their itinerant lifestyle had been cropping up for over a year.

"Sweetheart, you've only been to Nevada once, when you were a tiny baby. You might hate the place."

"Or love it. Gramma loved it, right?"

Anne motioned her daughter into the room, then led her to the fainting couch in the far corner and sat down. She pulled Zoey's little body into her arms and settled back against the worn, red velvet. The couch had been a wedding present from A.J. and Esther. If A.J.'s claim was true, the ornate piece of furniture once resided at the Mustang Ranch—one of Nevada's most notorious bordellos.

She stroked Zoey's baby-fine hair and kissed her ear. "Your grandmother Esther was a free spirit. She sought change like some people seek gold. She met my father at a dance she'd been forbidden to attend. Two weeks later, they eloped and I was born nine months after that."

Zoey snuggled close. When she sighed, Anne could feel the slight rattle in her chest. Bothersome, but no need for the inhaler, she decided.

"What happened then?" Zoey asked.

"Well, they moved around a lot because Daddy was a

salesman. But when I started school, he took a job in a hotel in Springfield, Illinois, so we could stay in one place. Mama worked there, too, on weekends while Daddy stayed home with me. She claimed it was her time off.''

Zoey fiddled with a button on Annie's shirt. "Then he died, and Grandma was very sad and you moved back to Maine to live with Great-Grandma and Grandpa Jensen for a couple of years, until she stopped being so sad and started living again and went looking for adventure.''

"Who's telling this story?" Anne teased.

"That's when she found Grandpa A.J. in Nevada, right?" Zoey asked with a barely stifled yawn. "They wrote love letters. And talked on the phone. Then one day, he showed up in Maine and took her home with him.''

Anne smiled against her daughter's crown. Her mother had loved to tell that story. "Nobody thought it would work out," Esther would tell people. "My parents begged me to leave Anne with them, but she's an adventurer— just like her mother.''

Anne knew that was a lie. In truth, she'd been terrified that her mother would forget about her, her grandparents would die, and she'd be left alone. She'd chosen Nevada out of fear, not adventure.

Zoey's body went boneless. Anne closed her eyes for a few seconds. She was so tired her joints ached, but she still had to finish packing Zoey's things then write a report for Roger. Penance of another kind.

She eased the sleeping child down carefully and covered her with a chenille throw. As she walked to the bathroom to pack her toiletries, Anne's thoughts lingered on her Nevada experience.

To this day, the most memorable moment from that period was the kiss she and Will had shared. Not only her first kiss, but her first French kiss. Will's tongue in her mouth. A breathless joining of heat and passion that even now brought a flush to her cheek.

She made a face in the mirror and stuck out her tongue. "You're a hard-luck case," she muttered. It was just a kiss. No hands under her shirt. Or down her pants. Just a stupid kiss that should have been washed from her memory years ago.

Anne opened the cupboard door and started to fill a zippered plastic bag with cosmetics. A small smile tugged up one corner of her lips. *Why do women remember things like that? I bet Will has forgotten it completely.* Will had been a year older and light-years more advanced, both socially and sexually. A single kiss would hardly have made much of an impression on someone like him.

He'd barely spoken to her after their encounter on the porch. Not that she'd given him much opportunity, Anne had to admit. Humiliated by his apparent rejection and mortified by her passionate reaction to his touch, she'd scurried the other way anytime she saw him approach.

And something had happened to Will at the national rodeo competition later that summer. She hadn't attended, of course, but she recalled the grim look on his face when he returned. Not long after that, Will set off to follow his dream of becoming the number-one cowboy in the country.

Anne left for college the following spring. Busy with her career, a difficult marriage and a sick child, she seldom found time to return to the Silver Rose. Despite the familial link, Anne and Will rarely crossed paths—until this past February. At her mother's funeral.

He'd arrived late. A gentle handshake had segued into a hug. Too numb to cry, Anne had blinked against the fine wool of his suit before he let her go. They'd mumbled

words of mutual despair, then she'd been whisked away
to catch her plane.

Now, virtual strangers, they were about to become business partners.

WILL CAVANAUGH had debated trying to slip out of the
post-event hoopla unnoticed. The PBR, or Professional
Bull Riders organization, was known to fine riders as much
as five hundred dollars if they failed to make themselves
available to the public after an event. And while Will
wasn't worried about the money, he didn't want to leave
the tour on a sour note.

Technically, he wasn't a competitor. He hadn't ridden,
but he had been introduced to the sellout crowd. His name
was still popular with fans. But fame was fleeting once a
rider was out of the spotlight.

Thanks to an overly cautious doctor, Will had been side-
lined for three months—minimum. If Walt Crain, an or-
thopedist specializing in sports trauma, had his way, Will
would be off the circuit for good.

"Consider yourself the Steve Young of bull riding," the
fifty-something doctor had said after interpreting the results of an extensive round of CAT scans and MRIs. "You
could wear two helmets, but nothing will erase that frac-
ture along here," he'd told Will, pointing to a faint white
line in the uppermost vertebra.

To Will, the spidery line didn't look any different from
the fifty or so other breaks and fractures he'd suffered in
the course of his career.

"Another poke and you could be eating Jell-O through
a straw for the rest of your life—if you're lucky."

Walt's frank, no-nonsense manner made him popular
with the riders—unless they were the recipients of the kind
of news he'd given Will. For the most part, riders and
doctors accepted that in a sport like bull riding, which
pitted the brute strength and wily contortions of a two-
thousand-pound beast against a man armed only with a

rope and spurs, riders would get injured. Broken bones, punctured lungs, and concussions were just part of the job. But Walt drew the line at suicide. "Giving you a green light to climb on the back of a bull would be like signing your death warrant, Will. I won't do it," he'd said adamantly. "It's time for you to think about retirement."

Washed up at the ripe old age of thirty-three, Will thought bitterly. It wasn't fair. Bull riding was the only job he'd ever done. He had a high-school diploma, and thanks to thriftiness instilled in him by his grandfather, a fairly healthy bank account. But he was still missing that golden ring, which carried with it the title of champion. A goal he'd been pursuing with single-minded focus forever since high school.

Now, thanks to one man, Will was being told he had to step away. He was angry, frustrated and itching for a fight, but he made sure none of that showed on his face as he strolled through the throng crowding the staging area just beyond the arena where the bull riding had taken place.

Will had been in New Orleans several times. The New Orleans Arena put on a good show—fireworks exploding overhead, pre-event activities on Bourbon Street, good media coverage. Will had watched from the chutes, helping as needed. He knew from experience that a pat on the back or word of encouragement went a long way when a young rider found himself airborne well before the eight-second buzzer.

As he looked around, Will wasn't surprised to see the largest crowd—kids and a bevy of women—clustered around Troy Jones.

Troy was twenty-three, green as his flashy trademark vest, but basically an intuitive rider with an ideal center of gravity. He was a good kid. Tonight, he'd drawn Rounder, a rank bull with more twists than a hunk of barbed wire. In bull-riding lingo, rank meant mean, nasty and hard to ride. The more difficult the ride, the better the score—provided you could stay on.

Troy had earned eighty-five points for his efforts. Combined with the score from his first bull, it was enough to ensure he'd take home a sizable purse. And by the looks of it, he'd also have his pick of pretty young women.

Lord knows, Will had partaken of his share over the years—both purses and girls. He'd never found the right one, though.

An elbow jostled him. Will put on his game face and turned, ready to sign his name to a hat, program or body part.

"Still pouting, I see." A small man dressed in Wrangler's, a black, western-style long-sleeve shirt and black cowboy hat grinned at him.

"Yeah, Doc, better call the *waaa*mbulance. I'm about ready to cry."

Walt Crain laughed.

"You takin' off tonight, Will, or joining the guys downtown?"

Will had considered staying. He enjoyed the lusty, life-affirming abandon of New Orleans nightlife. The music, the crowds, the liquor. A person could lose himself—and his worries—in the energy. But the chasm of uncertainty facing him didn't invite revelry. Besides, back in Nevada, his grandfather was chomping at the bit to hit the road.

"The sooner I get started, the sooner I'll be at the ranch," Will said, making up his mind as he spoke the words. He scanned the now-thinning crowd to judge whether or not he'd put in enough public relations time. Despite what his doctor thought, Will planned to return to bull riding, and he wanted to make his temporary exit on good terms.

Early in his career, Will had enjoyed the meet-and-greet. Bull riding drew fans from all walks of life. Most were positive, enthusiastic and respectful, and usually he found it a pleasure to stand among them. But too often lately, he'd experienced the humiliation of facing the crowd after landing on his butt two seconds into his ride. And he'd never forget the surreal feeling of signing autographs before catching a ride to the emergency room, where Walt was waiting to reset his broken arm.

Will was about to turn away, when a little boy—probably seven or eight, he guessed—ran up to him, an adult-size straw hat in hand. "Could y'all sign this hat for me?" he asked, his wide grin revealing several gaping holes where new teeth were starting to sprout.

Will dropped to one knee. "Sure will, son. What's your name?"

"Gooley Jompers." He glanced between the men sheepishly. "It's really George, but my kin all call me Gooley. My uncle says it'll make a good bull-riding name. Whattay'all think?"

Will had to suppress a chuckle. The boy was cute as a puppy and full of life. He didn't want to be the one responsible for squashing his dreams—that's what doctors were for. "I think Gooley is a great name. Has a real ring to it."

He uncapped his fine-line felt-tip marker and signed his name on the hat, in one of the few remaining blank spots. It didn't surprise him—or even hurt his feelings—that he wasn't the first to sign. He'd been the first in other years.

He shook the boy's hand solemnly. "You take care and study real hard in school so nobody can cheat you out of your money when you're a rich bull rider, okay? You never know when somebody will come along and tell you you can't ride anymore."

Gooley nodded as if the words were gospel, but a second later he bolted away with a quick, "Thank ya, suh."

Will watched him join his parents and stifled a bittersweet sigh. He liked kids and wouldn't have minded having a couple of his own, but the rolling-stone lifestyle of bull riding didn't lend itself to settling down. Hell, Will had barely even made it home to see his grandfather and Esther as often as he should have—which was one reason A.J. hadn't needed to do much arm-twisting to get Will back for the summer. Guilt was a powerful tool. So was not having anything else going on in his life.

He got to his feet with a soft groan. His left knee wasn't quite healed from the surgery he'd had six months earlier. Nothing serious—just a little nip and tuck to clean up some scar tissue and remove a bit of fluid.

Walt grabbed his shirtsleeve and tugged. "You're good with kids, Will. I've noticed before the way you take the time to talk to them at their level—not like some of the hotshots who only have time for the ladies. Especially the ones with big hooters."

Will started toward the locker room where his gear was stashed. Walt followed. "Maybe you ought to think about settling down and starting a family," the older man said.

"Maybe you should mind your own business." It irked Will to have his thoughts come out of Walt Crain's mouth.

Walt cuffed Will's shoulder lightly. "Son, you *are* my business. That's why I want to keep you alive. Now, go back to Nevada, find a pretty gal and have a couple of kids. Maybe a few years from now your son will be out there in that arena and you'll thank me for keeping you alive long enough to see that day."

Will snorted. Liking kids didn't automatically make a person a family man. He was a bull rider. First and foremost. And he would be back—just as soon as he paid this debt to his grandfather, the man who'd given him a home and raised him.

Because his grandfather had trained him to treat people civilly, Will turned to the physician and held out his hand.

"Look, Doc, I don't agree with your diagnosis, but until you say otherwise, I'm grounded. I'm heading home for the summer. But come next fall, I'm going to get a second—or third—opinion, because this is my life. I will be back."

Walt smiled enigmatically and winked. "Unless some sweet young thing sweeps you off your feet."

Will guffawed—the first time he'd laughed in days. He knew the likelihood of that happening was on par with his winning top-money-earner status this year. His grandfather had already informed Will that he'd be sharing the management duties of the Silver Rose with Anne Fraser.

"You'll be in charge of the land, the animals and keeping the city slickers from killing themselves. Anne will handle things back at the house," A.J. had explained.

Will couldn't imagine how his grandfather had talked Anne into coming back for the summer. From everything Will had heard about her over the years, Anne was as goal oriented and driven in her career of hotel management as Will was in his.

Despite their common history, Will knew surprisingly little about her. An executive of some hotel chain. Divorced, with a young daughter named Zoey. Currently living in New York City.

He pictured her as pretty but reserved. Shy. She'd had a difficult time fitting in when she first moved to the ranch. Will had tried to keep an eye on her, but his high-school rodeo team had been closing in on the state championship that year. Then there'd been his near miss at the title, and his disappointing showing at the Nationals. Life had taken a sharp turn in the opposite direction after that.

Will remembered kissing her once. He'd been attracted to her for reasons he couldn't wholly define, but she'd made it clear that he wasn't her type. She planned to attend some big-name college back East and couldn't wait to leave Nevada behind her. A cowboy didn't figure into her life then, and from their few brief encounters over the years, Will had no reason to imagine her opinion had changed.

"Like I said, Doc. I'll see you in Reno in September. Next year, that championship title is mine, and don't you forget it."

ZOEY FRASER PEEKED over the rim of the airplane's window. Her mother said the plane was too high up to see anything, and she was right. Just clouds. Thin wispy layers of gray and white.

She took a deep breath, mentally checking for any telltale sign that something was wrong. At eight-soon-to-be-nine, she was a pro at gauging her excitement level to avoid triggering an asthma attack, but this trip had her very excited. She felt in the pocket of her sweatshirt to make sure her inhaler was there.

"What will Maria do without us, Mom?" Zoey asked, glancing toward her mother, who'd been staring at the same page of her magazine for ten minutes. Zoey was pretty good at gauging her mother's moods, too.

"She already has a temporary job for the summer. Didn't I tell you that?" Mom asked, blinking repeatedly as if coming out of a dream. Zoey knew her mother was tired. And stressed. Who wouldn't be with all that was going on? This summer would be good for her—even if she didn't want to leave her job.

Her job. Zoey frowned. Her mother's job—and that ugly troll Mr. McFinney—was the reason Zoey spent more time with her nanny than she did with her mother.

Zoey couldn't wait to get to Nevada—it was a whole country away from Roger McFinney. Zoey didn't care if they ever returned to New York. It was an okay city, but her school was crowded and the older boys were mean and pushy. The girls were cliquish and it was hard to make friends. Two girls from her school lived in her building, but they were older. They talked about boys and worried about their weight and clothes. Zoey didn't care about any of those things. She wanted a dog, which her mother would never agree to as long as they lived in the city. She wanted to ride a horse, which she might get to do while living on a ranch. And more than anything, she wanted her mother not to work so hard.

The airplane gave a little bump and Mom reached out to touch Zoey's leg, as if to reassure herself her baby was okay. Zoey frowned. She wasn't a baby anymore. She would turn nine in July. She wondered if her mother would throw her a party. *Who would come? Did any kids stay at the dude ranch?* Summer birthdays were no fun, Zoey thought. Kids whose birthdays came during the school year got parties with lots of friends and presents. Zoey didn't care about the presents that much, but she'd always dreamed about having a big party with lots of fun games and a special cake.

Maybe I'll grow this summer, she thought. A ranch sounded like a great place to do outdoors things. Fresh air and exercise. According to Grandpa A.J., that's just what Zoey needed to beat her asthma. Zoey hoped he was right. She was tired of being sick. She'd visited the emergency room so often she knew which nurses hurt you when they took your blood and which gave candy suckers.

"How do you feel?"

Startled from her thoughts, Zoey frowned and looked out the window. "Fine." One part of Zoey liked it that Mom worried about her, but another part hated to be treated like a baby.

"Good. Sometimes the recirculated air really bothers me when I'm on a long flight. Do you want a drink of water? I brought two bottles."

Zoey knew that. She'd unpacked them during the inspection of their bags. The frowning man in uniform had spent five minutes examining Zoey's plastic zippered bag full of medicine bottles. Finally, he'd given her a sympathetic smile and let them pass.

It made her mad when people acted as if she was pathetic.

"Do you want to play cards?" her mother asked through a yawn.

"Sure. Old Maid?" Zoey produced the pack from her carry-on bag. They'd played hours of the game in hospital waiting rooms. As she dealt the cards on their fold-down plastic tables, she asked, "Can I ride a horse this summer?"

Mom picked up each card and immediately arranged it in her hand. "The horses are there for the guests, honey. The Silver Rose gives them a chance to practice their equestrian skills," she replied, a subtle emphasis on the second-to-last word.

Zoey rolled her eyes. Her mother loved to use big words to challenge Zoey's vocabulary. "Horseback riding," she supplied, because she liked knowing the answer.

"Very good. Can you spell it?"

No. "I could, but I'm on vacation."

"Oh. Sorry."

They looked at each other and laughed. Her mother winked. "You're a good sport. Thanks for putting up with me, pal."

Zoey's chest tightened, but it wasn't from asthma. She loved her mother, but she worried about her, too. Mom had changed in these past few months. Zoey didn't know if it was from her job or from Grandma Esther dying or what. But she had bags under her eyes—not that they made her less pretty. Zoey noticed the way men looked at her mother, even if Mom didn't.

That was another reason Zoey thought this move might be good for them. Maybe in Nevada, Mom would meet a man. Possibly even a cowboy. Which might not seem like her mother's type, but a cowboy would have horses, and riding a horse was Zoey's goal in life.

"You know, Mommy, someday I'll be gone."

Anne gave a horrified gasp.

"To college."

Without thinking, Mom laid down a card that played right into Zoey's hand.

"I win," Zoey said. Her mother was really easy to beat when she was distracted.

"You did that on purpose, didn't you, my sweet little cheat?" Mom's teasing tone made Zoey smile.

Zoey used her special Hello Kitty pen to draw a cross on her tablet, then put their names at the top of the two columns. After writing down the score, Zoey said, "I think you should get married again."

The cards went flying every which way, like germs when somebody sneezed. "Did you do that just to watch me pick up cards?" her mother asked. Her neck was scrunched up against the seat in front of her. "You'll have to get the Old Maid, I can't reach her."

Zoey squeezed into the space with no problem. She retrieved the card. "I said it because I don't want you to be lonely. To wind up an old maid." She looked at the image on the card in her hand. The cartoon figure had buck teeth, silly socks pulled up to her knobby knees, fat ringlets and big lips. "Maria says women who aren't married by the time they're thirty are old maids." She glanced at the card again. "Not that you look like one. You're beautiful. And nice. I think some man would like to marry you a lot."

Her mother chuckled. "Well, thank you for that endorsement." She tucked the Old Maid card back into the deck and finished shuffling. As she dealt the cards, she said, "You know, honey, I don't have anything against marriage. I loved your daddy to pieces when we first got married. But marriage is a lot of work, and I'm pretty busy with my job. And you."

Zoey could vouch for that. Some nights she was asleep before her mom got home. Maria was nice, but she wasn't as smart and fun as her mom. And she spent a lot of time playing blackjack on the computer—although Zoey didn't share that information with Mom. There were worse things than a nanny who gambled. Like after-school child care. Little kids with runny noses. Bad smells from wet coats and stinky feet in the locker room.

Zoey had been sick so much of that first year of school, her teachers had suggested holding her back a grade. Instead, Mom had hired Maria. No more before-school and after-school day care.

"I just think you should think about getting married."

Mom appeared to be concentrating on the game. "Okay."

"I'll learn to ride a horse and you'll look for a husband."

Her mother lowered her cards. Her left eyebrow rose in an arch. "We'll see."

Zoey took a deep breath to keep her excitement from getting out of hand. Her mom had sorta agreed to think about letting Zoey ride a horse—which, of course, had been the whole point of bringing up the idea of marriage. It deflected Mom's focus from the important topic. Not that marriage wasn't important, but Zoey knew her mother would never get married again. She was too busy to fall in love.

But, then again, like Grandpa said on the phone the last time they talked, "This summer is about fixing the past and getting a fresh start on the future. Who knows what will happen, kiddo?"

Her mother cleared her throat. "Your turn."

The chuckle in her voice made Zoey expect the worst. Sure enough, she had to pick up the Old Maid. But at the moment, Zoey felt too happy to care.

CHAPTER TWO

"WHAT A BEAUTY!" A. J. Cavanaugh said, running his hand along the fender of his 1998 Fairwinds motor home.

It wasn't beautiful. Not really. But the odometer read eighty-five thousand miles, and he'd bought it for a song. And Esther couldn't see what it looked like. Maybe she could, but he preferred to think of her spirit as resting peacefully in the bronze metal box on the passenger seat. Once they got to the Atlantic Ocean in northern Maine, he would release her ashes in the wind and set her free.

That was his mission. The motor home was gassed and lubed. It had new tires and brakes. He'd given it a thorough cleaning then stocked it with provisions, realizing belatedly that this wasn't a Conestoga wagon and he could stop and buy anything he needed along the way.

With luck, A.J. would hit the road in the morning. The girls—Anne and Zoey—were upstairs settling in. Will was due any time. The coming weekend would see the arrival of the first Silver Rose guests of the season, which in A.J.'s mind marked the beginning of summer.

"Grandpa, may I look inside?"

A.J. planted the heel of his boot in the loose gravel of the driveway and turned to look at the sprite standing at the open door of the motor home. He hadn't even heard her approach. A bit small for her age but bright-eyed and inquisitive, Zoey waited patiently for his answer.

Needs some fresh air and exercise, A.J. decided. A summer in Nevada might just be the ticket.

"Of course you can, sweet child. Hop aboard."

She gamely clambered up the metal step. A.J. followed.

"It's nice," she said, slowly spinning about to take it all in. She pointed at the wall-to-wall bed at the rear of the vehicle. "That looks cozy. You'll be comfortable there, won't you?"

"I will, indeed, Miss Zoey," A.J. agreed, watching her closely to see if she'd inherited any of her grandmother's wry humor and gusto for life.

She discreetly checked out the bathroom facilities then poked about the galley, asking questions nonstop. When she stepped to the helm to survey the view through the wide front windshield, she froze, her gaze dropping to the polished bronze box on the passenger seat. "Is that…?"

"Your grandmother's ashes? Yes, it is. This is her trip, so I put her where she can see everything."

Zoey's eyes grew round, and her bottom lip disappeared behind her two prominent new teeth. Too late, it occurred to him that Anne might not have explained about cremation. Zoey had been sick when Esther's funeral had taken place, so she might not understand the process.

He sat down at the built-in dining table and reached out to catch her delicate wrist in his hand. "Come're, sweetheart. Let's talk."

She came docilely. He picked her up and placed her on his knee. It had been a long time since he'd had a grandchild small enough to bounce on his knee. He hadn't realized that he'd missed the feeling.

"I don't know what your mama thinks about this trip of mine, but she came when I asked her, so I have to assume she understands. Your grandma and I made a lot of plans—"

"For when you got old?" Zoey asked.

"Exactly. But she got sick. It came on real fast and we weren't able to do some of the things we planned."

"Like take a trip," she said sagely.

He bussed the top of her head. "That's right. Now, some people when they die want their bodies buried in the ground so their friends and relatives can stop by and pay their respects. Grandma Esther thought that was a waste of time. She used to say, 'People have better things to do than put flowers on graves. I want my ashes sprinkled in the Atlantic Ocean.'"

"How did she get to be ashes?"

A.J. didn't believe in lying to children. "In a beautiful fire."

"Did it hurt?"

His heart clutched in his chest. "No, sweetness, it didn't."

She cocked her head and looked at the box. "Good." A second later, she hopped down, then walked to the seat and leaned across the space to pat the box. "Bye-bye, Grandma. Hope you like the ocean."

A.J.'s throat was too tight to speak, his eyes moist. He'd cried more tears in the past few months than in all his seventy-plus years. When he'd been told his only son and daughter-in-law had been killed in a car accident, A.J. had felt gut shot. But there had been so many demands on him at the time—two funerals, his wife's debilitating grief, his nine-year-old grandson—he never had time to feel sorry for himself. Not so with Esther.

"Zoey," an out-of-breath voice wheezed. "I've been looking all over for you. I thought you were resting."

A.J. rose as his stepdaughter entered the motor home. "My fault, Annie. We were jabbering away."

Zoey grabbed her mother's hand. "He's got Grandma in a box on the front seat. Wanna see?"

Anne's features froze in shock.

"Don't worry. He burned her up first."

Anne's gaze went from the seat to A.J. After a split second of horrified panic, she laughed. A.J. chuckled, too.

Anne stepped to her daughter's side and leaned over the seat. She, too, patted the box. "Nice job, A.J. Mom would love this view."

A.J. turned away and pretended to straighten some packages of instant oatmeal. He had enough provisions to last all summer, but the planning kept him from thinking about the long, lonely drive ahead.

As if sensing his anguish, Anne came up to him and put her arms around his middle, hugging him from behind. "This is a good thing you're doing. I'm sorry I gave you any grief about it. I really am glad to be here."

He squeezed her hands where they met at his belly. He'd put on a bit of a spare tire thanks to Esther's good cooking. Some of that weight had melted away from worry when Esther was sick, but after she passed, the church ladies and his neighbors' wives had kept him supplied with casseroles and cookies. He'd eaten some and relegated the rest to the freezer—in case Anne wasn't the cook her mother had been.

The guests who were scheduled for the summer were mostly repeats. All had been apprised of the change awaiting them and not one had canceled or expressed anything but sincere sympathy. He'd sent out letters offering to re-fund those who had paid. None had accepted. To anyone calling about vacancies, he spelled out the changes. To his surprise, the place was booked solid through the end of August.

A.J. knew the repeat customers would miss Esther's hospitality and friendship almost as much as they'd miss her cooking. He reckoned Anne was smart enough to handle the kitchen, or to hire someone who could, but he couldn't help worrying that nobody could truly replace Esther. He doubted Anne—even though she was beautiful and possessed a sweet, open smile when she wasn't worrying about something—would ever achieve the same personal touch her mother had had with people.

But that wasn't his problem. Anne would work something out. She was the most organized person he'd ever met.

"Thank you, dear," he said. "I don't feel like quite such a bully now."

She stepped away and sat down in the spot he'd vacated. "Did you have to do a lot of arm-twisting with Will? Or does the bull-riding circuit take the summer off?"

"It goes all year, for the most part. But Will landed wrong a month or so ago and banged himself up. The doctor wants him to rest up a bit."

She had a serious look on her face. He could tell she was concerned about sharing the managerial duties with his grandson. Before she could say anything, Zoey asked, "Do you have a horse I can ride, Grandpa?"

Anne's expression turned to horror.

"We have lots of horses, but before anybody gets on one around here, they gotta learn how to ride. Do you know how to ride?"

Zoey's thin shoulders lifted and fell. "Is it like riding a bike? I can do that. Mommy taught me. She has a scar on her elbow to prove it."

"*Mommy* has the scar?"

Zoey grabbed her mother's arm and lifted it like a boxer who has just won a match. "Right there. See? She tried to stop me when I forgot how to make the brakes work and we crashed into some boxes where the homeless people sometimes live. She landed on a wine bottle and it cut deep. We had to go to the emergency room, only this time it was 'cause of her, not me."

Anne confirmed the story. "Six stitches and a tetanus shot."

"Maybe horseback riding is safer. No wine bottles to fall on."

"But there are boulders and barbed-wire fences, and a horse is a lot farther off the ground than a bike," Anne said, her tone leaving no question how she felt about her daughter on horseback.

"Your mother is right, Zoey. Any sport is dangerous—until you're good at it. Even bicycle riding. If you're willing to learn how to ride a horse safely, I'm sure you'll be able to talk your mom into letting you give it a try." Anne's forehead furrowed and her lips compressed. "With supervision."

He almost smiled at the image of his rough-and-tough bull-rider grandson teaching the petite, feminine eight-year-old how to ride.

Anne rose. "Well, Zoey, we'd better get the rest of our stuff unpacked and survey the kitchen. Guests start coming soon. There's a lot to do to get ready."

Once the two were gone, A.J. slipped into the driver's seat. He glanced at his traveling companion. He could almost picture Esther's long, thick silver hair waving in the breeze from the open window, her round face smiling.

"Why are you always smiling, Esther?" he once asked.

"Because you've given me the best life anyone could ask for, Albert John Cavanaugh. And I love you."

A.J. wiped his leaky eyes with the back of his hand. "I love you, too, dear," he whispered.

WILL WAS GRATEFUL to reach the turnoff to the ranch before sunset. His drive had taken longer than expected thanks to a water-pump problem in Tonapah. Luckily, the local garage had had one in stock, and he had been on his way again after a three-hour delay.

He'd tried calling from the gas station, but no one had picked up, not even the service that handled Silver Rose bookings. The clock on the dash told him he'd missed dinner. His growling stomach agreed.

If Esther were alive, dinner would be warming in the oven, no matter how late he arrived. Will hadn't realized just how dear his grandfather's second wife had been to him until she was gone.

He'd barely made it back for the tail end of her funeral. The sad affair had been further hindered by the weather—a blizzard that had reached all the way to Denver and stranded him overnight at the airport. In lieu of a burial, mourners had gathered at the mortuary in town for a service and returned to the Silver Rose afterward for food and drink.

He only saw Esther's daughter, Anne, for a few brief moments before some high-school friends interrupted. It was the first contact they'd had in nearly fifteen years. Although Will had visited the old homestead often, his stay had never coincided with Anne's. She'd matured into a beautiful woman who hid her pain well. Only her eyes reflected the depth of her loss. He'd watched her comfort her mother's many friends and community members, without revealing her own grief.

It touched Will's heart to see how gentle she was with A.J. who, for the first time Will could picture, seemed truly overwhelmed.

A.J. was the rock in Will's life—the fortress that weathered every storm. To see the man so completely lost was unnerving. The coward in him wanted to leave just so he wouldn't have to deal with the reality that his grandfather was getting old.

Whether Anne was aware of it or not, she'd fulfilled the role of hostess just as her mother would have done, making sure every coffee cup—or whiskey glass—was full, gently directing the generous ladies of the church society as they fed the thirty or so people present. She comforted strangers who'd grown to love and respect her mother.

Deciding the activity kept her from dwelling on her mother's absence, Will kept in the background. But when he looked around an hour or so later, he realized that she'd disappeared.

"Where'd Anne go?" he'd asked his grandfather as things began to wind down. Will had already checked the kitchen and study. "Is she lying down upstairs?"

A.J. gave him a glassy-eyed look and shook his head. "She went home. Baltimore, ain't it? Or is it New York City? She's moved so many times I lost track."

"She left?" Will croaked. The fact that she hadn't said goodbye stung, but he wasn't sure why.

A.J., who was sitting sprawled in his favorite chair—the king's throne Esther used to call it—shrugged. "They all do," he muttered.

In Will's experience, leaving was inevitable, but it was usually Will who walked away. He'd yet to meet a woman who inspired him to stay put. Or maybe, as his pal Hayward once said, Will never gave one the chance to inspire him properly.

"She had to get home to Zoey," A.J. added. "Poor little mite was too sick to come to the funeral. Annie was caught between a rock and a hard place—trying to be a good daughter and a good mother at the same time."

The tiny bit of ire Will felt disappeared. He had no right to judge Anne. He barely knew her.

But guaranteed they would know each other better by the end of the summer, he told himself as he turned at the large, rough-hewn sign making the entrance to the Silver Rose.

The tires of his four-wheel-drive Chevy churned up dust as he raced down the mile-long driveway. Esther had dreamt of getting the lane paved one day. Will had suggested it once to A.J., who nixed the idea. "Blacktop will get chewed up in winter, and concrete breaks. With gravel, it ain't quite so slippery."

Made sense, Will had thought at the time. But A.J. wasn't the one trying to keep dust off the furniture. "Sorry, Esther," Will murmured.

The ranch, which had been in the Cavanaugh family since pioneer times, was a well-laid-out arrangement: house and garage on the left-hand side of the hub and barns and outbuildings to the right. In the middle of the circle was a sprawling cottonwood tree that had been climbed by generations of Cavanaugh children—fewer and fewer as the years went on. Will's father had been an only child and Will was an only child. A.J. had had two older brothers who were killed in World War II, leaving no heirs.

Will's grandmother was Boston born. Her family had been mortified by her decision to marry a rancher living on the edge of the wilderness and threatened to disown her.

At some point, her parents had forgiven her, but Will was pretty sure no one from that side of the family had come to her funeral.

Not that he remembered much from that time. His parents had been killed in a car accident and he'd come to live with his grandparents. But his grandmother wasn't the same woman he'd known. Sad and withdrawn, she'd died a few years later. "Grief sucked the light right out of her," his grandfather had said.

When A.J. remarried, it was something of a relief to have a woman in the house, even though Will took off not long after. But his affection for Esther had grown over the years. She was the quintessential grandmother—happy, welcoming and nosy in a caring way. She would spoil him rotten the whole time he was visiting, then send him off with a huge care package.

As Will neared the buildings, the first thing he spotted was an older motor home. Spotless and outwardly roadworthy, it appeared perfect for an old man on a mission. When his grandfather first introduced the idea of crossing the country alone, Will had tried to talk A.J. into waiting until Will could accompany him, but A.J. said it wouldn't be proper. This trip belonged to Esther.

Will still had some trepidation, but since A.J. hadn't asked for his opinion, Will didn't offer it. The only thing A.J. had asked for was three months of Will's life. A shiver tingled down his back as Will considered how providential his grandfather's call had been. Three months of healing might give him a shot at the Labor Day Buck-Off in Reno.

Talk about timing, Will thought. Rolling down his window, he took a deep breath of the brisk, pine-scented air. Nothing in his travels had ever compared to that smell. His heart felt full and excitement coursed through his veins. It was good to be home.

Not that he didn't expect to be chomping at the bit to leave by the end of August. Ranch life hadn't been enough to keep his father settled down and fulfilled, and Will was familiar with the restless yearning that struck him whenever he tarried in one place too long. He figured that was another reason he'd stuck with bull riding so long—the itinerant lifestyle suited him fine. No matter how tempting it was to put down roots, there was always another event up the road calling his name.

But three months won't kill me, he thought. *My co-manager, on the other hand…* Will scanned the yard for a sign of Anne or her daughter. A.J. had informed him last night that the two would be here when he arrived.

Will still couldn't quite believe that a city girl like Anne had agreed to spend the summer at the Silver Rose. Not only did the move seem out of character—she'd made it clear over the years that she wasn't fond of Nevada—but he imagined Anne would find it painful to step into her mother's shoes so soon after Esther's death.

As he pulled into a parking spot in front of the two-story white farmhouse, a movement on the covered porch caught his eye. Two figures—a woman and a child—occupied the glider that faced the road. The smaller one jumped to her feet and rushed to the railing. Will couldn't make out her features thanks to the shadows cast by the old-fashioned coach lights on either side of the door.

Even though daylight savings time had extended the evening by an hour, mountain dwellers knew that in these parts night fell like a stage curtain. Temperatures dropped dramatically in a matter of minutes and those not prepared could find themselves suffering hypothermia. Will ignored the chill when he stepped out of his truck.

"Hey, there," he called. "I made it."

He closed the door, leaving his gear where it was. Will already knew which cabin he planned to use for the summer. Esther always gave him his pick when he visited and he preferred to keep some space between himself and the house.

He stretched cautiously. He'd learned the hard way not to make sudden moves until his muscles were fully aware of his intentions.

A waist-high fence encircled a twenty-foot strip of lawn that Esther had valiantly battled to save from moles, gophers and marauding deer. When he reached the gate, an odd mix of carved wood and deer antlers, he lifted his arm in greeting. "Howdy, ladies."

Too late he remembered Rupert's Bastard—the bull he'd been riding in Fort Worth when he landed on his right shoulder, tearing his rotator cuff. He winced and let his arm fall to his side.

Maybe they didn't see...

"Are you hurt?" the little girl asked. She leaned so far over the railing that her mother tossed the book they'd been reading on the seat cushion and rushed to her daughter's side.

Will used his left hand to rub away the tingling sensation. The pain was less severe if he kept the shoulder moving. Driving for three days hadn't helped. "Naw, I'm fine," he said, closing the gate with the heel of his boot. "Just a bit on the stupid side. A smart person would have flown."

Stepping carefully to avoid the tulips that were just beginning to blossom in Esther's flower bed, he walked to where Zoey was standing, her small feet in sporty pink leather sneakers wedged between the rungs of the railing. "You must be Zoey. That's a great name, by the way. I'm Will."

Ignoring the twinge in his shoulder, he reached up to shake her hand.

Her smile revealed a mixture of mis-sized teeth and gaping holes. Her eyes were almost too big for her face, but she would be a looker in a few years.

Not surprising, he thought, shifting his gaze to Anne, who, despite the dark circles under her eyes and serious frown on her lips, was one of the most beautiful women he'd ever met. That fact had dawned on him at her mother's funeral, which had struck him as horribly inappropriate timing.

"Your grandfather was getting worried," Anne said. She was dressed in tennis shoes, jeans and a baggy NYU sweatshirt. Her straight, collar-length, blond hair was tucked behind her ears. "He expected you earlier."

Not much of a greeting, Will thought. He wasn't sure how to interpret that. Was she unhappy about this arrangement? Or just tired from travel?

"Hello, Anne," he said, touching the brim of an imaginary hat. "Good to see you and finally meet your daughter. I had water-pump trouble in Tonapah. Am I too late for dinner?"

He gingerly backed out of the flower bed—Esther had loved her plants—and mounted the steps. Anne and Zoey met him. In the light from the coach lamps, he could see Anne's smile and the hint of mischief in her eyes. *She has emerald-green eyes.* How had he forgotten that?

"We ate hours ago," she said. "A.J. barbecued half a cow. At least, I think it was beef. It might have been a brontosaurus."

Zoey laughed and shook her head. "Mommy, dinosaurs got eggstinct a long time ago."

"Extinct," Anne corrected. Winking at Will, she added, "Maybe it was a buffalo."

Zoey made a face. "Eouw."

Will rested his shoulder against the upright post. "I guess that means we're officially on ranch time, huh?" A.J. liked his meals at five, eleven and five. Surprisingly, the guests who stayed at the Silver Rose never complained about what had to be a change in their eating pattern. Of course, Esther wisely kept coffee in an insulated dispenser and various breads, rolls, cookies and snacks on hand at all times.

"Will we be adhering to that schedule while A.J. is gone?" Will asked, curious about how Anne saw their roles.

Anne rested a pretty, slim hand on her daughter's shoulder. "I don't know. Quite honestly, I haven't had time to think about it. And since I've been a guest here, I don't have any history to maintain. Do you?"

"Some," Will said, surprised by her candor. Knowing her background in hotel management, he'd expected her to come in with a rigid agenda.

Before he could elaborate, the screen door swung open on a squeaky hinge and his grandfather stepped outside. "'Bout time you got here, boy. I was ready to send out the dogs."

Will chuckled at the old joke. As an imaginative ten-year-old, Will had tried to train his grandfather's ragtag troop of cow dogs to be bloodhounds. While the experiment had been doomed to fail, the canine participants had stumbled across several of Will's hidden carcasses—G.I. Joe dolls swathed in chicken skin he'd filched from the kitchen.

Will closed the space between them and gave his grandfather a hug. Was it his imagination or had A.J. shrunk since he'd seen him last month on the way to Texas? "You know me, Gramps, a day late and a dollar short."

A.J. returned the embrace but, typical of a man of his era, quickly backed away. "At least you made it," A.J. said, his voice gruff.

"Sorry I worried you. My cell phone won't hold a charge. I tried a couple of times from a pay phone but nobody answered."

"We musta been outside. The girls were checking out my new home away from home."

Will gave in to the urge to look more closely at the mother and daughter standing to one side. Anne had positioned herself to shelter Zoey from the night breeze, her hands linked at Zoey's chest. Both were casually dressed, but the overall package looked expensive. That understated glamour, he decided, was what suddenly filled him with an odd uneasiness.

"How come the service didn't pick up?" Will asked, forcing his gaze back toward his grandfather.

"Mountain Phone got bought out by a bigger company. The gals that worked the reservation service got relocated—Phoenix, I believe. I been handling it myself and sometimes I forget to turn on the dang machine. That's something you and Anne can work out."

A.J. turned away and headed back inside. "Let's get you fed, then we'll have a meeting. I'm heading out early, so we'd best get our business talk out of the way tonight."

"Fine with me," Will said. A blatant lie. He'd been hoping to talk A.J. into sticking around a few days longer to give them all time to settle into their new jobs. Apparently that wasn't going to be the case.

He held back, waiting for Anne and Zoey to go into the house first.

Anne took her daughter's hand. "I promised Zoey she could take a bath in Grandma's tub. I'll be down as soon as I can."

Zoey followed docilely, but her gaze never left Will. When they parted company at the foot of the stairs, he gave her a wink. "See you in the morning, Miss Z."

Hurrying after his grandfather, Will glanced around the foyer and dining room. Nothing had changed since his last visit, although the whole place seemed a bit dustier and less vibrant than when Esther was alive. Still, the two-story ranch house reflected her vivacious spirit in its furnishings and color. He'd heard someone at the funeral refer to the decor as shabby chic. Will called it Early American Esther.

Will stiff-armed the swinging door into the kitchen and found his grandfather at the microwave. The interior light of the built-in appliance came on, and Will spotted a familiar-looking bowl on the turntable. Esther had loved her colorful food-storage containers but never scolded him if he failed to return them to her. A month after her funeral he'd broken down and cried after discovering half a dozen under the seat of his truck.

The bell dinged loudly.

A.J. handed Will a fork and knife. "Sit down. You know where the napkins are. Here's some beans. I put your steak on the grill when I heard you drive up. Still like it bloody, right?''

''You bet.'' In truth, Will's tastes had changed over the years. He ate less meat and more vegetables and salads, but he wasn't about to share that with A.J. In this part of Nevada, an inch-thick steak was a man's birthright.

Before sitting down, Will walked to the refrigerator and helped himself to a beer. He took a healthy swig then pulled a stool up to the counter, where a plate and drinking glass had been set out. While his grandfather tended the meat on ''the barbecue deck,'' as Esther had called it, Will let his gaze wander.

An innovative remodeling project nine years earlier had doubled the space, and added a sitting room and master bath to the second floor. New cabinets, marble countertops and top-of-the-line appliances—including an eight-burner stove—had been necessary for Esther to offer culinary lessons for those guests who chose not to accompany the cowboys into the field. To A.J.'s surprise, she'd developed quite a following over the years. In some cases, even the husbands stuck around for a class or two.

Is Anne planning to cook, too? Will wondered.

''What's wrong with your truck?'' A.J. asked, returning to set out a loaf of homemade bread and the butter dish.

Will grabbed a serrated knife from the wooden block. The bread was probably a gift from some concerned neighbor, he thought as he slathered a slice with butter. ''Same ol', same ol','' Will said, tearing off a chunk with his teeth. He'd had his jaw wired shut a year ago to help the bones knit. His bite still wasn't quite right. His dentist wanted him to wear a retainer or some molded guard at night, but Will wasn't that desperate. He just chewed a bit slower, taking care that his teeth didn't grind. ''That hunk of junk has been a lemon since the day I bought it,'' he admitted with a rueful smile.

A.J.'s shaggy white eyebrow arched, but he didn't say the words Will deserved to hear: "I told you so." Instead, he returned to the deck. As the door closed, the smell of barbecued meat rolled in on a gray cloud.

Will appreciated his grandfather's restraint. Three years ago, after a particularly lucrative ride that brought him just over fifty grand, Will had called to ask A.J.'s opinion before he bought the vehicle. "Sounds like more truck than you need," A.J. had said with his penchant for understatement.

Will bought the lifted, turbo-charged four-wheel-drive, anyway.

"Sure is a looker," A.J. had said when Will came by to show it off. "Looks as though it'll cost you plenty when all's said and done." Then he added, "But at least it won't ask for alimony when you dump it."

His grandfather's pithy jest proved prophetic. The darn thing ate tires as if they were made of pizza dough and guzzled gas like a wino. Will planned to sell it this summer. Surely he wasn't the only foolish cowboy in the world.

Will ladled a scoop of beans onto his plate. The calico-colored mix was made up of five or six different varieties in a tomato sauce. His first bite made him moan with pleasure. "Mmm…" Was that chipotle pepper he tasted? Just a subtle bite, but delicious.

A.J. returned, the screen door banging behind him. He carried a charred steak so large the edges hung over the rim of the plate. Anne was right—it could have been buffalo.

"Sorry I was too late to eat with all of you," Will said, mopping up more of the beans with his bread.

A.J. set the platter beside Will's plate then drew up a second stool. "The rest of us ate at a normal time."

Will repeated his apology then added, "These beans are great."

"Joy McRee made them. Didn't you used to date her daughter?"

"Judy? Kind of. Took her to the prom. Is Joy available to hire?"

A.J. gave him a funny look. "That's the same thing Anne said. Maybe you two aren't as different as you think."

When A.J. had first proposed this arrangement, Will had argued that he and Anne came from opposing schools of business—college and corporate versus remedial and country. A.J. hadn't bought it. "You don't have to agree on everything. Look at me and Esther, for pity's sake. We hardly ever started out at the same place, but sooner or later we found a way to work things out.

"You and Anne just have to keep the place afloat long enough for me to do what I gotta do. When I come back I'll probably put it on the market and settle into some old folks' home."

The idea had struck Will as so abominable he'd been momentarily speechless. Apparently, A.J. had interpreted Will's silence as approval, because he'd forged ahead with his explanation of how he envisioned the summer. "Anne's a city girl. She doesn't know squat about running a ranch. And you aren't exactly what I'd call a people person. Me, neither. That was Esther's strong point.

"The way I see it, if you and Anne can take care of your own business and stay out of each other's pockets, everybody ought to get along just fine. Think you can handle that?"

Put that way, how could Will say no? He'd never backed down from a challenge. And if he and Anne were able to keep the place running smoothly, maybe A.J. would return with a more positive outlook. Will couldn't picture his grandfather in any kind of retirement facility. A vital, active man like A.J. would shrivel up and die without something to keep his interest. And Will wasn't about to let that happen.

ANNE SLOWLY DESCENDED the wide, carpeted stairs. Zoey was sound asleep, her breathing surprisingly even, only the slightest rattle in her chest. The steamy bath had helped, and her mother's jetted tub was a child's delight. Zoey, overly tired from the time difference, had balked at getting out.

They'd avoided a tantrum, but the diplomatic effort had depleted Anne's reserves. She longed to crawl into her mother's four-poster bed, but the day wasn't over.

Anne tried to make her mind blank. Normally before a business meeting, she would have been making mental notes, eager to stake out her territory from the get-go. But Zoey's brief disappearance earlier in the day had unnerved Anne.

A child raised in the city knew the hazards, the predators. Life in the country—especially a ranch miles from town—presented a different set of pitfalls. Anne would need to watch Zoey carefully, and the weight of that responsibility felt like an elephant on her back.

Anne hadn't been surprised to find her daughter at A.J.'s side. Zoey loved men, and Anne almost wept when she thought of Barry Fraser, who was living in Japan with his second wife and seemingly happy to have little or no contact with his beautiful daughter.

Maybe a summer surrounded by a bunch of cowboys would be a good thing, Anne thought, although the memory of the eighteen months she'd lived on the ranch in high school didn't fill her with hope.

As she neared the ranch's office, she breathed in the smell of coffee and immediately perked up. Her mouth watered and her step became a bit jauntier. Six months of trying to wean herself from caffeine had done nothing to erase the craving.

The thought of stirring cream into the pungent black brew was so distracting she almost missed Will's remark. "A division of power might work in government—hear me, *might,* but I'm not sure two people can run a place like this without creating friction."

A new image replaced the picture of her lovely café mocha. Two bodies in a passionate embrace. Friction of another sort. Her cheeks burned and she shook her head to erase the thought. *Good Lord, have I been without a man for so long I've turned into a sex fiend?*

Exerting the kind of control she prided herself on, Anne walked into the well-appointed office. Her mother had fretted over the decor, anxious to create a feeling of comfort and elegance. Floor-to-ceiling bookshelves bracketed the rock fireplace, and hardwood flooring emphasized the room's spaciousness. Persian rugs, a distressed-leather sofa against the wall and two chairs at angles in front of A.J.'s massive desk completed the look. Tucked unobtrusively behind the door stood an oak cabinet that held the computer and operation center for the ranch.

"We're like two peas in a pod," Esther had crowed with triumph when she called Anne to describe the finished product. "A.J. has his space—nice and tidy—and I can close the doors on my mess so we're both happy."

Anne joined the men. "Sorry it took so long. Zoey was overtired, which made bedtime difficult."

"Is she breathing okay?" A.J. asked.

Anne wanted to hug him for asking. He truly was a dear man. She could understand why her mother had called him the love of her life. Esther had been quick to point out that her second marriage in no way detracted from the first. "I don't want you to think I didn't love your father," she once told Anne. "But George and I were just kids when we married and had you. We loved each other, but A.J. and I have a different kind of love. Older. Wiser. We fill in each other's gaps."

"She's doing great. Her air purifier is up and running and I changed the bedding this afternoon, so she should be fine. Thanks for asking. And I really appreciate you giving us the master suite. We could have gotten by with a single room."

A.J. made a scoffing sound. "You'll sleep better having her next door but not in the same bed. And you're gonna need your sleep. This is a busy place once the guests start arriving."

That thought made the butterflies in Anne's belly flutter. She hadn't worked one-on-one with the public in years. "When exactly will that be? I looked over the calendar," she said, motioning toward the computer hutch, "but I couldn't quite decipher the code."

A.J. snickered. "Your mother had her own method. I left everything alone thinking you'd want to do it your own way. The guest list is a file marked Coming."

Oh, dear, Anne thought.

A soft chuckle to her left made her hope she hadn't said the words aloud. She looked at Will, who'd politely risen when she walked into the room and was still waiting to return to the pewter leather chair with its matching hassock.

"Sit down," she said, hurrying forward. "Please. It's late and I'm sure you're tired from your drive."

She quickly lowered herself into the chair adjacent to his. Once she was settled, he sat, kicking out his legs to recline slightly. His boots were clean and polished and his ankles crossed, exposing the plain leather upper of his boot. Nothing showy.

It struck her that Will didn't fit the image she had of a

professional cowboy. For one thing, he wasn't a big and burly guy. An inch or so under six feet, he seemed fit and lean, but not overly muscular. And aside from the boots, his clothing was what ninety percent of her male acquaintances wore outside the office—broken-in jeans and a Henley T-shirt. Only the ornate belt buckle at his waist—an oval of highly polished silver and gold with some inscription she couldn't read—lent a distinctly western flair.

"Coffee?" he asked in a low, raspy bass that must have been tuned directly to her hormones.

Anne heard, "Sex?"

A spot in her lower belly buzzed, her breasts tingled, and her heart skipped a beat. She couldn't find a single word in her vocabulary to give in reply.

Will cocked his head and lifted the steaming mug in his right hand as if to communicate by sign language.

Mercifully, Anne's brain kicked in. "No, thank you. I've been trying to kick the habit."

"Bad timing," he said with a sympathetic grin. "According to Gramps, we go through more coffee around here than at an AA meeting."

"I'm a tea drinker now. Herbal mostly."

He shook his head as if the idea was too far outside his ken to grasp.

Anne turned to A.J. "So, what have I missed? Are you still planning to leave in the morning?"

Will answered. "I tried to talk him into sticking around another couple of days, but he's a stubborn mule." The gentle rebuke was softened by his tone, which seemed filled with genuine fondness.

A.J. rose from his chair behind the desk and walked to an oversize map of the United States, which had been tacked to the wall with colorful pushpins. He pointed at the state of Maine. "I've got a long way to go." She sensed at the edge of his determination a hint of despair.

Anne realized just how little thought she'd devoted to
A.J.'s grief. Torn between a sick daughter and a deceased
mother, Anne had stuffed her anguish onto the back burner
and handled the funeral as if the whole thing was happening to someone else. In the months that followed, she'd
devoted her attention to work, rather than deal with the
pain that hovered on the perimeter of her consciousness.

Maybe, she thought, if I'd stuck around and helped with
grief counseling, this whole pilgrimage could have been
avoided.

"A.J.," Anne said, too tired to move, "I don't want to
sound like a broken record, but I know from experience
that transitions are smoother when the previous management oversees the change of command. Even a day or two
would help."

He shook his head so forcefully that his oiled silver hair
fell across his forehead. He swiped it back. "I told your
mother spring. If I wait any longer it's gonna be summer."

She might have argued the point, but he didn't give her
a chance. Instead he returned to the desk and picked up a
sheaf of papers held together by a thick black clip. When
he handed them to her, Anne recognized the logo on the
cover page. "Sign these and drop 'em off at the bank. You,
too, Will. The manager suggested using two-signature
checks. That way everybody knows where the money
goes."

He returned to the map and glanced at it as he spoke.
"And I set up a power of attorney for you both with my
lawyer. Stop by his office, too. Sooner the better, I
reckon."

Anne's hand trembled as she perused the official-
looking documents. "A.J., do you think it's wise to leave
everything you hold dear in the hands of two novices?
Shouldn't there be some kind of safeguard?" She spotted

the line that listed the types of accounts. "At least, hold back your savings."

He sighed weightily. "You and Will are my only heirs. If you run the place into the ground, then you get less when I die. If you decide to sell it off while I'm gone, then I won't have nothin' to worry about when I get back."

The defeatist tone was so *not* A.J. that Anne couldn't speak.

Will reached across the space between their chairs to take the papers from her numb fingers. "Don't worry, Gramps, we won't let the place fall apart. The Silver Rose will be here for as long as you want to run it."

Anne wished she shared her new partner's confidence. She could hire staff, revamp the Web page, update the reservation system and handle the guests once they started arriving, but could she manage all that plus keep her daughter safe, hold on to her real job and prevent her head from exploding?

Possibly, but what was she going to do about the crush she still had on Will Cavanaugh?

CHAPTER THREE

AN UNFAMILIAR SOUND—the murmur of male voices—entered her dream. Anne tried to interpret the words, but the harder she focused the more awake she became. Suddenly, her eyes blinked open.

Daylight.

Panic sent a spurt of adrenaline through her veins. She sat up and looked around, trying to remember where she was. Her fingers tingled as she swept back the covers. The chill of morning made contact with the prickle of sweat under her arms, producing a shiver.

Anne never slept past five. Her day was jam-packed from start to finish. Oversleeping meant playing catch-up.

She leaped out of bed as if she were in her own room. Her left foot landed on an uneven mass, and when she tried to hop away from the obstacle, her right foot became entangled in the bulky covers. With a strangled cry, she careened forward, her hands slapping the bare oak floor. The handmade rug she'd noticed last night had gotten pushed aside by her suitcase, which she'd left open beside the bed.

Her flannel pajamas provided little protection against the rigid plastic rim of her weekender. Too tired last night to finish unpacking, she'd planned to tackle that first thing. She'd even set her alarm to go off early.

''Why didn't the buzzer work?'' she muttered, disentangling her feet and scooting sideways so she could examine her wounds.

The faded yellow and pink daisy print of her pajamas showed a few spots of blood, and Anne gingerly pulled back the material, exposing her shin.

She'd live, but the inch-long scrape wouldn't go well with her shorts.

She blotted the blood with a tissue she found in the pocket of her robe, which had followed her to the floor, then glanced at her trusty travel clock on the bedside table. Even at a distance she could see that she'd forgotten to push the On button.

With a huff of frustration, she rose, ignoring the twinge in her shoulders and knees.

The sound of an engine revving joined the rumble of voices. Anne didn't want to miss telling A.J. goodbye, so she snatched up her robe—a space-saving jersey number that had seen better days—and hobbled toward the door. She paused at the French doors between her room and Zoey's.

In preparation for their visit, A.J. had pushed Esther's sewing machine into one corner and installed a white, wrought-iron daybed for Zoey to use. Cozy and utterly charming, the room was every little girl's dream. Knowing Zoey needed sleep to help her body acclimate to a new time zone, Anne decided not to wake her.

When she touched the pounded-brass doorknob, Anne recalled her conversation with Will the night before. She'd assumed that Will would be occupying one of the upstairs rooms, but he'd informed her in no uncertain terms he'd already picked out his cabin at the far end of the compound. "I need my space," he'd told her after A.J. had retired to spend his first night in the motor home. "I'm not housebroken."

When Anne expressed concern about having strangers down the hall from where her daughter was sleeping, Will had promised to install a self-closing hotel lock. If she hadn't been so tired, Anne would have argued that losing the revenue from one cabin, which rented for twice the rate of a single room, could adversely affect their bottom line. But given her ridiculous attraction toward him, she'd finally decided the extra distance might be good.

Realizing she was barefoot, Anne scanned the room for her slippers. The spacious suite faced east, and a watery blue light filtered through the miniblinds. Anne had been grateful to discover that her mother had kept fussy window treatments to a minimum upstairs. Curtains, carpets and down-filled comforters were attractive dust catchers that could aggravate Zoey's asthma.

Not spotting her footwear, Anne decided she could handle cold feet for a few minutes. She walked into the hall and looked around to get her bearings. A.J. and Esther had undertaken some remodeling since Anne lived here. The hallway seemed wider, and they'd added a skylight, which provided enough light to see by without turning on switches.

The old farmhouse was functional and had served the Cavanaugh family well over the years. Anne's mother had added a badly needed dose of style, although Esther's tendency to collect *treasures* warred with Anne's inclination to reduce clutter. The housekeeping staff would stay busy.

Anne hurried downstairs, thankful for the wool carpet runner. Its Oriental design was a dramatic blend of red, black and amber. She paused at the foot of the stairs to cinch the fabric belt at her waist. Morning light filled the entry, which was painted an unusual shade of tarnished gold. Her mother's choice of color scheme wouldn't have been Anne's pick, but she had to admit the effect was warm and oddly welcoming. A cathedral ceiling and refurbished chandelier added to the room's expansive feeling. The front door stood open; a hunk of firewood kept the exterior screen from closing.

To avoid lingering on the flagstone flooring, Anne dashed across the foyer, her goal the rubber welcome mat. As she crossed the threshold, she spotted Will charging headlong up the steps, a battered thermos in his right hand and a half-eaten chocolate doughnut in his left. Only his quick reflexes kept Anne from winding up on the floor.

"Whoa," he said, wrapping the chocolate-doughnut hand around her shoulders and pulling her against him when she overcorrected.

Her senses weren't prepared for the impact of Will Cavanaugh first thing in the morning. Fresh air and fabric softener mingled with coffee and chocolate—two of her favorite vices.

She looked up, too dazed to move. His chestnut-brown hair looked damp and springy. An unruly lock spilled across his forehead. She was close enough to see the line left by his razor where it trimmed his sideburns. When he grinned, a whiff of spearmint toothpaste made her wiggle free. She hadn't brushed her teeth yet.

The sparkle of laughter in his medium-blue eyes could have been because she was obviously disconcerted or because he read her mind. Either way, he had Anne at a disadvantage and that was a bad way to start the morning—and a new job.

"Sorry," she said, stepping back. "I didn't want to miss A.J."

"He sent me in to wake you up and fill his thermos," he told her, before he polished off the doughnut. "I'll take my time."

His generosity made her instantly suspicious. In her business, men were usually most considerate when they were setting you up for something, Anne thought as she hurried across the painted porch to the steps. She had no idea what to expect from this partnership, and last night, she had been too tired to set boundaries. She and her new partner needed to take a meeting—a serious heart-to-heart.

The wording made her miss a step. She landed flat-footed on the bitterly cold concrete sidewalk. *Is that frost?* A shiver ran through her as she saw the flattened-out grass in the fenced yard.

"Anne," a voice called from behind her.

She looked over her shoulder.

"It got down to thirty degrees last night," Will said, holding up a pair of sneakers in one hand. "Too cold to go barefoot."

She remembered leaving her shoes by the back door. *Thoughtful and considerate. You don't see that much anymore,* she had to admit as he pitched the shoes to her in a graceful arch. They landed on the grass a few inches away.

"Nice shot," she said, bending down to pick them up.

Will's eyebrows wiggled playfully. "I knew all those horseshoe tournaments would come in handy someday."

He disappeared inside before she could thank him. Anne looked at the shoes, just slightly scuffed from landing toe first on the grass. If she were honest, she'd admit that she found his thoughtfulness even more unnerving than his smile. She couldn't remember the last time a man went out of his way to see to her needs.

Another shiver hit her—one that had nothing to do with the brisk morning. She was going to have to be extra cautious, she decided. They had a very long three months ahead of them and she wasn't going to screw it up by getting her heart broken by a love 'em-and-leave-'em cowboy.

Anne was well aware of Will's reputation. Her mother had despaired of him ever falling in love and settling down. "He's a rolling stone—just like his daddy," Esther once bemoaned. "So far, he's barely even slowed down long enough to gather a little dust, let alone moss."

Pushing aside all thoughts of Will, Anne crammed her icy feet into her shoes. Tiny bits of sand and debris stuck to the soles of her feet, making it difficult to walk. Slowly, she made her way to the driver's-side door of the boxy camper. Engine idling, the motor home resembled an oversize refrigerator on wheels.

A.J. sat stiffly in the captain's chair, facing forward, but his gaze was on her. Had he witnessed her encounter with his grandson?

"I overslept."

"You needed it. Gonna take a few days to get acclimated."

His deep scratchy voice was comforting. She was going to miss him. "Do you have to leave today, A.J.?"

His chin turned toward the right as if consulting his copilot. "Yep. Time to hit the road. You saw my map— we got a long way to go."

In their business meeting last night, A.J. had used one arthritic finger to trace his intended course all the way across the country, pausing at the important stops. Important to Anne's mother. Anne had been too tired to really take it in, but a few of the names rang a bell or two. A distant relative in Jackson Hole, Wyoming. Another in Detroit.

When he pointed to a spot in Minnesota, Anne remembered hearing her mother wax poetic about stepping across the source of the Mississippi River. And she couldn't deny that her mother loved American history, especially the Civil War. But Anne wasn't sure why that mattered now. Her mother was dead.

Anne reached up and put her hand on the window. "I know it's a long way, A.J., but would another day or two really make a difference?"

He looked at her, his expression serious. "Yes, dear, to

me it would. I made your mother a promise, and I'm through letting her down.''

Anne's heart twisted. She understood, but an old fear—probably easily traced back to her abandonment issues—made her cry, ''A.J., are you sure this is what Mom would have wanted? She loved this place. What if Will and I can't get along? We could really screw things up.''

An odd grin pulled at the corner of his mouth. ''Same complaint the boy just got done bellyaching about.'' He looked straight into her eyes. ''I'll tell you what I told him. You need him to run the ranch, and he needs you to handle the guests.'' He winked. ''Hate to think what he'd do if somebody complained about his cooking.''

Anne smiled despite herself.

A.J. covered her hand with his. ''You need each other, Annie. Just like I needed your mother. Sometimes we disagreed about how to do something. Sometimes there was nothing but hot tongue and cold shoulder for dinner, but we still managed to keep our guests happy. If you can't find a middle ground, then keep out of each other's way.''

His words echoed last night's sentiment, but this time his tone was uncompromising. Anne had been in business long enough to know a reality check when she heard one. She needed to suck up her fears and tell him goodbye. She rose onto the very tips of her toes and looked across the console to the brass box. Her throat tightened and she blinked back the sudden rush of tears. ''I'll do my best,'' she whispered.

''I know you will, dear girl. That's why I asked you to come home.''

Home. The word did her in. Esther had been *home* to Anne—the reason she left the safety of her grandparent's house in Maine to travel to the unknown wilds of Nevada. And no matter where she moved, Anne had always known she could count on that maternal compass point.

She dropped back a step and covered her face with her hands, struggling to keep her feelings boxed up. She might have managed to stifle her tears if a hand hadn't suddenly touched her shoulder.

Will had materialized at her side. A strong arm pulled her to him. A second close encounter in less than ten minutes. She didn't think this kind of emotional demonstration boded well for their working relationship, but Anne needed a shoulder—any shoulder. She'd been too busy handling things to cry at the funeral. Too busy with work and her daughter once she got home. Now, the reality of her loss hit hard. Her mother was leaving her forever.

He didn't say a word, but his hands were gentle and kind. Once, Anne thought she felt his lips brush the side of her hair above her ear. When he took a deep breath, so did she and found she'd stopped weeping.

Blinking against the residual tears, she searched in the pocket of her robe and miraculously came up with a second tissue. She blew her nose then wiped her cheeks with her sleeve. "Sorry," she murmured, unable to look him in the eye.

"It's okay. A.J. said this was going to be hard on you."

How had he known when she hadn't? She looked at her stepfather. His eyes were filled with kindness—and a hint of moisture, too. He reached out the window and brushed the back of his hand against her cheek. "You know how much she loved you. I'm only taking her ashes way, Annie. Her spirit will always be here when you need her."

Anne felt a second wave of sadness surface but she bit down on her lip and nodded. "I know," she said in a strangled peep.

He cuffed her shoulder lightly then reached a bit farther to shake hands with Will. Their arms touched and Anne felt a sensation pass through her. A run-for-the-hills sensation. But that wasn't possible. She was stuck here. For the summer. Surrounded by sensations.

Will nudged her with his elbow.

"Huh?" she mumbled, realizing A.J. had spoken to her.

Her stepfather's eyes twinkled with that same devilish glint she'd spotted earlier in his grandson's eyes. "I said, you and Zoey ought to take a day or two to get acclimated. Higher altitude, thinner air. Less blood to the brain."

Hey, Anne thought, her spirits lifting. *Maybe that's my problem. I'm not crazy, I'm oxygen deprived. Well, something deprived.*

Nodding, she said, "Good idea. I didn't sleep well last night."

A.J. settled back in the captain's chair. "Esther left a bunch of boxes in the attic. Dress-up stuff for Zoey. She said you used to love to dress up and have tea parties when you were a little girl."

A gossamer image of cloche hats and stoles made of mink pelts with beady glass eyes brought a return of weepy feelings. "Mom always bought the coolest things at Goodwill—just for fun." *When was the last interruption-free playtime Zoey and I spent together?*

"And I'll call the contractor about the locks, Gramps," Will said, reminding Anne of her snit last night.

Slightly defensive—Anne knew A.J. and Will felt she was being overprotective—Anne took a step back. Her mother often bragged about not having a lock on the door of the house, but Anne didn't live in that kind of world, and she wasn't about to sacrifice personal safety for some misplaced code of the West.

"Bill Crenshaw is a handyman who helps me out once in a while," A.J. said. "His number is by the kitchen phone. And you'll find Joy's number there, too."

Joy McRee. A possible cook and a longtime friend of Esther's, whom Anne vaguely remembered meeting at the funeral. Anne prayed this arrangement would work out. "I'll call her today," Anne said.

A.J. gave a nod then put the motor home in gear. Anne backed up to watch him make the sweeping turn into the main circle, but Will hollered, "Wait" and threw himself in front of the slowly moving vehicle.

Anne's heart bounced violently against her chest. What kind of crazy person tried to stop a motor home with his body? Oh, yeah, the kind who hopped on the back of a giant bull.

A.J. hit the brakes.

"Your thermos," Will yelled.

He trotted back to the gate, where the metal container sat balanced on a post. His dress resembled yesterday's attire—snug denim jeans and boots—but today's shirt was a faded blue chambray. The top two buttons were open, exposing a white undershirt.

He moved with surprising grace, Anne thought, given the punishing nature of his profession. Anne knew she'd be hobbled and limping if she had suffered even one or two of the litany of injuries her mother had attributed to Will over the years.

A second later, A.J. waved goodbye and the vehicle rumbled down the gravel driveway.

She watched until it turned onto the country road that would connect with the highway. Her tissue had turned to a soggy lump in the palm of her hand. Her chest hurt and her sinuses felt prickly. She doubted she could be more embarrassed.

Then she looked at Will. His face didn't betray his emotions—he was a guy, after all. A rough, tough bull rider. But she sensed that he wasn't a bit happier about this situation than she was.

Their gazes met, and for a moment Anne recalled her nervousness when she faced her husband that first night of their honeymoon. For the two weeks prior to the wedding, they'd been so busy they'd barely kissed. Then suddenly they were alone. And married. For better or worse.

As it turned out, mostly for worse. Six years of power struggles. Some hers, some his. Very little qualified as better—except for Zoey.

"Breakfast? I don't know about you, but I'm starved," Will said, turning toward the house.

Now, Anne decided, would be a good time to lay down some rules. For one, she wasn't a short-order cook. But before she could speak, Will did.

"I make pretty decent scrambled eggs, but I don't do froufrou stuff like omelettes, okay?"

He waited for her, holding open the bizarre gate—the one her mother had claimed was a work of western art.

Anne's stomach answered for her, loudly enough to make her blush. Not only was she famished, but she honestly couldn't recall the last time a man had offered to cook for her. "Okay."

As she hurried past him, she asked, "What happened to that half a cow A.J. served you last night?"

He shrugged. "Gone. Along with the bread and beans. And the midnight bowl of ice cream. Fast metabolism."

"I think I hate you," Anne said, trying not to scowl. "Now that you mention it, I seem to recall my mother referring to you as a walking garbage can."

He let out an attractive hoot. "That sounds like Esther."

Anne felt a tiny prick of jealousy. Although it wasn't his fault, in some ways Will had had a closer relationship with Anne's mother than Anne had. "Do you know how many women would kill to be able to eat like that?" she asked, stepping to the grass to let him take the lead. She suddenly felt ridiculous in her tacky robe and sneakers.

He hesitated as if going first broke some rule of cowboy etiquette. "Yes, ma'am, I've had that inequity pointed out to me more than once," he said, leading the way with obvious reluctance.

Anne followed a few steps behind, trying her best to keep her gaze off his lean backside. But when she heard a marketing jingle from her distant past—"Wrangler butts drive me nuts" in her head—she realized her focus was fixed on the manufacturer's label on Will's back pocket.

When he held the door open for her to enter the house first, Anne breezed past him and dashed for the stairs. "I'll get dressed then be right back down. We can talk over breakfast. Establish some kind of ranch-slash-guest parameters, job descriptions, hiring strategy, budgets."

Anne didn't need to look back to know he was watching her. As much as she wanted to deny it, something existed between them. Unfinished business? Thwarted lust? First love? *No, not that.* But something. She felt it, too. But that didn't mean anything was going to happen.

And now was the time to nip it in the bud. *This isn't high school,* she told herself as she dressed.

True, Will was even more gorgeous than she remembered. And yes, a woman would have to be comatose not to feel the allure of his laughing blue eyes and sexy smile, but Anne had no intention of giving in to her fantasies. She and Will Cavanaugh were partners for the summer. In running a guest ranch. Nothing else.

WILL HAD ALWAYS thought the Silver Rose's kitchen was the heart and soul of the ranch. Esther had made it so. Will couldn't picture Peg, his "real" grandmother, anywhere other than in the corner bedroom that had once been Will's father's.

A.J. once told Will that if he had it to do over again, he would have made Peg go to a psychiatrist. Unfortunately, back then, clinical depression wasn't openly discussed or treated—at least in this part of the world.

"She went from her Bible to her deathbed in three years," Will overhead A.J. tell a friend. "Peg was the type who needed answers face-to-face, so she went to heaven to ask God why he took her son."

His grandfather's obvious despair over losing Esther had concerned Will, making him fear that A.J. might give up, too. Maybe that explained why Will didn't put up more resistance to this trip. In most ways, his grandfather's mission seemed a healthy, positive thing. The urgency bothered him, but Will figured time took on a different meaning when you reached A.J.'s age.

He walked directly to the deep stainless steel sink, which overlooked the fenced backyard. Several straw-covered raised beds were waiting for Esther to fill them with flowers and vegetables. A partially obscured glass greenhouse and potting shed occupied a spot close to the garage.

A.J. had mentioned that Esther left behind written instructions for planting and plant care. Will wasn't a farmer, but he'd be willing to help Anne with the garden, if she wanted to give it a try. Any kind of physical labor would help him get back into shape—his main goal for the summer.

He cocked his head to listen for Anne's step on the stairs. Now, there was a possibility he honestly hadn't considered when his grandfather had suggested this arrangement. True, he'd known for some time that she was single and lovely, but it wasn't until he accidentally touched her that he realized the old fire was still alive.

Heaving a sigh, he shook his head. Better he keep his mind on business. Will was going to need Anne's help this summer. He doubted that he possessed any hidden proclivity for hotel management—that took someone with more education than he could claim—but Will could hold his own where ranching was concerned. And he wasn't really all that bad with people, despite what his grandfather thought.

Although Will was considered a loner because he rarely joined in the bar scene after an event, he got along well with other riders. Novice bull riders knew they could approach him for advice. He didn't mind coaching the new generation, but he always traveled alone.

Some bull riders partnered up to split costs. When Will first started out, he shared everything with three friends from high school. Eventually, Will's wins outpaced the others' and his buddies drifted away. For a while, Will traveled with his pal, Hayward Haimes—a crazy, bowlegged rascal who never failed to make Will laugh. Divorced, with two kids who lived in Tennessee with their mother, Hay was a hoot. And a damn fine bull rider, until an accident claimed his life.

Will shook his head. He didn't like thinking about Hayward. Fate had a lot to answer for with that one.

He looked around the kitchen. It was spotless, just the way Esther had liked it. She had been the kind of cook who routinely used every pot in the cupboard to concoct a recipe, but at night, everything needed to be in its place.

Will remembered coming in late one night and catching her in a cleaning frenzy. When he had offered to help, Esther had shooed him away. "I make-a the mess, I clean-a the mess," she had said with a truly awful Italian accent.

The countertops were slabs of rose-flecked gray marble. Will recalled his grandfather grumbling about the cost. Esther had cheerfully retorted, "This will outlast us by centuries, my dear." For all his gruff noises to the contrary, Will knew A.J. would have done anything to make Esther happy.

The walls were mostly white with wallpaper borders. Sepia photos of the ranch occupied the far wall. Will remembered Esther telling him the pictures served as an icebreaker for new guests. "Photos are a great way to get stories flowing."

He washed his hands and dried them on a soft towel, which he tossed on the counter, then he crossed to the industrial-size refrigerator directly across from the sink. A separate freezer and ice maker were located in the laundry room/pantry, which had been added to the building the year after Will moved out.

He set out what he needed—eggs, bread and butter— then headed to the dining room for a cup of coffee. Doc had suggested Will cut down on caffeine, which reminded him of Anne's comment last night. After just one week of deprivation, Will decided he'd have better luck trying to fly without a plane. Besides, Will figured, since he didn't smoke or chew, he was entitled to one vice.

A.J. had prepared this particular vat. It smelled strong. A little framed disclaimer on an ornate gold tripod read: "Help yourself, but if the well runs dry, you die." The antique oak sideboard was wide enough to hold a separate pot for hot water and a frilly basket filled with teas and instant cocoa, as well as a dispenser of fancy creamers and sugar packets. Will ignored the girlie stuff and filled a man-size mug.

"My mom drinks tea," a voice said.

Will had to double-clutch the cup to avoid dropping it. Several drops of hot liquid splashed on his wrist; several others stained his sleeve. He looked at the culprit who'd snuck up on him.

She didn't appear dangerous, just sleepy. A tiny little thing with tufts of hair sticking out as if anchored with gum, she rubbed her eyes with her knuckles and yawned so wide Will could see her tonsils. Her mouth made a sucking sound.

Will didn't have a lot of experience with children. The only child he'd ever spent any prolonged time with was three-year-old Riley, the son of a woman Will had dated for a few months last year. By the time Will figured out he and Riley's mom weren't the least bit compatible, except in bed, he'd grown amazingly attached to Riley.

"Good morning, Miss Zoey. I'm fixing breakfast. Are you hungry?"

Her green eyes blinked wide, exactly as her mother's had a few minutes ago. Only Zoey actually expressed her disbelief. "You cook?"

"Yes, ma'am, we cowboys have to fend for ourselves sometimes, so it's learn to cook or starve."

She watched him take a sip of coffee. "My mom doesn't cook much. She usually brings stuff home. I can make mac and cheese in the microwave and soup cups. And peanut butter sandwishes. Do you like peanut butter sandwishes?"

He smiled at her sweet mispronunciation. "Yes, ma'am. One of my favorite things. I like 'em with bananas."

Her eyes went round. "Me, too."

"Cocoa?"

"Yes, please."

Nice manners. Very refined. Except for her hair, everything about her seemed neat, orderly and perfect. Which struck Will as not kidlike enough for his taste. Somehow he knew her mother would disagree.

He poured hot water into a cup and added a packet of powdered mix. "Too hot," he decided. "Better add some milk. Follow me." Together they headed for the kitchen.

Once he had the brew ready for her, he set the cup on the counter near the stove and hefted her to a spot a safe distance away from the gas burners. She was light. *Too light for her age?*

Her peal of glee made him smile.

"Whoever heard of blue dogs?" he asked, poking at one of the much-repeated images on the leg of her flannel pajamas.

After taking a sip of cocoa, she said, "I like blue sometimes, but pink is my favorite color. What's yours?"

Did he have one? "I don't know. I'll have to think about that. What's your mother's favorite color?"

"Sage green, but she only wears black. It's a New York thing," Zoey said with wisdom beyond her years.

Anne hadn't been wearing black this morning. Her pajamas were a pale, feminine fabric with tiny sprigs of flowers on a white background, and the peachy robe had hugged her body contours far better than he had any business noticing.

"Where's Grandpa?" Zoey asked.

Will bent over to select a frying pan from the lower cabinet. "He took off about fifteen minutes ago," he said, searching for a lid.

When he straightened, he glanced sideways and saw Zoey's face awash in tears. Her nose was red and flowing and her chest heaved, but no sound came from her mouth. She was in obvious distress.

Will tossed the pan and lid on the stove as he rushed to her side. "Zoey, honey, what's wrong? Are you choking?" Suddenly, he remembered: asthma.

She tried to answer but the words came on a wispy sputter. Her skin changed color to a hue matching her pj's.

He picked her up and ran to the foot of the stairs. "Anne," he hollered. "Come quick. Zoey's not breathing."

Almost before he was done speaking, Anne appeared at the top of the stairs. She looked at the child struggling for breath and disappeared, only to return a few seconds later with a plastic apparatus in hand. Dressed in tan slacks and a white blouse, she raced down the stairs so swiftly her feet barely seemed to touch the carpet.

"In there," she said, leading the way to the living room. "The couch."

He carefully laid the child down. Anne sat beside her and pulled Zoey into a sitting position on her lap. She held the molded-plastic instrument to her daughter's lips and coaxed a response. "Breathe, honey. You can do it."

Zoey's eyes were partially rolled back in her head. Will watched in agony, his heart beating as if he'd just gone ten seconds on Little Yellow Jacket, one of the toughest bulls on the circuit. He debated calling an ambulance but didn't want to interrupt the connection he felt between Anne and her daughter.

Zoey's small chest rose; the inhaler made a spritzing sound and a moment later a tiny sigh came to his ears. Anne repeated the process, and as if by magic, Zoey's color returned to normal. Her face was bathed in tears and sweat, though. Her pajamas stuck to her in places. No wonder she was skinny, Will thought. Asthma attacks were a lot of work.

Anne looked at him as she gently swabbed her daughter's face with a tissue she must have had in her pocket. "What happened? Did you spray a cleaning product nearby?"

He shook his head. "No. I gave her cocoa, but she only took a sip. We were talking. She asked about A.J. I told her he'd already left."

Anne made a small sound of dismay. She hugged Zoey and rocked back and forth, crooning softly. "Oh, sweetheart. I'm so sorry. You wanted to tell Grandpa goodbye, didn't you?"

Zoey nodded.

Anne kissed her cheek. "I should have woken you up. But you were sleeping so peacefully I thought you needed your sleep."

Will started to withdraw, but Anne reached out and touched his sleeve. "Thank you for your help," she said.

"Help?" Will wanted to kick himself for not realizing

Zoey would have been upset. "I didn't do anything. In fact, I probably made it happen."

Anne shook her head. "No, you didn't," she said firmly. "Zoey did. She knows that her emotions can trigger an attack. She's worked with a biofeedback counselor and a respiratory specialist. She knows how to handle disappointment, but sometimes—like all of us—her emotions get away from her. Right, honey?"

Zoey swallowed and nodded. "Sorry I scared you, Will."

Will didn't scare easy, but if he were honest, he'd admit this episode had shaken him badly. "No problem. Who's hungry for eggs?"

They followed him, Anne carrying Zoey this time. Will kept up a running discourse to cover the fact that he really wanted to head for the hills. Zoey was a sweet kid. He liked her, but an unschooled cowboy who knew nothing about children—especially asthmatic children—could be hazardous to her health.

When Anne suggested they meet in A.J.'s office after breakfast to discuss business, Will declined. "I promised Gramps I'd take care of those locks right away. Maybe later?"

Anne shrugged. Will could tell she saw through his excuse.

When they finished eating, Anne said, "Zoey and I will clean up. We need to get rid of any toxic cleaning products, so we don't have any accidents in the future. Most of Zoey's breathing difficulties are brought on by environmental causes." She took his plate and walked to the sink. "And it's so unnecessary," she said. "It's amazing what you can do with hot water and lemon."

Will gave Zoey what he hoped was an encouraging smile, then left. He really did need to meet the locksmith, but after that he and Anne would set up a division of power. One that would keep Will out of the house and out of their lives.

"WAIT HERE and I'll bring the boxes down," Zoey's mother said, her hand on the rope railing of the ladder that had unfolded from a trapdoor in the ceiling of the upstairs hallway.

Zoey loved this house. It was everything their apartment wasn't—big, and cluttered, inviting exploration. "I wanna go up," she said, trying to duck under her mother's arm. "Maybe there's a ghost."

"It's probably dusty, honey. You've already had one attack this morning. Let's not press our luck."

Our. Zoey hated it when her mother acted as if her asthma belonged to both of them. Her mother wasn't sick all the time. She wasn't the one who was a freak. Who was so pathetic even her daddy left so he wouldn't have to hang around her.

"Please, Mommy…"

To Zoey's immense surprise, her mom took a deep breath and let it out with a sigh. "Okay. Grandma was a pretty methodical cleaner. It might not be that bad. But if you start feeling the slightest bit wheezy…"

Zoey nodded with exuberance and started to climb. "Can I go first?"

She heard a chuckle follow her up the steep steps.

The attic was dim and mysterious, with deep corners and stacks of boxes. A square shaft ran from the floor to the ceiling in the middle of the room. Zoey stood up and turned in a circle, trying to see everything at once.

No ghosts, unless they were hanging in the shadows of the rafters. Some of that pink cotton candy–looking stuff could be ectoplasm. That was a word she'd learned last week. The thrill of being someplace so new and different made her breath a bit raspy. She slowed her breathing.

"This is too cool," she whispered, walking straight to a big trunk with a humped back. It was green, like the color of her friend Brigit's sister's hair last summer. "I wonder what's in…" She opened the latch and pushed up the lid. Pretty stuff. White and silky. Maybe somebody's wedding dress. "Mommy, come see."

Her mother scrambled crablike to reach her. "I swear this place has shrunk since the last time I was here," she said, looking around with that look, as if she could catch the dust before it got to Zoey's nose.

"I feel fine, Mom. Look at all this cool stuff." She buried her hands in the watery-feeling cloth. She suddenly remembered a time when her daddy had lifted her up to put her hands in a tank where the lobsters lived. They were kinda mean-looking and she'd been afraid, until her mother pointed out the bands around their claws.

Later, the waiter brought her father a plate with a strange red object on it. Zoey hadn't realized what it was until she saw the bands around the claws. Then she'd cried so hard she stopped breathing and ruined the whole night. Her dad left them not long after that. He went across the ocean to live.

"…your grandma's wedding dress," her mother was saying as Zoey put the sad thoughts out of her mind. "Her second one."

"Grandma was married twice?"

Mom pulled the dress partway out of the box and held it to her chest. "You know that, honey. She married A.J. after my daddy died, remember?"

"Oh, yeah. I forgot." Zoey dug a little deeper and came up with a funny hat with a long train. "Look at this."

She put it on her head, fluffing out the net stuff so it fell over her shoulders like the long hair she dreamed of having one day. "Isn't it pretty?"

Her mom got a funny, sad look on her face. "You are

so beautiful, Zoey Elizabeth Fraser. This dress might be back in style by the time you get married. Let's put it away and find those other boxes A.J. mentioned.''

Zoey thought the dress looked more like her mother than her. It was simple with little pearls that sparkled. Zoey planned to wear something much fancier than this when she got married. After she finished veterinary school and explored Africa. ''Maybe you could use it, Mommy, the next time you get married.''

Her mother laughed—not so much a happy laugh as a like-that-will-ever-happen laugh.

''You could, Mom. You're not that old.''

''Thanks, dear,'' she said, reaching for another box. ''Wonder what's in this one.''

Ignoring the obvious attempt to change the subject, Zoey said, ''Brigit's mom dates.''

''Brigit's mom doesn't work my hours.'' Her mother pulled out a denim hat, the kind that drooped on the sides like a long-eared dog. ''I remember this hat,'' she exclaimed. ''Mom embroidered the flowers on it. I thought I was so cool.'' She put it on.

Zoey cocked her head to study it. Her mom was cool. Not everybody could wear a silly hat like that and not look stupid.

''Brigit said her mom might marry this new guy. He's a doctor. Not the gross kind, but the kind who fixes people's ears or something.''

''Good for her,'' Mom said, returning to her search in the box. ''Oh, here you go. This is right up your alley. *Très* chic.''

She produced a sleeveless dress with wide diagonal stripes of blue, green and orange. The slinky material slipped right over Zoey's head. ''And look—shoes to match,'' she said, holding up a pair of white, patent-leather sandals on top of four inches of cork. "Platforms. I wonder where she got these."

Zoey kicked off her tennis shoes and put her left foot into the shoe. It was too big, but her mother tightened the straps across her toes and tied the rough, leather thread around her ankle. She had to use her mother's shoulder for balance when she tried on the right shoe. "Neat," she said, feeling grown-up. "Where's a mirror?"

"Downstairs. Let's haul these boxes down to your room so we can really go through them. There may be a ghost or two around here, yet."

Zoey knew Mom didn't mean it. She was talking about the memories the clothes brought back.

Impulsively, she put her arms around her mother's neck and hugged her. Hard. She was starting to tell her she loved her, when a deep voice said, "What's going on up here?"

Zoey let out a little yelp and tried to spin around. Her shoes wobbled sideways, and she dropped into her mother's lap. Anne pointed to the hole in the floor that led down the ladder. Will's head was poking out like a ghost without a body—or maybe God. He looked serious. Maybe he thought she might go into another coughing fit.

Then he looked at her mother and his face changed. The lines around his eyes went sorta soft and fuzzy; he tilted his head like he wanted to see more of her. He smiled.

He likes her, Zoey realized. Her heart speeded up.

She looked at her mother and saw that her cheeks were pinker than usual. "Wow," Zoey whispered. She didn't know what this meant, but for some reason, the weight on her chest felt a little lighter.

CHAPTER FOUR

"FIRST, the lawyer, then the bank. Right?" Anne asked as Will's ostentatious yellow truck neared the edge of the unincorporated crossroads community—dead center in the path of urban sprawl inching its way south and west from Reno.

The area had changed dramatically since Anne had lived here. Not only did new businesses dot both sides of the roads, but so did housing developments that seemed to have sprung up overnight. The crush of cars as they approached the Galena Junction Shopping Center made her want to turn around and race back up the mountainside.

Anne's mother had lamented that growth was as inevitable as death and taxes but had better side effects, like first-run movies and a new school. "Mom told me there's a new high school around here," she said, trying to spot any familiar landmarks.

"Yep. Galena High. No more long bus rides for these kids," Will said. "Esther sent me a clipping."

Anne turned in her seat. "She kept you apprised of local news?"

He grinned wryly. "Not exactly. The article was on the same page as a photo of a buddy's wedding. I think it was to remind me that life was passing me by."

His tone was sardonic, not critical, but in her mother's defense, Anne said, "She was a big believer in marriage." *Another reason Anne had felt like a failure after Barry left.*

"Tell me about it. If she knew ahead of time that I was coming home, she'd invite some single girl over for dinner."

"Really?" *She never tried setting me up.*

Anne studied his profile. In the bright, early-afternoon light, she could see evidence of his physical and often dangerous job: a crescent-moon scar above his right eyebrow, a silvery line along his jaw. Despite—or perhaps because of—the flaws, he'd matured into a truly handsome man. No wonder her mother had tried fixing him up.

Scanning first left, then right, he said, "I can never remember which way to turn. My memory sucks."

He made an apologetic grimace and looked in the rearview mirror. "Sorry, Zoey. I gotta watch my language."

"Huh?" Zoey's head popped up at the sound of her name. Anne could tell she was too engrossed in the book about horses that she'd found in A.J.'s library to pay attention to the adults in the truck.

"Nothing, honey. The town's grown so much, neither Will nor I know where we're going, but we'll stumble across the lawyer's office eventually." She leaned forward to peer out the window. "Isn't it the next street up? By the light? Wait a second. Did that sign say Community College?" she exclaimed. "When did that go in?"

Will filled her in on what he knew of the area's progress, but Anne didn't listen too closely. She was still curious about her mother's matchmaker activities. Whom among the local populace had Esther considered right for Will? And why had she bothered plotting? He didn't seem overtly lonely or pathetically single, like a few of the men she'd dated.

"This is where we turn," she said as they neared an intersection.

"All right," Will said with a nod. "Good navigating."

The praise pleased Anne more than it should have, especially considering Will's quick escape after breakfast. Some men didn't handle illness well. Barry, for instance. As Zoey's attacks had worsened, her father had found ample reasons not to be around.

Anne didn't plan to get involved with any man who couldn't make her daughter's welfare a priority—a high price to pay for a wife. Which was why she didn't expect to marry again until after Zoey went off to college.

College. Her new position at WHC would provide the kind of financial security that would allow Anne to plan for her daughter's future. Although Anne earned a decent salary, the cost of living in New York and having a nanny left little extra.

She turned in the seat. "Hey, Zoey, after I get the reservation system organized and hire our staff, we'll make a trip to the library to check out some books," Anne said, raising her voice to be heard over the country music on the radio. "Your teacher passed out a summer reading list, right?"

"I don't know. Maybe," Zoey mumbled, lifting her book to block their connection.

Was she pouting because I cut short our dress-up party? Anne wondered. This trip had been Anne's idea, not Will's. It was a spur-of-the-moment decision based on her reaction to the look he'd given her in the attic. That glance had left her flustered and in need of an escape. Signing papers in town had seemed like a safe diversion.

Unfortunately, she hadn't realized that they'd be riding together in his truck. A.J. had given Anne the keys to her mother's almost-new Toyota Forerunner, but he'd neglected to mention that it had a manual transmission. Anne had driven a rental car on recent visits, and Esther had been too sick to drive, so the subject hadn't come up. Now, Anne realized she had two choices: ask Will for driving lessons or hire him as their chauffeur.

Will hadn't seemed to notice her dilemma, apparently assuming that since he needed to sign the papers, too, they'd ride together. But Will's truck was proving more claustrophobic than the attic. The extended cab was bigger than a full-size car, but every square inch exuded testosterone—like its owner. In the built-in cup holder sat a sixteen-ounce insulated mug from "Joltin' Joe's," which sported red kisses and risqué slogans she hoped Zoey couldn't read from the back seat. A visor organizer held a pen, an empty case for sunglasses, a map and a metal tin of mint candies. A dusty cell-phone charger was clamped to the dash. As far as she could tell, the unit wasn't turned on.

"Doesn't your phone work in the mountains?" she asked, reaching for hers to check the signal. She hadn't tried using it at the ranch.

"I hate phones," he told her. "I check the messages every few days, but I'm not much of a talker."

They pulled to a stop at the light. Rumbling at an idle behind a luxury sedan, the truck dominated the smaller car, which was by no means little. Anne had never ridden in such an assertive vehicle.

Will put on the blinker then reached overhead for the mints. He flicked open the lid with his thumb and offered her one, but Anne declined, strangely unnerved by his dexterity.

"How 'bout you, Miss Z?" he said, reaching over the seat.

The stretching motion emphasized his powerful shoulders, even through his butterscotch-colored suede jacket.

"Sure, thanks." Zoey eagerly claimed the candy.

"What if A.J. needs to reach you?" Anne asked, her voice sounding oddly breathless. "Maybe you should carry that phone. Just in case."

The light turned green, but Will looked at Anne a second longer before stepping on the gas. "He never has," he said, his tone serious, as if the question of A.J. in distress hadn't occurred to him. "Gramps doesn't talk much. Your mother, on the other hand…"

The gentle teasing made Anne smile. Esther had loved to gab. It broke Anne's heart to recall the number of times she'd cut Esther off to focus on work-related nonsense.

"My ex didn't carry his phone, either," Anne said, grabbing at any straw to distract her from the guilt she felt. "He was worried about his sperm." The word slipped out accidentally, and Anne peeked over her shoulder to see if Zoey was listening. Fortunately, the little girl's focus was on her book.

Will tipped his chin to look at her over his sunglasses, which had slipped down his nose. His shock was obvious. Whether at the implied health risk or the personal nature of her revelation, she wasn't sure. Either way, embarrassment turned her cheeks hot.

Anne went for a diversion. "Is that the place?" she asked, glancing from the address on the stationery on her lap to a faux Colonial with two overtrimmed mulberry trees in the front yard. A discreet sign read: Johnston, Johnston and Johnston, Attorneys-at-Law.

The truck rocked as it swung into the parking lot. Before the shifter made it to P, Anne had her door open. She slid the three-foot drop to the ground and straightened her black wool DKNY jacket, which she'd added to her tan slacks and white blouse—her best stab at a professional look. After checking her lipstick in the side mirror, she reached for her purse and briefcase.

"Open the door, Mommy," Zoey said, leaning over the front seat.

Anne studied the glossy yellow paint job. "Where's the handle?"

Will hurried around the truck bed. "I'll get that for

you,'' he said, squeezing a cleverly hidden latch in the door frame. Zoey emerged like a princess, resting her hand in Will's as he helped her jump to the pavement.

She stepped away from the truck and looked around with wide-eyed interest. "Funny trees," she said. "They look like Grandpa's hands."

Will made a surprised sound. "You're right, Miss Z, they do. Arthritis is an occupational hazard for cowboys. Even some of the younger guys have knuckles that look almost that knobby."

Beaming, Zoey turned and skipped up the walk. Anne followed, pleased by Will's praise but praying he'd overlook her gaffe.

He fell into step beside her. "Cell-phone infertility, huh? Maybe you could explain that to me sometime," he said, his voice laced with mirth.

Her face warmed. "Check it out on the Internet. Barry seemed to think there was cause for concern." She kept her chin up and didn't look Will's way as she added, "And so far, Zoey doesn't have any stepsiblings."

"How long has he been re-married?"

"Almost three years." The day after Zoey's sixth birthday, Anne had come home from work—alone, thank God, since Zoey was on a day-camp field trip—and heard Barry's message on her machine. *"Anne…Zoey, I just wanted to let you know that Kiki and I got married today. It was a little impulsive. No guests, kiddo, but we'll celebrate when you come for a visit. Love you, honey. Hope everything is going well for you, Anne. Bye."*

Anne couldn't claim she hadn't seen it coming—Barry was the kind of man who needed a woman in his life. He just didn't appreciate her once she had a ring on her finger. Their divorce had been civil but fraught with tension because Barry had made noises about wanting shared custody. Why, Anne had no idea, because once the final papers were signed, he moved as far away as possible and started a new life—one that didn't include his daughter.

"Can we get ice cream after this?" Zoey asked, hopping from one foot to the other on the building's porch.

"Good idea," Will said, reaching around Zoey to open the door. "I was just thinking the same thing."

Anne didn't believe it—she'd have pegged him as a cold beer kind of guy. But she didn't say so. She owed him that much. He could have given her a much harder time about her bizarre, personal revelation.

He let Anne lead the way to the reception area. Although the exterior resembled a house, the interior decor cried serious business. The "living room" consisted of a receptionist's desk, a buff leather love seat and two wing-back chairs upholstered in navy plaid. In the curve of the bay window, a play area for children had been set up.

Anne and her daughter exchanged a nonverbal question and answer, then Zoey walked to the alcove. Anne saw her dive into a beanbag chair and come up with a copy of *Nickelodeon* magazine.

Good, Anne thought, she hasn't been reading enough lately. Too much television and computer games. Both were pacifiers that Anne employed all too readily when she was swamped at work. That, too, was going to change this summer.

She turned to the woman sitting behind the large, U-shaped desk, which sported a built-in computer stand and chest-high filing cabinets to one side. Blond. Early thirties. A bit overweight, but nicely dressed in a lavender colored sweater set that enhanced her voluptuous assets.

The woman looked up, her gaze flitting over Anne like a bee with a choice between a weed and a big juicy patch of clover.

"Oh, my Lord, it's Will Cavanaugh," the woman exclaimed, jumping to her feet with such force the chair she'd been sitting in skidded backward and hit the wall with a bang. She charged around the desk on a perfumed breeze and wrapped Will in a bone-crunching hug.

To his credit, Will looked shocked and a bit overwhelmed. Maybe such overt fan adoration wasn't common in bull riding. "Hi…um…" Anne could tell he was searching for a name. His eyes appealed to her for help, but she didn't have a clue. The woman looked slightly familiar but she could have been one of the many mourners at Esther's funeral.

Anne shook her head.

"I'm sorry," he said, extricating himself from her hold. "I'm coming up blank for a name. I've been knocked on my head so many times, my memory isn't what it should be."

The woman stepped back. Her grin said she wasn't offended. "Linda Pilster. I married Grant Pilster. He was two years ahead of us. I used to be Linda Guardilargio when you knew me."

Will reached out and shook her hand politely. "Linda, of course." He motioned toward Anne. "You remember Anne Fraser, don't you?"

Now it was Linda's turn to look confused. She smiled a hello, but immediately went back to Will. "Are you in town for the reunion?"

Anne hadn't felt this invisible since her first board meeting, when she was a glorified gofer. She shifted her briefcase to her left hand and checked her watch. When she looked up, Will's gaze was on her.

"Actually, Linda, we're here to see A.J.'s lawyer. Anne called for an appointment."

Apparently realizing she was in breach of her duties, Linda scuttled back to her desk and sat down, drawing her appointment calendar into view.

"The Silver Rose. Good grief, where is my head? It's

all this crazy class reunion stuff! I'm losing it." She tapped her forehead then looked at Anne. "You're Esther's daughter, aren't you? I'm sorry I didn't recognize you. It was so hectic at the funeral we didn't really get a chance to talk. Everyone was impressed by how well you handled things. You were behind us in school, weren't you?"

"A year," Anne said, finding it difficult to keep up with the woman's scattered thought processes.

Linda picked up the phone and punched a button. Her acrylic nails sported little yellow flowers. She spoke into the receiver then hung up. "Dick will be right out," she said. "He's A.J.'s lawyer."

The muffled sound of magazine pages being turned filled the awkward silence. Linda leaned across her desk as if to touch Anne. "I want you to know how sad I was to hear about your mother. She was an amazing woman." Her smile was sincere but her perfume was so strong Anne actually backed up a step. She was grateful Zoey was across the room.

"Thank you."

Linda took a deep breath and let it out. "Esther helped our family a lot when my mom first got sick. You wouldn't believe how many trips it took to the specialist in Reno before they found out what was wrong. Your mother was there when they told us Mom had lupus."

Anne winced. An old friend from college had been diagnosed with lupus. She was doing remarkably well, but Anne knew the prognosis was never great. She reached out and squeezed Linda's hand. "I'm so sorry. How's she doing?"

Linda blinked, obviously embarrassed to have brought up the difficult subject. "Pretty good. She's in a nursing home now."

"Is she nearby?" Anne asked, making a mental note to

send a card or flowers. *Your mother would have visited,* her conscience whispered.

Linda swallowed. "Yep. It's why I moved back. To be closer to her and to help Daddy. He's lost without her. I swear, he's more helpless than my kids. At least *they* know how to run the dishwasher," she said with a forced laugh.

Just then, a fifty-something man in a conservative flannel suit came from the hallway to greet them. After reassuring Anne that Zoey would be safe in the waiting area, he ushered them to his office. Two bracketing generations of Johnston lawyers—one A.J.'s age, one Will's—dropped by to introduce themselves. All three were pleasant, professional and obviously related.

Since Will and Anne's business was cut-and-dried—just a matter of witnessing their signatures and assuring the senior Johnston that neither Will nor Anne had any intention of running his old friend's business into the ground— they were soon back in the reception area.

Linda was nowhere in sight. Zoey tossed aside her magazine and joined them. "I'm hungry."

Anne ruffled her wispy curls. "When aren't you hungry?"

They were just about to leave, when Linda caught them. "I just talked to Janice Graham, Will. She's head of the reunion committee. She said they sent your invitation to your grandfather, but we all know how hard Esther's passing was on him, so you might not have gotten it. How 'bout I fax you a copy?"

Anne was almost positive he blushed. He scratched his chin. "I appreciate it, Linda, but don't bother. I'm here to help Gramps this summer. And Anne and I are going to be swamped once the guests start arriving."

Anne's mouth almost hit the floor. His casual inclusion of her name gave the distinct impression they were connected in a way that went beyond business. Or had she imagined it?

The speculative gleam in Linda's eyes told her that was exactly what she was thinking. Before Anne could set the record straight, Zoey yanked on her sleeve. "Can we get our ice cream now, Mommy?"

Will put both hands on Zoey's shoulders and steered her out the door. "You bet, Miss Z. The Dairy-Doo is on the way to the bank."

Anne might have lingered to explain that theirs was strictly a working relationship, but she couldn't take another minute of Linda's perfume. Besides, did it matter what people thought? She and Will were practically related. Only a complete idiot would contemplate something sexual between them.

An idiot, huh? And who might that be?

Anne ignored her inner voice and dashed to catch up with her daughter, who was bent over laughing. Anne's heart gave a funny stutter. When was the last time she had seen Zoey laugh with such abandon?

Will spotted her and gave a slight nod and mischievous wink.

When was the last time a man's wink made my knees weak?

Anne was honest enough to admit she didn't want to know the answer to either of those questions.

THREE HOURS LATER, Will lowered the tailgate of his truck and faced the two-dozen brown-paper grocery bags lined up like feed sacks.

"Better to stock up now than face intermittent trips to town," Anne had announced after leading a Pied Piper caravan of clerks with carts through the parking lot. After their visit to the bank, Will and Zoey had passed the time in the arcade two doors down from the grocery store while

Anne shopped for the "food items to get us by until we hire a chef."

He'd volunteered to assist in the shopping, but Anne had insisted he'd be doing her a bigger favor by entertaining Zoey. "Zoey hates to shop for groceries, don't you, honey? And the process takes twice as long and costs three times as much when a child is along."

Zoey had agreed wholeheartedly, taking his hand to lead the way to the arcade. Will hadn't expected her to warm up to him so fast after their awkward start that morning, but apparently little girls didn't hold grudges—although she'd exacted revenge by gleefully crushing him at every video game he tried.

Will figured the exercise in humility had cost him about thirty bucks. Which, glancing at the bags of groceries, was about a tenth of what Zoey's mother had spent.

Guests have to eat, he reminded himself. And the first arrivals would be checking in in three days.

He wrapped his arms around two bags and headed toward the back porch. Anne had left the door ajar. Zoey had needed to use the bathroom right away—a possible reaction to her mega-Pepsi and double-dip ice-cream cone. The two had hurried inside without looking back.

At times, Zoey acted like a normal kid, full of mischief and nervous energy, but at others, she seemed wilted—a delicate flower deprived of sunlight and water. Despite his intention to keep a safe distance, Will had enjoyed spending time with the little girl. And her mother.

Unfortunately, after their stop at the law office, Anne had retreated into a distant reserve. No more slips about her ex-husband. No more shy smiles and provocative blushes. Had he ever met a woman who blushed more becomingly?

He set the bags on the counter then returned to the truck.

As he walked along the garden path, he reviewed their first day in business.

Lawyers? Check.

Banking? Check.

Groceries? He wrapped his arms around a second load. *Check.*

Attraction toward Anne? He hesitated. *Double check.*

Will wasn't blind or completely obtuse. He knew that part of the tension between him and his new partner was sexual. But only an idiot mixed business and pleasure, especially with a child in the picture. A lovely, fragile little girl who already had a lasso around his heart.

He trudged up the steps, feeling weighted down by something far heavier than two bags of food. For a man who'd gotten stomped on by more bulls than he could remember and had slept with more women than he cared to recall, Will didn't have a clue how to handle this situation. Run for the hills sounded like a good idea, but he'd just signed his name to a card at the bank that required him to endorse every check Anne issued. If he made himself scarce after the Silver Rose guests arrived, he'd cripple the business.

"Just set them anywhere," a voice said, startling him from his musings. "I'll put things away."

He tripped over the threshold and bumped into Anne, who was waiting to exit. "Sorry," he mumbled, trying to ignore the pleasant sensation of her arm touching his. He'd abandoned his jacket hours earlier.

"No harm," she said.

"There're only a few bags left. Why don't you start unpacking," he said.

She reversed course. "Good idea."

"Where's Zoey?"

"On the computer." She gave a little laugh. "You'd

think two hours at an arcade would have satiated her thirst for conquering lands and enslaving peons, wouldn't you?''

He chuckled. Before petering out on the drive home, Zoey had regaled Anne with the humiliating story of trying to teach Will how to play Cossacks, a video game that defied his tactile abilities and apparently required a more bellicose nature—like an eight-year-old girl's.

''Nothing like getting shown up by a four-foot Hun.''

Anne smiled. ''Don't let it get you down.'' She snickered softly. ''I never win, either.''

Will resisted the impulse to hug her out of sheer gratitude. He returned to the truck for another load so he wasn't tempted to admit that her admission eased the ridiculous irritation he'd felt at being beaten by a child. Maybe if he hadn't scratched eight out of the last nine times he was on a bull, something so trivial wouldn't have bothered him. But it did.

He juggled the final three bags and shouldered the tailgate closed. Whistling the new Dixie Chicks tune, he entered the house. ''Um, Anne, could you help me out? I got lazy, and this bag…'' He felt the lone plastic bag start to slip through his fingers.

Anne made a sound of distress and swooped down on him. She caught it in time, but her proximity—a grocery bag apart—made him freeze.

She backed away a step, her cheeks pink. ''It has the cleaning products,'' she said, holding up the sack as if to explain her embarrassment. ''Even nontoxic cleaners could set off an attack if we broke the bottle.''

Will set the bags on the counter and began stacking cans to put away. ''Maybe you could give me some Web sites to check out about asthma,'' he said, pausing to examine one label. *What the heck are hearts of palm?*

''I could, but why?'' she asked, her tone suspicious.

Will shrugged and scooped up his load to carry to the

pantry. "To be more informed. In case we're alone some-time—me and Zoey—and something happens."

The look she gave him said that would never happen.

"Zoey asked me to teach her how to ride a horse," he told her, hoping he wasn't breaking a confidence.

"What did you say?"

"That you'd have to okay it."

Her shoulders lost their defensive set. "Good. Thank you."

Will chuckled. "You must have a pretty low opinion of me if you think I'd put her on a horse without checking with you. I don't even plan to let an adult near the barn without a written liability disclaimer."

Will had heard A.J. grumbling in recent years about the cost of insurance and the convoluted codes an operation like the Silver Rose was forced to follow.

Anne walked across the room to hand him a piece of paper. "When I was in the office getting Zoey settled, I found this in the fax machine. Linda from the lawyer's office seems pretty determined to get you to the party."

He looked at the large print announcing a celebration in June. He had a pretty orange and white one just like it that A.J. had forwarded to Will's post-office box in Dallas. He hadn't replied because, as he told Linda, he wasn't inter-ested. This invitation looked different, though.

"There's a note on this for you," he said, following her back to the counter, where she was unloading bags.

"I saw it." She juggled two giant bags of pasta. "Freezer or pantry? I don't know if we have bug problems or not."

Will shrugged. "Me neither, but I somehow doubt a bug would dare show its antennae in your mother's kitchen."

She smiled before disappearing into the pantry. Will un-loaded the rest of the items then started folding the fleet of paper bags scattered on the floor. ''Linda's note says they'd love your help. Are you gonna volunteer?''

Anne returned. She looked around, hands on her hips. ''We should probably buy staples at the warehouse chain stores and see about getting perishables delivered every week,'' she said, ignoring his question. ''I'm hoping our new chef will have some connections. Did I tell you she's coming in for an interview tomorrow?''

''Do you mean Joy McRee? She used to cook for the rodeo association's fund-raising barbecues. She's great.''

''Apparently she's been helping Mom for a couple of summers when they had some kind of special event planned. She also asked if we intend to keep offering Mom's cooking classes. Do you have an opinion on that?'' Anne asked, transferring jugs of milk to the refrigerator as he handed them to her.

Whole. Two percent. Skim. Soy. *Soy?*

Will watched her find a place for everything.

He swallowed his question and answered hers instead. ''Not exactly, but I blundered into one by accident last summer. Esther was teaching a group of women—wives who didn't want to help with a roundup, I think—how to make pan-fried gravy and biscuits. I was their guinea pig.''

Her lips twitched as if she wanted to say something sassy but chose the high road instead.

''So?'' he asked again. ''Are you going to call Linda back?''

''No.''

He waited for her to elaborate. When she didn't, he slid a package of cheese across the slick counter to get her attention. ''Why not?''

She crammed it into a shelf. ''It's your class. You volunteer.''

''But I'm a...'' Her eyes narrowed and he changed the sexist blunder he'd been about to make. ''I'm a bull in a china shop when it comes to anything creative.'' His face started getting hot. "I just thought this might be a way for you to make friends.''

The arch in her eyebrow told him she knew darn well what he'd been about to say. She shrugged. "I'm only here for the summer. Why get involved?''

Will agreed, but just to be contrary—and because something about her sentiment bothered him—he said, "Meeting new people doesn't necessarily mean a lifetime commitment.''

Anne had her back to him as she examined the jars of spices in the cupboard beside the stove. "True. But even superficial associations require time. I don't even go to the same hairstylist more than once, because I don't want to hear his or her life story any more than I want to tell mine.''

Will understood. Lately, it had become a chore to extend a hand of friendship to the new kids who showed up on the circuit. Some of Will's buddies argued that it wasn't worth the effort to get to know these hotshots because they'd be gone after a season or two. It took more than skill to ride bulls; it required heart. A lot of newbies were only in the sport for the money. If the big bucks didn't pan out, then neither did they.

But, regardless of how fast the turnover, Will still made himself available to the up-and-coming riders. And he had a long list of good friends to show for it, just as Anne's mother had.

Maybe Anne was just shy, he decided. "I think you'd like Linda,'' he told her. "You have things in common.''

Her muffled snort sounded skeptical.

"Really. I finally figured out who she is. Your mother had her to dinner a year ago when I stopped here on my way to Salt Lake City.''

Anne turned to look at him. "Like a date?''

"Like dinner. But we sat around talking afterward. She's divorced. She has a daughter about Zoey's age. And an older child. A son, I think. Her ex is a real jerk. Had a gambling problem and left her with a bunch of debt. And, as she said, her mom's pretty sick."

Anne frowned, but her green eyes looked compassionate. "She seems like a nice person, and I was truly touched by the kind things she said about my mother, but I don't plan to contact her, Will. I don't have time."

Will heard the finality in her tone, but he couldn't let it go. "Maybe not in your real life, but you'll have spare time with this job. When your mother ran this place, she still managed to maintain a very active life in the community. Are you saying you're not as organized as Esther?"

Her shoulders stiffened. "I'm saying I don't plan to go out of my way to meet people this summer. When I'm not working, I want to spend my free time with Zoey. Do you have a problem with that?"

"No." He paused. "Well, actually, yes."

She picked up the molded-cardboard container that held eighteen eggs and gave him a flinty glance. "Tough."

He bit down on a grin. He didn't know why he was baiting her. This wasn't any of his business, but he enjoyed ruffling her feathers. He leaned against the counter and crossed his arms. "You know, Anne, I think you might be a bit of a snob. People in high school thought so, too."

She fumbled the carton, nearly dropping the eggs. She faced him, eyes flashing. "That's ridiculous. This whole conversation is ridiculous. You're taking me to task for avoiding a short-term relationship with a woman I've barely met and that means I'm a snob? You're crazy."

He threw back his head and laughed. "That's a given. I ride bulls."

"Why are you arguing with me? I'm an adult. I don't

need you to arrange play dates for me. If I want to make friends, I will.''

''You just said you won't.''

She crammed the carton into the nearly full refrigerator and slammed the door. ''I don't plan on it, but I could if I wanted to.''

''Maybe you have an inferiority complex.''

Hands on hips, she growled, ''Now you're a psychologist? Hmmph, maybe those frequent falls on the head did permanent damage.''

''What are you guys fighting about?''

Anne whipped about, bumping into the stove with a grunt. Will put out a hand to steady her, but she hopped out of reach. ''Hi, honey, we were just talking.''

Zoey didn't look convinced, but she let it go with a shrug and asked, ''Can I have an apple?''

Anne nodded toward the fruit basket she'd left on the counter. ''Wash it first.''

Zoey took the apple to the sink. She sent Will a curious sideways look. ''So what were you *talking* about? When I get to start my riding lessons?''

Will knew this wasn't the right time to broach that subject. He stepped close enough to tousle her hair then headed for the door. ''Speaking of horses, I've got to find someone to shoe the darn beasts.''

Zoey's bottom lip popped out, but the twinkle in her eye told him she got the message.

He paused at the door and asked, ''Should I come back for dinner or are we saving all this food for the guests?''

Zoey answered. ''Mommy hates to cook on days that she goes shopping. Grocery day is grilled-cheese-sandwish-'n-soup day.''

''Sounds good to me. Are we keeping A.J.'s schedule?'' he asked Anne, who looked a bit dumbfounded by the conversation that hadn't included her.

She sighed. "Do we have to?"

"No. You're in charge here. You get to set the rules."

Anne and Zoey exchanged a look. Will could almost see the silent communication pass between them. He didn't envy many people, but he'd have given just about anything to share that kind of connection with someone.

"Six," Anne said.

Zoey nodded and chomped into her apple.

Will smiled and left. Those two were something else. Something special. But from what he'd gleaned from talking to Zoey, they both could use more friends. Which was something he might just be able to arrange.

ANNE WAS IN HER ROOM preparing for bed when the phone rang. She picked it up hesitantly. What if it was that classmate of Will's? Anne couldn't understand why Will seemed so insistent that she get involved with this ridiculous homecoming party. It wasn't her class. She probably wouldn't even hear from her class next year.

"Yes?" she said cautiously.

"Annie? How did your first day go?"

"A.J.," she cried with delight. "Fine. It was good. How are you? Where are you?"

"Not quite as far as I thought I'd be, but I found a nice little campground near Winnemucca and decided to pull in. Had a bite to eat and now I'm getting ready to call it at night. But I got to thinking that I left without telling Zoey goodbye and that just didn't feel right. Can I talk to her?"

"Absolutely. She'll be so happy you called. She's turning into a prune in Mom's tub." A.J.'s gruff laugh made her blink back tears.

"Did you and Will get much done today?"

"We signed the papers at the lawyer's and went to the

bank, then I did a little grocery shopping—although Will will probably claim I bought out the place.''

"Good for you. Mary Jane will be happy to know we're back in business.''

Anne assumed Mary Jane owned the store. Her checkout clerk had been a jovial older woman, but Anne had kept her eyes on the digital display to avoid conversation. "I started reorganizing the office," she said, feeling strangely guilty about her unfriendly attitude. Maybe Will was right. Maybe she was a snob. "I hope you won't be totally confused when you take over.''

"I'm always lost on that computer. That's why your mother handled the books. I'll have to hire someone after you're gone.''

That worried Anne. She knew how easy it was for an unscrupulous person to rip off older adults, especially someone like A.J. who was used to being able to trust his wife implicitly. Anne would have to add "hire a new office manager" to her list of things to do. She'd need to make certain the person was extremely trustworthy. "Joy McRee is coming tomorrow. She sounded very capable on the phone. Maybe she'll be able to step into my shoes when I leave.''

She opened the bathroom door to a billow of steam. "Zoey, honey, dry off. It's Grandpa.''

Zoey let out a squeal of delight. "Gimme, gimme.''

Anne waited while Zoey splashed out of the tub and wrapped herself in a big, fluffy towel. She plopped to a sitting position on the mat and held out her hand for the cordless phone. Anne closed the door to let them talk in private. She was really touched that A.J. thought to call. He was such a wonderful man. He'd always treated Anne as if she was just as dear to him as his grandson. Who was going to be the death of her this summer.

Will was crazy. And opinionated. At dinner he'd made

it clear he thought Zoey should be allowed to learn how to ride. "Taking care of a horse is a big responsibility. Gramps gave me my first horse right after my parents died. He said I needed to think of something besides myself."

It had broken her heart to picture Will as a sad little boy crying against the neck of a horse, but that didn't mean she was ready to let her daughter spend time with large, dusty animals.

"Mommy, Grandpa wants you."

Anne retrieved the phone. "Get dried off so you don't catch a chill, hon." Closing the door, she said into the phone, "It was so sweet of you to call, A.J. She was pretty upset this morning."

"I know. Zoey told me. Probably scared the pants off my grandson."

Anne pictured the look of horror on Will's handsome face. "He handled it very well." *Then hightailed it out the door.*

"Good. Speaking of the devil, could you do me a favor and get him on the phone?"

Now? "Um, I don't think the portable will reach that far. Can I have him call you back?"

"I guess so. I'm at a pay phone. I'll give you the number and he can call me here in say…fifteen minutes or so."

Anne scribbled the number on the back of the first piece of paper she saw—the flyer that Linda had faxed this afternoon. "Okay, A.J., I'll get Zoey ready for bed then run to his cabin."

She started to hang up, but he added, "I'm glad you got out some today. You need to take time to relax. Maybe look up some old friends."

She swallowed her immediate reaction and mumbled a polite goodbye. Despite what Will thought, she did have friends. A few. From college. None who came to mind locally, but that wasn't because she was a snob. Shy, maybe. Introverted, perhaps, but she could live with that.

If Will couldn't? Well, tough.

She checked on Zoey, who was rescuing drowned dolls as water drained from the tub. "Hurry, honey, I have to run to Will's cabin. Get your jammies on and pick out a book to read when I get back."

In the foyer, she grabbed her jacket from the coat tree. She wasn't completely certain she knew which cabin was Will's, but the new outdoor lighting guided her in the right general direction.

A yellowish glow in a window of the most remote cabin became her beacon. She paused at the stoop to take a deep breath to relieve the stitch in her side, then mounted the step and rapped on the door. "Will, it's me."

She tried a second time but there was no answer. Too cold to wait around, she tested the door. Most hotel-room doors locked automatically. This one opened without hesitation. She poked her head in to see if he was asleep. Nope, the room appeared vacant.

Maybe he's at the barn. Anne walked to the desk beside the window. She'd leave him a note. If he didn't return in time, she'd call A.J. and make arrangements for them to talk the next day.

She'd just located a pen, when the white noise in the background that hadn't quite registered in her mind stopped. Curious to the cause, she lifted her head to listen. Comprehension dawned the same moment the bathroom door opened. *He's in the shower.*

Her eyes widened. Correction, *was* in the shower. Now he stood wonderfully, gloriously naked in the middle of the room.

CHAPTER FIVE

"WELL, GOD BLESS it, you're not supposed to be here," Will exclaimed, grabbing blindly for something to cover his nudity.

Unfortunately, the only thing in reach was a pair of chaps draped across the back of a chair. Chaps were made for function not modesty. Exasperated, he turned the stiff leather leggings sideways, pinning the ends together at his hip. A decorative suede fringe in his trademark silver bordered the outside edge of each leg and hung almost to his knees, like a hula skirt. Strangely, this embarrassed him more than standing around in his birthday suit.

"What's wrong? Is Zoey…?"

Anne shook her head. "No, she's fine." Her cheeks were crimson—whether from the cold night air or from seeing him naked was anybody's guess. Maybe a combination of both, he thought, because she definitely appeared discombobulated. She swallowed twice and made a motion toward the desk. "I…I was leaving a note."

Her gaze dropped to his feet then traveled upward, never quite making it past his chest. Will bunched the leather as tightly as possible with his roping hand to free up his other hand to swipe away beads of water trickling down his pecs. "Why?"

The word came out more sharply than he'd intended. She gave a startled little shiver and blinked. Her cheeks went a shade brighter. *Not the cold. Definitely not the cold.* "A.J.'s at a pay phone. Wants you to call him back. Tonight."

She looked away, as if finally deciding that yes, he truly was naked and she'd better do the right thing and leave. Will bit back a grin. Seeing Anne flustered was almost worth the peep show. Unfortunately, he'd noticed the way her gaze zeroed in on the matching scars on his shoulders, stiletto-like mementos of a not-too-distant surgery. He wasn't naive enough to think she'd find them glamorous.

"I'll be there as soon as I get dressed. I can change in the bathroom if you want me to walk you back."

She shook her head and opened the door. "I'm fine. I got here in one piece. I can get home. Zoey's waiting for me to tuck her in."

Apparently as an afterthought, she paused and added, "I'll leave the number on A.J.'s desk, okay?"

"Got it."

With the door partly closed, she called out, "Nice chaps, by the way. Very impressive."

Her amused tone made Will look down. And swear. The widest part of the design was to the rear, and the fringe didn't cover quite as much as he'd hoped it would. As the door clicked shut, he started laughing. To Anne's credit, she was cool under pressure. She might have blushed, but she didn't run.

Damn, he liked a woman with spunk.

Twenty minutes later, Will tiptoed upstairs. He didn't want to wake Zoey, but A.J. had asked him to give Anne a message. In the back of his mind, he wondered if the old man was trying to do some long-distance matchmaking. He doubted it—that was more Esther's style than A.J.'s—but it was possible his grandfather hoped Will would hang up his spurs and settle down.

The idea wasn't new. Last summer, well before she took ill, Esther had asked Will if he had ever thought about taking over the Silver Rose when she and A.J. retired. He'd blithely replied, "You bet, Esther. Right after I win the title of World Champion." And while the circumstances had changed with her death, Will's goal hadn't. He fully intended to help his grandfather as best he could, but that didn't include giving up his life's dream.

Besides, Will thought, swallowing the bad taste in his mouth, Gramps will never retire. The Silver Rose is his life. *Isn't it?*

At the landing, he turned left and walked the short distance to the master bedroom. The door was ajar; light spilled across the threshold. Although turnabout would have been delightful fair play—the thought of catching Anne in a towel made his heart rate increase and palms sweat—he knocked softly and called out, "Anne?"

She emerged from the bathroom towel in hand, dabbing her freshly scrubbed face. The rest of her was dressed in sweats. Unfortunately.

"Hi," she said, moving toward him. "I wasn't sure if you were still here or not. Is everything okay?"

"Pretty much."

A small sound from Esther's former sewing room made her put a finger to her lips. "Come," she whispered, nudging him back into the hallway. She dropped the towel on the bookcase where her mother kept family photos and led the way to a small settee in the main corridor.

She sat down, leaving room for Will to join her on the bench seat. The antique looked too dainty—and chummy—for his taste. He leaned against the wall a foot or so away. The overhead light fixture bathed the hallway in a golden hue that made Anne's freshly washed complexion even more luminous than usual. She peered up at him with an expectant look.

He wondered if he should say something about their

close encounter of the naked kind. "I'm not an exhibitionist. I hope you know that."

She put one hand to her cheek and smiled. "That was my fault entirely. How come there aren't autolocks on the doors of the cabins?"

Will shrugged. "Gramps hates carrying keys with him. He opted to provide small safes in each room instead of hassling with master keys and whatnot. Haven't you heard him say that a locked door is an affront to the code of the West?"

She smiled. "Come to think of it, yes. But I thought that only applied to not locking the front door of *this* house. Are the guests okay with it?"

"Seem to be. They keep coming back."

Neither spoke for a minute, then Will said, "Gramps wanted me to apologize to you for this morning. For leaving so abruptly. He was especially upset with himself for not waiting until Zoey got up."

Anne smiled. "So I gathered. They talked on the phone, and I think everything is okay between them. Zoey included him in her prayers tonight." She started to add something then seemed to change her mind. Instead, she said, "It's as much my fault as his. I'm not used to including other people in our lives, and I didn't expect her to be so upset."

"Is she asleep?"

Anne nodded. "Nothing like a good long soak in a bubble bath. That's where I'm headed next." Her gaze dropped to his shoulder. "You know, anytime you want to use the jetted tub, feel free."

Will was surprised by the offer. And pleased. "Thanks."

His good mood evaporated when she added, "I couldn't help noticing your scars. Are you in pain?"

He pushed off from the wall and shoved his hands in

his hip pockets. "Not really. I dislocated my left shoulder in Albuquerque when a bull stepped on it, and since I was going under the knife, the surgeon decided to scope the other side to fix an old tear."

She winced. "Sounds like a pretty dangerous job."

"Bull riding is considered an extreme sport. The higher up you get in the level of competition, the greater the risk."

"*Extreme,*" she repeated. "I hadn't realized bull riding fell into that category. Makes sense, though. One man taking on a thousand-pound bull."

"Actually, professional stock averages around twenty-two hundred pounds," he said, instantly wishing he hadn't.

Her eyes went round and her mouth formed an O.

To his complete surprise, her next question wasn't "Why would anyone be crazy enough to do that?" but "What does it feel like?"

He took his time answering. "You know those kids' toys with little colored chips that you turn round and round…?"

"A kaleidoscope," Anne supplied. "Zoey has one at home."

He nodded. "Sometimes a ride is like that. All you see is a rush of color and crazy impressions. The crowd noises blend together. You don't even feel the bull. Everything happens so fast it's a blur.

"Other times, every second is slow-mo. Each image is as clear as a photograph. Valley, peak, twist right, spin left, airborne, dirt." He slapped imaginary dust from his thigh. "Either way, afterward, you get up, grab your rope and starting thinking about the next ride."

"How does a person get started down that road? You don't just wake up one day and say I think I'll ride giant beasts for a living. Do you?" Her tone was curious not condemning.

"I began riding calves when I was six years old. Any more, I think you have to be older, but my dad busted broncs, did team roping and rode bulls at rodeos all over the state, and my mother was a barrel racer. Rodeo was a way of life. After they died and I moved to the Silver Rose, Gramps rigged up a bucking barrel to keep me out of my grandma's hair. After she passed away, A.J. started taking me to rodeos."

She nodded. "I remember. I went to visit my grandparents in Maine shortly before you left for the Nationals."

Will shook his head. "Where I came in second in my age group. I had the most points going into the competition, but scored a zero on my last ride for touching the bull with my free hand." The disappointment of that heartbreaking loss had been the driving force behind Will's decision to turn pro instead of taking four years off to go to college.

Her eyes widened in a way that told Will she was recalling something from the past. "That's right. Mom said you were inconsolable, but I wasn't so sure. I heard rumors about nonstop parties."

Parties to hide the anger, booze to dull the pain. "At the time, I felt cheated," he said, chuckling at the enormity of his youthful pride. "I was absolutely positive I was the best bull rider in the country and I'd been robbed of my rightful title by a fluke."

"Nothing wrong with your ego," she said with a grin.

"Nothing that time and experience didn't cure. I was so sure I had what it took to be champ, I decided college would be a waste of time. So I went directly into the circuit so I could qualify for the pro tour."

Anne looked down at her hands folded in her lap. "I...um...checked the national standings on the Internet," she said. "You were right up there at the top. Until you got hurt."

Will was too shocked at first to reply. More from habit than pain, he rubbed his shoulder. Finally, he spoke. "I started off thinking it was just a matter of time before I made my fortune and won the title. But here I am still in the running for the gold ring—only the pack of contenders has gotten bigger, better and younger. And while I'm on medical leave, they're earning the points I need to stay on top."

Anne rose and stretched. She rolled her neck as if she'd been carrying the weight of the world on her shoulders. It took all his willpower not to touch her. *Just a friendly massage. That's all.* He stuffed his hands deeper in his pockets.

"I know what you mean. I'm this close to getting the key to the executive washroom," she said, illustrating her point with a quarter inch between her thumb and index finger. "But instead of making career points, I'm hanging out in Nevada for three months."

He was curious about her life, her goals. "Do you like your job?"

"Does anybody?" Without waiting for an answer, she added, "I like parts of it, but overall it's not exactly what I'd planned." She gave a wry chuckle. "In college I pictured this fabulous career in hotel management. I'd travel extensively, save my money and eventually buy an exclusive little inn in Greece or Bermuda. Instead, I'm caught in the corporate eddy, fighting my way to the top of the food chain."

"If the feeding frenzy is getting to you, you could always stay here and run the Silver Rose for A.J.," Will said.

Her shocked expression made him feel like an idiot. He knew nothing about her world. His suggestion was probably on par with suggesting Donald Trump run a Mc-Donald's franchise.

She straightened the framed Frederic Remington reproduction on the wall behind the settee. "A.J. might be putting the property on the market this fall. Even if my promotion comes through, it'll be years before I can afford to buy a place of my own."

Hiring a manager was one thing, but selling the place…?

Will frowned. "I'm hoping that was just the grief talking, but if he did sell, I'm sure Gramps would let you buy on contract to deed, so you could pay him over time."

Anne's forehead crinkled. "That would hardly be fair to you."

He liked it that fairness was important to her, but he decided to be blunt. "I've done all right for myself, Anne. I took A.J.'s advice and invested my winnings in land. No houses, just land. All rented. The income makes up for times like this, when I'm not riding."

"Smart."

"Thank you."

"You're welcome, but it doesn't change the fact that A.J. is your grandfather by birth. I'm merely an interloper by marriage. The Silver Rose is your heritage." She said the last with a hint of reverence. He wondered why but decided to leave such weighty talk for another time. Their first day in business together had been a long one.

"My heritage is in need of one heck of a lot of work. A.J. should have kept a couple more hands on duty during the off-season, but he tends to try to do too much himself. Now, we're playing catch-up. The toolshed collapsed from the snow last winter. Part of the barn's roof blew off in a storm. The horses all need to be shod. And the dogs have worms. Don't ask how I know that."

She made a face and backed away from him. "Don't worry. I won't. And I'll keep Zoey away from them."

He snickered. "I already gave them deworming medicine. They'll be fine in a day or two. Also, I discovered two new litters of kittens if you want a house cat.''

Anne looked horrified at the prospect. ''Cat dander is one of Zoey's worst allergies. No indoor animals. Ever.''

Another dumb idea, dufus. ''Got it.''

She looked at him with a questioning tilt to her chin. ''I didn't mean to sound quite so dogmatic. Zoey can be around outdoor animals as long as she remembers not to rub her face after touching them, but cats seem to believe any space belongs to them, including beds and pillows. That would be very counterproductive to Zoey's breathing.''

''I understand. I'm glad you told me. Like I said before, if I knew more about what triggers an attack, I'd feel more comfortable around her.''

''I plan to update the Silver Rose's Web page tomorrow. I'll print some asthma articles for you while I'm online.''

''Thanks.'' He started to leave.

''Will, do you have a Web page? You know, for your riding?''

He paused at the top of the stairs. ''No. I'm a Stone Age relic. Never got into computers. But some of my friends have wwws. I'll make a list of their names if you want to check them out.''

He touched the brim of an imaginary hat then left. On the walk back to his cabin, he rehashed their conversation in his head. He figured he'd won a couple of points and lost a few others. Such was life, but what really confused him was why he cared. One quick summer, two people with really different lives. Not a favorable combination at all. No matter what her blush did to his libido.

ANNE SPENT the following morning in the office. A bush that had yet to leaf out blocked the room's only window. The ugly brown stalks reminded Anne of prison bars, and the heavy velvet drapes, while classy, contributed to the gloom. What would A.J. say if they accidentally appeared in the burn barrel? What if she painted the walls a warm yellow and boxed up all of the rustic knickknacks? Would he accuse Anne of defiling her mother's decorating legacy?

Maybe, she thought. Or maybe a fresh look would encourage him to spend more time in the office. She planned to ask Will his opinion as soon as she saw him. At least, paint was a nice safe subject, unlike the highly personal topics they'd covered the night before.

What on earth had possessed her to blurt out her dream? *An exclusive little inn in Greece or Bermuda.* Get real. That fantasy went down the tubes along with her marriage. Although her new job would mean a salary hike, Anne wasn't in a position to buy a home, let alone a hotel. Unlike Will, who could casually claim to own property— "land, no houses"—Anne was the stereotypical renter. That was something she desperately wanted to change, once her job allowed her to stay in one place longer than a year or two.

Thinking about Will brought to mind the image of his accidental nudity. He hadn't seemed overly embarrassed about the incident when they talked in the hallway. And Anne hadn't given it much thought, either, until she woke up in a wild tangle of covers, caressing her pillow like a lover. Even now, she could detect a distinctive tingle in places she could have sworn had lost the ability to tingle.

"I'm bored."

Anne looked across the room. Zoey stood in the doorway, Game Boy in hand.

"I'm just about done here, honey," Anne said, saving the changes she'd made to the Silver Rose Web page. She'd freshened up its look and streamlined the booking process. Although the current season was filled solid, cancellations had been known to occur. Now there would be a way to announce immediate vacancies and to contact people on a waiting list.

"It looks like a nice day. How 'bout some fresh air and exercise?"

"Horseback riding?" Zoey said, brightening.

"Gardening."

"Mom." The multi-syllable word was accompanied by a loud sigh.

Anne turned off the computer, jumped to her feet and charged around the desk. "Come on, lazybones. I bet I can plant more peas than you can."

Zoey never passed up a challenge. She pitched her hand-held game toward the couch and pivoted, her thick-soled shoes screeching against the oak flooring. "Nuh-uh," she cried and took off like one of the young colts Anne had seen frolicking in the pasture.

Anne had been thinking about the garden ever since Will mentioned it on their way home from town. He said Esther had left behind a how-to list. Anne didn't know the first thing about gardening. The only greenery in her apartment was silk—easy maintenance, no allergens. But Will's casual remark about Esther's "creamed peas and new potatoes" had triggered a memory: her mother teaching Anne how to make white sauce.

If she closed her eyes, Anne could almost inhale the fragrant steam from the butter and milk thickening in the pan. She recalled the shared sense of urgency as they'd stirred the mixture nonstop so it wouldn't get lumpy. Then, when the glistening white sauce was the desired consistency, Esther let Anne add the fat green jewels they'd picked from the garden that very morning.

Anne wanted to give Zoey that kind of *from-scratch* memory. And that meant planting a garden. The dirt and pollen were problematic, but if they worked early in the morning, Zoey might be able to handle the exposure. Anne had to try. Peas would be her first stab at a generational legacy.

With a chorus of "eeks" and "eouws" echoing in the rafters of the little shed, the two city girls battled past spiderwebs and dead bugs to load a garden cart with what Anne hoped were the proper tools of the trade—a rake, two hand trowels, an assortment of seed packages and the laminated instruction sheet written in her mother's clean, spare printing. Anne even found her mother's sun hat hanging on a post. After giving it a thorough shaking, she tied the faded scarf material under her chin. The straw crown sported several mice holes, but the brim was solid, if crooked.

"Oh, Mommy, that hat is too funny," Zoey said with a laugh.

"It beats age spots. I choose function over fashion."

"I'll say."

On the potting bench Anne found two sets of brand-new gloves, which she recognized as part of the Christmas gift she'd sent her mother. She blinked back tears as she pulled on a pair, then backed out of the shed, towing the wagon.

The sun was directly overhead. Around the Silver Rose compound the forest loomed—stately Jeffrey pines sharing space with various deciduous hardwoods just starting to leaf out. In the distance, a trail of silvery-barked aspens with iridescent-green buds marked the path of the creek that fed A.J.'s personal fishing hole.

The bright spring sunshine made Anne regret not going upstairs for her sunglasses, but she didn't want to risk losing Zoey's enthusiasm. "Isn't it a glorious day?" she said, pausing to take a deep breath of the clean, pine-scented air.

"Uh-huh. Can I plant carrots?" Zoey asked, examining an open seed packet. "I like carrots best."

Anne consulted the garden bible. On one side was a

hand-drawn map with a list of what fruits and vegetables went where. Adjacent to the A-frame greenhouse where someone had started a dozen flats of flower and vegetable seedlings were three raised beds about three feet wide and eight feet long separated by spongy, bark-lined corridors. Two hillocks were positioned at either corner, and a designated border with lattice for climbing plants followed the extra tall, deerproof fence.

As Anne looked around to get her bearings, she saw that her mother had prepared for winter by covering several of the raised beds with straw. Metal stakes proclaimed the intended usage. She spotted the word *zucchini* atop one mound and *melon* on the other.

Consulting the map, she said, "I think carrots belong in that small box beside the gate."

They headed there together, the wheels on the wagon making a cheerful squeaking sound. A moment later, they stood side by side assessing the box. Delicate green fronds poked through a layer of mottled straw. Zoey used her hands to brush aside the mulch. "These are pretty. Are they weeds?"

Anne consulted the chart, which included a rough sketch of each plant. Had her mother gone to this effort for A.J.? Had she known last fall that she might not be around come spring? Anne shook off the depressing thought. "Actually, honey, I think those little plants are carrots. Read this and tell me what you think."

Zoey sat on the edge of the box and read aloud: "Thin winter carrots in early spring. Taste like candy."

Anne and Zoey looked at each other. "Yeah, right," Zoey said. "Grandma was funny."

Anne silently agreed, but in her mother's defense, she bent over and attempted to pull one of the thin green shoots out of the soil. It snapped off cleanly right at the top of the infant carrot. "Oops."

Zoey's nimble little fingers probed beneath the damp soil and wiggled the miniature vegetable out of its home. "Wow. It's a teeny-weeny carrot."

"Made for teeny-weeny bunnies, perhaps?" Anne teased.

They took turns examining it. "It smells like a carrot. Should we eat it?" Zoey asked.

Anne shook her head. "It's covered with mud."

A foot away was a faucet wrapped in insulated foam; a hose sat coiled like a snake at its base. Zoey took the carrot to the impromptu sink and washed it thoroughly then returned, holding it aloft like a slick, wet Olympic torch. She thrust it at Anne. "You first."

Anne's mouth went dry. The only carrots she'd ever eaten came in plastic bags. Stalling, she pinched off the threadlike white root then bravely bit down. As she chewed, her saliva glands went into overdrive. It was sweeter than any carrot she'd ever tasted. Anne closed her eyes to savor the flavor. "It's like eating sunshine," she said, popping the remaining morsel into her mouth without thinking. "Delicious."

Zoey let out a shrill cry of outrage. "Mommy, you ate the whole thing." Tears erupted from her eyes and spilled down her cheeks.

"Oops. Sorry, sweetie. But, look," she said, redirecting her daughter's attention to the planter box. "There's a zillion more, and we'll never have big carrots unless we thin them. And eat them." Like candy, Anne heard her mother add.

Zoey's tantrum ended as quickly as it had begun. Sniffling, she wiped her cheeks with her muddy hand. The black smear resembled war paint, but Anne kept the observation to herself.

They both turned to the carrot patch and set to work

thinning. Every few minutes one of them would wash a handful of the candied treats and they'd munch and crunch.

Between bites, Zoey tried to teach Anne a song she'd learned in school. Appropriately, the lyrics were about bugs and slugs, but Anne was so lulled by the sun and the warm breeze she couldn't concentrate. Before she knew it, they had a basketful of minicarrots and a freshly weeded planter box. And, best of all, Zoey hadn't had an asthma attack.

They were sitting on a convenient wooden bench plotting their next move, when the clippity-clop of a horse's hooves filled the air. Zoey jumped up, spilling the carrots she'd been hoarding on her lap. "Look, Mommy, it's Will. Hi, Will, want some carrot candy?"

Anne knelt to pick up the fallen produce. From beneath the shaded brim of her floppy hat she could study Will sitting astride his large brown horse. Anne didn't know enough about the breed to be able to identify the exact make or model. It was a horse. It was big. And Will looked as if he belonged in the saddle.

Broad, muscular shoulders housed in crisp white cotton. His western-style shirt, neatly ironed, was tucked into snug Wrangler's. At his waist, the requisite buckle sparkled in the sunlight. Her mind recalled snippets of some talk she'd once attended called "Archetypes and the Modern Woman." The feminist lecturer theorized that "the cowboy" was a classic image that spoke to a woman's need to conquer new frontiers.

Frontier schmontier, Anne thought, her heart beating an erratic tempo. Try just plain sexy.

"How are you ladies doing this fine morning?" Will said, looping one leg over the horn of the saddle. He pushed his yellowish-white straw cowboy hat back and flashed them a million-watt smile. Anne wondered if he

had groupies—legions of adoring female fans who followed him from bull-riding event to bull-riding event.

"Josey here just got her new shoes and wanted to show
them off," he said, running his hand along the horse's
neck in an affectionate way.

Anne swallowed. Those hands had touched her in a similar way in her dreams.

"Hi, Josey. I'm Zoey," the little girl said, cramming the
toes of her Sketchers between the slats of the fence. She
pulled herself close enough to touch the horse's nose, but
Josey made a snuffling sound and arched her neck.

Zoey wobbled, almost losing her balance. Anne's instinct was to run to her, but she forced herself to wait.
Once she saw that her daughter wasn't going to impale
herself on a fence picket or topple beneath the feet of a
newly shod horse, she transferred the carrots to the bucket
and stood up.

"Baby carrots," Will exclaimed, leaning over as far as
his precarious position would allow. "Gramps mentioned
a winter garden, but to tell the truth, I wasn't paying attention. Got any to share?"

Anne offered him the pail. "With dirt or without?"

"Doesn't matter," he said, giving her a playful wink.
"Lord knows I've eaten my share of dirt over the years."
He grabbed a handful and sat back in the saddle. "Josey
would be happy to eat any of the tops you're throwing
away, Miss Z."

Anne watched him rub each little carrot between his
thumb and middle finger before popping it in his mouth.
He chewed with gusto. "Mmm, dang, these are good."

Anne still had the taste of carrot in her mouth, but suddenly she was ravenous for something more substantial
than a root vegetable.

Zoey bumped into Anne as she raced back to the carrot
box where their discarded tops littered the ground. Anne

realized she was staring. But not at Will's hands. As the heat rose in her cheeks, she dropped to one knee to help gather the now-wilted greenery.

"Can I feed her? Can I?" Zoey asked, clutching her bounty.

Anne watched Zoey approach the fence again. On her face, fear battled with yearning. Anne understood those diametrically opposed emotions all too well.

Josey apparently spotted the leafy-green bouquet and stepped closer to the fence. A single click from Will dampened her exuberance, but it was obvious she had high hopes the greens were meant for her. "Go ahead and hold them out," he told Zoey, returning to his original position in the saddle. "Just be sure to let go when she takes them. Her teeth are a long way from her eyes. She might accidentally get a finger if you're not careful. Josey loves carrots but isn't partial to fingers."

Anne clasped the bucket to her chest. Her baby's hand looked awfully small compared to the horse's mouth, and Josey's teeth resembled cogs in a garbage disposal. Anne was set to intercede until she looked at Will. Every single ounce of his attention was trained on her daughter.

She held her tongue. And her breath.

"Nice horsey," Zoey said, lifting her arm.

The green fronds shook like a wand in the hand of a fairy godmother with palsy. Josey didn't have a problem with that. Her large mouth opened; the stems disappeared.

Zoey clapped with joy. Anne quickly counted all ten fingers.

Before she could breathe a sigh of relief, Will asked, "How 'bout a quick ride with me, Miss Z? Just to the barn and back. I need to give the horseshoer a check."

Anne's initial protest was drowned out by her daughter's exuberant delight. "Oh, Mommy, please. I've never been on a horse and Josey likes me 'cause I fed her carrottops. Please.''

Anne wished she could be angry with Will for putting her in this position, but in all honesty, she'd known this showdown was coming. She'd already made up her mind that Zoey wasn't going near a horse without riding lessons and the proper safety equipment, but only a ridiculously overprotective parent would deny her daughter a chance to ride with an experienced cowboy. ''Okay.''

Zoey hugged Anne fiercely. ''Thank you, Mommy. Thank you. I'll write about it in my journal tonight.''

''Super. You promised Grandpa you'd write every night, remember?''

Zoey bounced back. ''Before, I didn't have anything to write about. Now, I do.''

Anne rolled her eyes and caught Will staring at her. He coughed and flexed his heels so the horse moved parallel to the fence. ''If you boost her up, we'll mosey around this area while you write out the check,'' he suggested. ''I can add my signature when I get to the barn.''

Anne took off her muddy gloves and dropped them in the wagon. A second later, her daughter was sitting astride the large brown horse, which now looked even bigger. Anne made herself ask, ''How much and to whom?''

He gave her the name and dollar amount and Anne dashed inside to write out the check. It was a simple task, except her hand was shaking so badly her signature was barely legible. She sat down in A.J.'s chair and took a deep breath.

How would my mother handle this? Anne asked herself.

The answer seemed obvious—in a manner exactly opposite to the way Anne was inclined to do things. Anne and her mother had disagreed constantly about parenting issues. Although she had never come right out and said it, Esther had implied that Anne tended to coddle Zoey.

"Risk is a part of life, honey," Anne could hear her mother saying. "You have to let Zoey try new things. She might get hurt, but at least she lived bravely."

Brave. Esther was without a doubt the bravest woman Anne had ever known. Her mother had courted risk, while Anne hid from it. To be precise, Anne assessed it carefully, assigned an acceptable loss factor and made an informed choice.

Anne knew that her mother had admired Will for following his dream, despite the toll bull riding took on his body. And while Esther had been supportive of Anne's choices, she had seemed faintly critical, too.

"You've done well for yourself, Anne, but are you happy?" Esther had asked toward the end.

Sorta. Kinda. Not really.

Then do something about it, a voice whispered.

Suddenly, Anne felt a strange sense of peace. She knew without the slightest doubt that she could trust Will to care for her daughter as if she were his own. And Anne also knew that if she was ever going to practice a little risk taking in her own life, now was the time.

Not with Will, per se—that would be just plain foolish—but in response to his challenge. Her mind made up, Anne rose. As soon as she returned to the office, she'd find the piece of paper she'd used last night to write down A.J.'s number. No doubt Linda would be surprised to hear from her.

ZOEY WAS IN LOVE.

The second her legs hit the saddle and her fingers wrapped around the stiff, coarse hair of the horse's mane, she knew she'd found heaven.

It didn't hurt that behind her Will's big, solid body made her feel safe. He seemed to be part of the saddle and he moved with the steady, easy rocking motion of the horse as they walked in a circle around the grassy yard at the base of the big tree.

"Have you tried out our swing, yet, Miss Z?" he asked, motioning to the black tire suspended on a long rope.

She shook her head. "Mommy said she needed to test it first. To see if it could handle my weight."

He didn't say anything for a few seconds. "Your mommy is smart. That rope has been hanging there for more years than I can remember. It could be frayed up high. I'll test it myself. That way, if the rope breaks, I'll hit the ground and not your mom. I'm used to hitting the ground."

She turned sideways just enough to look at him. "How come? Do you fall down a lot?"

"Sometimes, honey, it feels like that's all I do. I ride bulls for a living. Sorta like in a rodeo. Do you know what that is?"

"Of course. I'm not a baby."

"Sorry. I didn't mean to offend you. I just figured you might not have seen one since you live in a city. Although one of our biggest bull-riding events takes place in New York City."

"That's where I live. We used to live in New Jersey. And Pittsburgh. And…I forget. A bunch of places."

She leaned forward to stroke the horse's neck. "Does Josey like to be petted?"

"Yes, she does. Gramps told me Josey is a favorite with the people who come to stay here because she's gentle, but she can haul a…a lot of stuff when she has to."

"What kind of stuff?"

His mouth opened, but instead of answering he made a clicking sound and Josey lifted her head. The horse gave a little skip and Zoey grabbed for the funny-shaped knob in front of her. "There's your mom. Hang on, sweetie. We're going to try a trot."

The bouncing gait made Zoey's teeth rattle and her vision blur. Her insides felt jumbled and jittery. Not in a bad way, but she checked her pocket for her fast-acting inhaler, just in case.

They stopped abruptly in front of the gate where her mother was standing. She wasn't wearing the goofy hat, thank goodness. Her hair was messy in a cool way and she was smiling. A happy smile.

"How do you feel, honey? Are you having fun?"

Zoey ignored the first question. She was sick of people asking how she felt. "I love horseback riding. Can we buy a horse, Mommy? I'll take care of it. Really. I will."

Both adults laughed, which would have made her mad except she noticed the look her mother gave Will—friendly and nice. Zoey's breath stopped. *If Mommy likes Will, she might trust him to give me riding lessons.* Oh, man, Zoey thought, this could be great.

Suddenly, she had so many things to write in her journal she was almost sorry it wasn't bedtime.

CHAPTER SIX

As WILL CLOSED the door of his cabin behind him, he paused to look around the Silver Rose compound. He couldn't believe a week had passed since his grandfather's departure. Their first guests of the season had started arriving the previous Saturday. Four by land—two couples driving shiny SUVs, which were parked in a designated strip close to the cabins—and two by air. Will had played chauffeur, greeting Ms. Gustaffson and Mr. Taylor at the Reno airport. Unfortunately, they had arrived on different airlines and at different times.

Will was beginning to hate the drive to Reno. That, he told himself, was why he'd agreed to give Anne driving lessons this morning.

With a resigned sigh, he started toward the house. His reticence didn't stem from a reluctance to spend time with Anne. On the contrary, he enjoyed their contact, hit-and-miss though it was. They'd both been swamped with hiring personnel and prepping for guests, but her hastily scribbled notes and quick exchanges while signing checks had demonstrated her knowledge of the business.

She was a good judge of people, too. For instance, Anne hadn't hesitated to hire Joy McRee as head chef. It didn't hurt that the woman had shown up with a basket of cookies and a list of menus for the week.

"Joy is going to save my butt," Anne had confided at dinner the night before last. "I've overseen bigger kitchens, but it's been years since I actually cooked for a large group. And Joy's even willing to handle the bunkhouse, too. Plus, she's talking about expanding Mom's 'Old Time Cooking Lessons' to include men.''

Will liked the sound of that—anything to take some of the entertainment pressure off his back. He truly had no idea how his grandfather, a hermit at best, juggled all the responsibilities that came with running a ranch and entertaining a bunch of city slickers as well.

''Oh, William,'' a voice hailed. ''Just the man we need.''

Will put on his PBR meet-and-greet smile then turned to face the couple marching toward him. The tall, thin woman and her several-inches-shorter husband were in their late fifties. Both wore hundred-dollar cowboy hats and handmade boots.

''Howdy,'' he hailed. ''Isn't this a glorious Nevada morning? What can I do for you folks?''

''Buddy was wondering if you could teach him how to ride bulls,'' the woman answered. Will had noticed she did most of the talking.

''Got a hankerin' for a couple of broken bones, Bud?''

The man shook his head. ''Not exactly,'' he said. ''More like a photo op. We couldn't help but notice that rigging you have behind the barn. A bucking barrel, I believe it's called. Cherish thought it would make an excellent picture to show the guys back home.''

''A simulated ride,'' Cherish added, waving her compact digital camera. ''We could add the bull later.''

Will smiled. ''Wish I'd thought of that. Could have saved myself a couple of surgeries.''

They set up a time that would provide the best light, then Buddy and Cherish waved goodbye. Since today was a ''free day'' on the ranch, the pair had opted to join a group visiting Virginia City, the historic Comstock Lode boomtown that was a favorite of tourists.

As he resumed his walk, three cowboys on horseback, each shadowed by a novice cowpoke, trotted past. Whenever possible, Will tried to pair beginning riders with experienced ones. Tomorrow his crew was scheduled to move the Silver Rose herd from his grandfather's land to a leased field a few miles away. The three-hour job would probably take six thanks to their extra *help,* but Will figured that went with the territory.

And, fortunately, none of his hired men was likely to complain. Like Anne, Will had been blessed to have job applicants with Silver Rose experience on their résumés. In cowboy terms, that meant they showed up, named the ranchers they'd worked for then unloaded their gear in the bunkhouse.

He glanced at his watch and picked up the pace. Anne liked schedules, he'd noticed. Her housekeepers, three high-school girls, had an allotted time to complete the rooms before Anne followed with a checklist. Somehow, Will doubted that Esther was that detail oriented. But, so far, he'd heard nothing but positive comments from their guests.

The real test would come next week when every room was filled. Between dropping off existing guests and picking up new ones, they had six trips to Reno scheduled. Hence the driving lesson.

"It isn't fair that you do all the picking up and dropping off," Anne had told him Sunday night as he'd lugged their newest guest's massive suitcase up the stairs. Gina Gustaffson, a history teacher with a passion for architecture had been delighted to learn that she would be staying in the main house instead of a cabin. A.J. had cut her a deal on her two-month booking.

"I love the ranch house," she'd exclaimed with a thick Boston accent. "Classic turn-of-the-century function versus form. I plan on working on my book while I'm here.

It's called *From Log Cabin to Brothel—The Western Way of Building*.

"Your mother was so helpful last year, Anne. She'd drop me off at the library, then pick me up in time for happy hour at the local saloon."

Somehow Will couldn't picture Anne swigging a cold brew at the Alibi Bar and Lounge. Nor could he picture her behind the wheel of Esther's SUV, but that was her intention.

"Hello," Will hollered as he entered the kitchen. With any luck, there'd still be a leftover doughnut or two. He'd missed breakfast at the bunkhouse because of a plumbing problem in cabin six.

"Hi, Will," a youthful voice called. Zoey waved from her perch on a stool in front of the prep counter. She sported an oversize white apron wrapped under her armpits and tied at her chest. "I'm learning how to make sour-cream raisin cookies and debil-delight fudge today."

He walked to her to accept the hug she offered.

"Debil?" he repeated, patting her head. They hadn't spent much time together this week—no repeat horseback rides—and he found he missed her bright smile and spontaneous affection.

She nodded, her tongue worrying the gaping hole where her bottom teeth were just coming in. "It has a *b* in it, not a *v*."

"How come?"

"'Cause this fudge is so *good*," a gruff voice answered, "the devil thought it might hurt his reputation."

Will glanced over his shoulder as Joy McRee walked into the room. A squat woman with thick arms and a cap of silver curls, she looked as though she could wrestle a bull to the ground with sheer willpower. Anne followed a pace behind, two travel mugs in her hands. "'Morning, Will. Right on time," she said, offering him one of the fragrant brews. "Thanks so much for doing this. Are you hungry? I can probably find you a couple of Joy's fabulous doughnuts."

Hungry? He was starved. But something about Anne's brisk manner told him she was in a hurry to get this lesson behind her. "This'll do, thanks," he said, taking the cup.

When she turned to address her daughter, Will covertly studied her. Conservative tan walking shorts. Crisply pressed white shirt with sleeves rolled back to the elbows. White, heelless flats and no socks, which drew his focus to her shapely calves and perfect knees. Had he ever in his life noticed a woman's knees?

Realizing he was staring like a randy teen, he took a sip of coffee…and scalded the roof of his mouth. He couldn't prevent the flinch and looked around to find Joy eyeing him speculatively.

"Are you sure you have everything you need, Joy?" Anne asked, crossing to the message board beside the phone. A set of keys attached to a tooled-leather key bob sporting the distinctive Silver Rose brand—two intricately entwined silver initials making up a flower motif—dangled from a hook. "We could stop at the store while we're in town."

"Got eggs, butter, flour, chocolate and a few secret ingredients that only me 'n Zoey know about," the cook said, wrapping her pudgy arm about the little girl's shoulders.

"Which you intend to share with the guests who've signed up for the class, right?" Anne asked, her tone worried.

"Mebbe," Joy said with an exaggerated wink. Zoey giggled and tried to copy the wink.

Anne's smile looked wistful, and Will wondered if she was wishing Esther were the one giving Zoey a cooking lesson.

"Now, git going so Zoey and I can plan our business," Joy said, pointing toward the door. "If these turn out, we might give Famous Amos a run for his money."

"Okay," Anne said. "You have my cell number if you need me. You took your pills this morning, right, honey?"

Zoey made a huffing sound and turned her back on her mother. "Yes."

Will gave the little girl a playful tap on the nose. "Save me a cookie?"

Her cheek-to-cheek grin was accompanied by a fervent nod.

As Will followed Anne outside, he thought about Zoey's obvious bid for independence. Anne was a wonderful mother, but somewhat overprotective, in his opinion. Zoey seemed pretty healthy despite her asthma issues, and Anne had admitted to him that Zoey's condition seemed to be improving with age. But neither matter was any of his business. He needed to remember that.

At the garage, Anne reached inside the walk-in door to hit the automatic opener. A.J.'s '83 Ford F–100 truck and Esther's Forerunner sat side by side. Will housed his monster truck at the barn. Out of sight, so it wouldn't scare the livestock, some wise guy had joked.

"So," he said, taking a sip of coffee. "I gather we're still going to town today?"

Anne pulled a pair of sunglasses out of an organizer-type purse. Her mug was pinched to her side as she juggled keys, a sheaf of papers and the shades. He would have offered to help, but she seemed intently focused. When she was ready, she answered, "Yes. I told Linda I'd drop off the revised menu for the banquet. I could have faxed it, but since I need practice parking, I thought we could stop at the law office."

Her lips pursed pensively. He couldn't help noticing that her lipstick was an evocative shade of wine. "That's not too ambitious, is it? Should I stick to the back roads a while longer?''

Will had no doubt Anne would catch on quickly, and the longer he spent in her company, the more he would think about things that he really shouldn't. "You'll do fine," he said, meaning it. "But you might want to let me back out of the garage."

Anne handed him the keys. "No argument there. Find me a nice straight stretch of road. Preferably somewhere flat, like in the desert."

The leather key bob held residual warmth from her hand. Will pinched the molded-plastic grip of the key and started for the driver's-side door. "Okay, let's do it."

Twenty minutes later, he pulled to a stop on the gravel shoulder of a deserted stretch of highway with high-desert terrain in every direction as far as the eye could see. "This should work. No walls. Just sagebrush and a few scrub cedars to slow you down if you accidentally go cross-country."

He took a sip of coffee and placed the mug in the cup holder. After setting the emergency brake, he tapped the leather-covered shifter to make sure it was in neutral then opened the door and got out. Anne met him in front of the vehicle.

"Ready?" he asked.

She lifted her hand in a mock salute. Her saucy smile made him want to kiss her.

Bad idea. Bad idea, he silently repeated, pausing with one hand on the passenger-side door. Her image had been flitting about in his dreams the past couple of nights. So far, Will had managed to attribute this attraction he felt for Anne to their forced proximity. Somehow he doubted the narrow confines of this car would help matters.

"Are you afraid?" she called. "Or trying to remember if your life insurance is paid up?"

Chuckling, Will climbed in. "I ride bulls for a living. I guarantee there's nothing you can do that will be rougher than that. Do you want to go through the shift pattern again?"

She swallowed then placed her hand on the shifter. "Yes, please."

"Push the clutch all the way to the floor and hold it," he said, reaching across his body to use his right hand, too. Her skin was soft, her fingers small and breakable. He tried to keep their contact to a minimum as he guided her through the gears, but even that slight touch made him want more.

"Got it?" he asked, his voice hoarse.

"I think so." Did she sound a bit winded, too?

Will secured his seat belt and picked up his travel mug. "Now, put it in first gear and slowly release the clutch while giving it gas."

Her first attempt resulted in a stalled engine and a splat of coffee on his shirt. Anne apologized profusely, but Will was too distracted by her blush to care about his shirt.

The next try was better. Half an hour later, she was driving like a pro.

"You're a quick study," he said as they approached the outskirts of town.

"You're a good teacher."

Will doubted that. Given their close quarters and her evocative scent—he wouldn't call it perfume, exactly, but whatever it was reminded him of apple pie and fresh air— Will could barely keep his mind on the lesson at hand.

"Do you mind if I open the window?" he asked.

Anne shook her head. "Go ahead. It's warm in here."

Understatement. His internal thermostat was on well done.

"Actually, I'm feeling pretty comfortable with the mechanics of shifting, but the real test will come when I hit traffic.''

Will coughed. "Please don't use that word."

She glanced sideways. "Traffic?"

"Hit."

Her laugh reached deep inside him and sparked to life something he'd forgotten he possessed—the ability to be silly. Anne was fun to be around. Why hadn't he known that?

"Right or left?" she asked as they reached the intersection. "I can't remember."

"Right."

He watched her intently study the traffic, anticipating when to work the clutch and how much brake to apply. Ten minutes later they were safely parked in front of the lawyer's office.

"We did it," she cried, leaning over to turn off the key.

"You did. I was a mere passenger."

She swiveled in the seat to face him. "Will, don't undervalue your contribution. You're a wonderful teacher. Gentle and patient. And you explained the mechanics of the operation in a way that made sense to me, an automotive illiterate. I couldn't have done it without you."

He didn't know what to say so he said nothing. She smiled again then reached behind Will's seat for the paperwork he'd seen resting on the floor. Her stretch brought her breast in contact with his arm. Two layers of cotton and her bra separated them, but Will felt the touch much deeper.

Without being too obvious, he opened the door and got out.

"Are you going in?" Anne asked, returning to an upright position. She didn't appear to have noticed his discomfiture. "I should warn you, Will. Linda is determined to get you to the reunion. You'll be fair game if you walk through that door.''

Better than dwelling on an attraction that could only lead to trouble, Will thought. He didn't do affairs, especially when there were kids in the picture. He'd learned that lesson the hard way. Plus, he wasn't about to do something that might wreck his relationship with A.J. ''Actually,'' Will told her, ''I'm kinda curious about what you two are planning.''

That wasn't a complete lie. For a woman who eight days earlier had insisted she didn't have time for friends, Anne seemed to have jumped into this reunion gig whole hog.

She picked up her purse and got out, locking the door behind her. Will's door was shut but not locked. Anne shook her head. ''Old dogs, new tricks, right? I'm a chronic locker.''

''There are worse habits,'' he said, ushering her toward the law office.

Linda wasn't at her desk, but her delighted squeal a minute later proved she was in the building. She hurried into the reception area. Dressed in a black skirt and another sweater set—or was it the same one?—she hugged Anne and bussed Will's cheek. ''The menu!'' she exclaimed when Anne handed her the papers. ''Excellent. Did you bring the music list, too?''

Anne pointed out two sheets obviously printed from some Internet site. Linda scanned both pages. ''Oh, wow, this is great. Peter Gabriel, U2, Guns N' Roses, Pet Shop Boys… I hate to admit this, but I love the music of the eighties.'' She gave them a sheepish smile.

''Me, too,'' Anne said. ''Sting, with or without The Police. And anything by Dire Straits.''

''Dire Straits,'' Linda exclaimed. ''Didn't you love 'Money for Nothing'? She started singing—or rather, mumbling and humming the tune, since she obviously didn't remember the words.

A buzzing sound cut her off and she dashed to the desk. Intrigued by this new revelation, Will asked, "Are you a deejay, too?"

"Not even close," Anne said with a grin. "I put together the music list for a themed party at one of our hotels a couple of months ago. I had the Web sites saved on my laptop, so I told Linda I'd print out some titles for her to give the deejay they hired."

"You two wanna go to lunch?" Linda asked before pushing the button on her phone. "Grady's Grill is still open."

Anne shook her head. "I'd better get back to the cooking class. I'm not sure how well Zoey will handle the flour and spices. Thanks, though. Maybe next week." She seemed to consider her words then changed her mind. "Actually, next week is our first full house. I might not survive."

Linda put the phone to her ear, covered the mouthpiece and whispered, "Call me." To Will, she gave a stern look and said, "Send in your registration."

Will flashed a peace sign then followed Anne to the door. Once outside she seemed to hesitate, as if she had something serious on her mind. "You know, Will, I owe you an apology."

"For what?"

"For being so defensive when you suggested I call Linda. She's a lovely person, and I'm enjoying our friendship."

Will knew it wasn't easy for her to admit this. "Good. I'm glad you two hit it off. Does that mean you're going to the party?"

She shook her head. "Heavens, no."

"Why not reap the rewards of your labor?"

She shrugged and started toward the parking lot. "Linda asked me to go with her, but then she mentioned that her older brother would be going, too. That sounded a little bit too much like a date."

"What's wrong with a date?" Will asked, trying to place Linda's older brother. He seemed to remember she had two. One was a real loser.

Anne laughed as if he'd delivered the punch line to a joke. When he didn't laugh, too, she sobered and said, "I've found them to be an exercise in futility. Most men don't want the same things women want."

"Namely?"

"Love, joy, commitment, family."

He knew a lot of guys who put sex, fun, pleasure and freedom far ahead of the items on her list but felt compelled to defend his sex. "Beware of rash generalizations, Anne. They can come back to haunt you."

She didn't look too worried. "Maybe," she said, unlocking her door. "But I'm only here for the summer. Why bother...?" Will could tell by her blush that she caught the familiarity of the refrain. Letting out a sigh, she leaned over to unlock Will's door, but he'd already opened the unlocked door and started to settle into his seat.

Her shoulder connected with his ribs, and he made a grunting sound.

"Oh, dear, did I hurt you?" she asked, pressing her hand to his side. Her delicate fingers kneaded the flesh beneath his shirt in a gentle, butterfly-like touch. Will's breath hissed but not from pain. His reaction to her touch was too immediate, too male, for such cramped quarters.

"I'm fine," he said, brushing her hand away. Too long without a woman's touch, his body's response was natural but unwelcome. He didn't want Anne to think he was the same randy cowboy she'd known in high school.

Anne sat back. "Okay, then. A quick stop at the hardware store before we head back home, right?"

The hardware store? Damn. He'd forgotten about his promise to fix the leaky sink in the upstairs bath. He almost cursed his grandfather for teaching him such practical skills.

She waited, the engine idling.

"Yeah, fine," he said. A promise was a promise.

BY THE TIME they reached the Silver Rose, Anne was ready to call her first driving lesson a complete failure. True, she'd driven the car with some success, but something had gone amiss between her and Will. She wasn't sure what. On the way to town, he'd been very hands-on—helping her shift, prompting her to remember the clutch, praising her for getting it right. For most of the trip home, he'd kept his focus out the window, answering her questions with a barely audible yes or no.

Anne didn't like moody men. Toward the end of her marriage, Barry had driven her crazy with his temperamental mood swings. She didn't plan to put up with that kind of attitude in the workplace.

She pulled the car to a stop in front of the mailbox.

Will's head came up, and she felt his gaze follow her as she retrieved the thick wad of envelopes. Once back inside, she sorted them aloud. "Bill. Advertisement. Credit-card application. Bill. Check. Postcard from A.J."

Will lowered his window all the way and shifted his body to lean against the door. He looked as though he wanted to be as far away from Anne as possible. "What's it say?"

She studied the scenic shot of the Grand Tetons then flipped the card over and scanned the text. "I'll read it aloud but not until you tell me why the silent treatment for the last fifteen miles."

He took a deep breath and let it out. "I'm sorry, Anne. I didn't mean to be rude. I put close to forty thousand miles on my truck last year. When I'm driving, it's usually just me, my thoughts and the road."

"You're not upset about something?"

"No. Well, actually, yes. I'm worried about filling Gramps's boots once the guests arrive. He said my job was taking care of the herd, but obviously there's more to it than that."

Anne could sympathize with that, and she felt a little sheepish for attributing his silence to her. "I've had my share of nervous butterflies in my tummy the past few days, too. Maybe we should put our heads together and brainstorm."

His Adam's apple rose and fell. "When?"

"Tonight? After dinner? It's movie night."

Will's lips twitched. She couldn't explain why, but his smile made her want to smile back. Or touch him.

"Ah, yes," he said, "a classic kung fu movie with kung pao chicken. I overheard the couple from Santa Cruz discussing it. They couldn't wait."

Offering a themed dinner and movie once a week had been Anne's idea. She had yet to see if it would pan out.

"I just signed up for an online DVD service. Joy is having a blast planning future menus to go with certain movies. Pizza and pasta for the *Godfather* series. One of A.J.'s western barbecues to go with *Unforgiven*. The only one I refused to consider was *Silence of the Lambs*."

He made a face, but his chuckle let her know he wasn't appalled. "Speaking of A.J., what does his card say?"

Anne drew it from the stack on her lap and read aloud: "'Dearest family, reached Jackson Hole last night. Couldn't believe how much the place has changed. Esther wouldn't have cared much for it—too many people. But the mountains are mighty pretty and the nip in the air reminds me of home. Yellowstone tomorrow. Love, Gramps. P.S.—bought Zoey a bear cub. Stuffed.'"

Anne groaned without thinking.

His questioning look made her explain. "Stuffed animals are problematic. The fake fur is a dust catcher and they don't wash well."

Knowing she probably came off as an overprotective worrier, Anne changed the subject. "A.J. sounds a little disillusioned, doesn't he?"

Will shrugged. "Nothing stays the same. Nobody knows that better than A.J."

"True, but it's easier to hold on to our illusions from a distance than face them point-blank."

Will looked at her for a few seconds, then nodded. "Can't argue with that." He nodded toward the paper sack by his feet. "If we hurry, I might be able to get the sink fixed before our guests return from their outing."

Anne could take a hint. Obviously, Will didn't want to spend any more time in her company than absolutely necessary. Okay. She could live with that. In fact, she'd probably pay for this driving lesson with a week of steamy dreams. What a shame her libido couldn't fixate on a more suitable subject—like some unattainable movie star. Will was just as handsome as Russell Crowe, but far too close for comfort.

She stepped on the clutch and put the car in gear.

WILL WALKED to his grandfather's desk and sat down. Anne would be joining him in a minute and he needed to get his head focused on the business at hand. Ever since their driving lesson that morning, he'd been castigating himself for reading too much into Anne's friendly attitude. She was loosening up around him and that was good—for business. It didn't mean she was interested in him as a man.

The door opened, and Anne slipped in, her hands full.

Will quickly raced around the desk to help. The aroma of freshly popped popcorn and melted butter made his mouth water. He relieved her of a grease-stained paper bag and reached for one of the bottles pressed tightly to her chest, but decided against risking the touch.

As he closed the door, he heard the sound track of a movie playing in the living room. "Is Zoey watching the show?"

"Yeah, it's summer. She can stay up later as long as she doesn't get run down."

With a mischievous smile, she held up two amber bottles.

"Beer?"

His shock must have been obvious because she grinned sheepishly. "Root beer. I'm not much of a drinker."

That didn't surprise him.

She walked to the middle of the room and looked around. "I thought we could sit on the floor. Keep it casual. Formal business meetings can be counterproductive to creative energy. We want to keep this fresh, right?"

Fresh? "Um...okay."

Anne flashed him a grin then set the pop bottles on the desk. "Let's move these chairs out of the way," she said, leaning over to push on the rolled arms of the smaller leather chair.

Will set down the greasy bag and rushed to help. "Careful. Those are heavy. You'll throw your back out and then where will we be?"

"Don't worry. I'm stronger than I look," she said, grunting from the effort.

"Well, you're full of surprises. Root beer and popcorn aren't exactly what I pictured when you suggested this."

She pulled the cushion from the chair and dropped it on the rug in front of the fireplace. "Actually, whatever you imagined is probably right. I'm usually very staid and conservative—'' A blush accented her rueful grin. "Actually, I think *anal* is the word." Motioning him to bring the popcorn, she collapsed in a cross-legged pose on the cushion. "But I'm trying to be more like my mother this summer. Doesn't root beer sound like an Esther idea?"

"Esther would have brought real beer."

Her laugh went belly deep. It made him want to kiss her.

Instead of the shorts she'd had on earlier, she wore loose drawstring pajama bottoms and a sloppy khaki sweatshirt that revealed a white tank undershirt. Her feet were bare. She looked sixteen.

"Come on," she said, prompting him to join her. "We've only got two hours to come up with a plan."

He started to comply, trying to decide whether or not to kick off his boots. "Oh, wait," she said, pointing to the desk. "Could you grab those papers for me, please? And the colored marking pens."

Will put the popcorn bag between his cushion and hers, then returned for the writing utensils. Fearing he might have donned socks with holes in the heels, he opted to leave his boots on. After settling himself with far less grace than Anne displayed, he took a healthy swig of his soda, ruing its lack of alcohol.

"Let's start with the basics," Anne said, selecting a neon-green pen from the pile. "We've got our staff in place. We have history on our side. How hard can it be?"

"History?"

She nodded. "I was thinking this morning, that we could poll returning guests for their Best Silver Rose Memories. I could tell them we want to put together a memory book for A.J., then we could pilfer as we like."

Will nodded. "That's a great idea, Anne. Gramps would be really touched."

She frowned. "Um...I hadn't actually planned to do a book, but I suppose I could. Or maybe a video. Does A.J. have a camcorder?"

"Yes, although he might have taken it with him. Esther and Gramps came to a couple of events and recorded my rides."

"Really? I wonder if the tape is around. I'd like to see you in action."

"No, you wouldn't. I'm pretty sure the last one shows me getting hung up then stomped on." Instead of a pleasant weekend escorting his family around Fort Worth, he'd been stuck in the hospital getting MRIs and CAT scans.

Anne took a handful of popcorn and shoved the whole thing in her mouth. Another surprise. He had her pegged as a nibbler—one kernel at a time. When she finished chewing, she asked, "How long ago was that?"

"Last fall."

"Hmm. So, let's brainstorm. All we have to do is keep eighteen couples and the occasional single happy for twelve weeks. How hard can it be?"

Her upbeat manner made him smile, but Will had a feeling guest services was going to be the easy part of this partnership.

In broad, fluid strokes, Anne jotted down her ideas. "Joy suggested we put on a weekly ice-cream social. I found two hand-crank ice-cream freezers in the pantry. Maybe if we buy one more electric unit, we could handle the demand." She wrote that down, then added pink ice-cream cones. "And what if we invite some local cowboy poets and storytellers to give a presentation? Joy said she has several names."

"How much would they charge?" Will asked, sampling the salty snack. "I don't remember seeing anything in the budget for performers."

Anne nodded. "True, but usually that kind of artist has

audiotapes or books to sell, and they're grateful for the exposure."

"Good point. Something like that could easily take care of one day a week. And your dinner-and-movie night appears to be a big hit, so there's another day covered."

Her cheeks colored slightly. "Thank you. Joy gets most of the kudos. It was my idea, but she ran with it."

Will liked the way she shared the credit. Will liked her. Period.

"Oh," Anne said, waving a fistful of popcorn. "The last time he called, A.J. asked if we'd planned a barbecue yet. A weekly old-fashioned barbecue would be great, wouldn't it? Outside when the weather is nice. Or in the barn. It could be our big Saturday-night send-off."

Will wiped his fingers on his jeans then picked up a red marker to add her suggestions to the pad. It amazed him how in sync their minds were. Before long they had ten items on the list.

Anne flipped onto her back. "Some of these ideas are great, Will. Like turning a trail ride into a high-meadow picnic."

Her enthusiasm was contagious, but Will felt compelled to warn her of the downside. "Don't forget that we're billed as a working cattle ranch. A lot of the guests plan to participate in the day-to-day business of ranching. We can offer a few special events, but mostly we just need to feed 'em and work 'em."

Anne closed her eyes. "I wish it were that easy where I come from."

Will kicked his legs out in front of him and eased back on his elbows. Their bodies formed an L on the Persian rug. "I would have thought the hotel business was easier than a B&B," he said truthfully. "You only have to feed people if they come to your restaurant."

She opened her eyes and stared at the ceiling. "WHC

has venues all over the world. A fluctuation in the dollar or a strike in Japan or a monsoon in China can compromise our bottom line. We don't just think up a new idea and implement it. First, we need market studies, focus groups and earnings projections. It's complicated.''

Complicated. What in life wasn't? Will had a very big complication in mind at the moment.

He reached out and took a lock of her hair between his fingers. The color, he decided, was actually a multitude of shades, ranging from white blond to reddish gold. She turned her chin, slim eyebrows arched in question.

''I want to kiss you.''

Her mouth dropped open, but Will could tell this wasn't an invitation. ''That's not a good idea, Will.''

''Why?''

She sat up but didn't scoot away. ''For a number of reasons, but the first that comes to mind is that we tried this before and it didn't go anywhere.''

Will didn't reply, because that wasn't the answer he'd been expecting. ''You don't remember, do you?'' she asked, her tone slightly miffed.

Will remembered, but before he could say anything, Anne prompted, ''High school. A few weeks before your graduation. There was this unusual heat wave, and A.J. hadn't installed central air yet. My room was stifling so I was reading on the porch. You came up to the house for something. We shared a soda. We talked. You kissed me. Then you left. Something about a date with your former girlfriend.'' She shrugged. ''No big deal.''

''If it wasn't a big deal, why are we talking about it?''

She sighed. ''Okay. I'll admit, I was a little heartbroken for a few days. I'd been nursing this crush on you for months, so when you kissed me, I thought...well, it doesn't matter. But later, when I saw you and Judy in school, and you were laughing and I...''

"You thought we were laughing at you?" he finished. "You pegged me as a kiss-and-tell kind of guy?" Will was more put out than he thought possible. Why should he care about something that happened—or rather, didn't happen—fifteen years ago?

She made a supplicating gesture. "I didn't know many boys, Will. I barely knew you—even though we'd lived in the same house for six months. You were so far above me in the high-school caste system I'm surprised you even acknowledged me in the hallway."

Now he was pissed. "You're saying I snubbed you?"

"No. But our paths didn't cross too often."

"Because you ate lunch in the library instead of hanging out in the commons. And you rode the bus instead of riding with me. I did offer. Remember?"

She had a shocked look on her face. "How do you know where I ate lunch?"

"I knew. Gramps asked me to keep an eye on you when you first moved here. I tried to be friendly, but you'd run the other direction anytime you saw me coming. I decided you didn't like me." He shrugged. "Not that I blamed you. You were a Level One kid. Smart track. French Club. I was a jock—worse, a cowboy jock. It's not like we had a lot in common, but I still kept an eye on you."

She moved into a fully seated position, her legs to one side. "I didn't know that."

Will sat up, too. They were only an arm's length apart, but he made no move to touch her. Maybe the old barriers were too great to overcome.

After a moment of awkward silence, Anne said, "I didn't dislike you. I was afraid of you—your popularity, your visibility. Maybe I even envied you a little, but I always thought you were a good person."

He made a skeptical sound.

Her cheeks colored again. "A little wild, I guess. But underneath all the hoopla I thought you were nice."

"Hoopla?"

"Scads of friends, rodeo events, people phoning day and night. Girls," she added with a chuckle. "Mom used to shake her head and say, 'Girls didn't behave that way in my day.' I wondered if she thought I was weird because I never called any boys."

"She knew you were shy. And you were busy studying, too, Miss Straight-A-Summa-Cum-Something-or-Other."

She blushed and looked down. "I guess."

He brushed the back of his hand across her cheek and lifted her chin. "For the record, there never was a Judy. Other than one date at the prom, we were just friends. She was an excuse I made up that night to leave. I didn't forget that kiss, Anne, but I wanted to."

Her lips formed the word *why?* but no sound came forth.

Oil from the popcorn glistened at one corner of her mouth. He was tempted to lick it, but instead he answered her question. "Because kissing you made me think about sticking around. I even picked up an application for college from the guidance office."

"Really? Why didn't you go?"

"Because of my loss at Nationals," he said bluntly. Even now his ignominious defeat—the sense that he'd not only let down himself and his team, but also his father's memory—twisted in his gut.

Anne moved back. "Second place isn't exactly losing, Will."

"It was to me. That loss put everything into focus, or so I thought."

"You didn't even make it back for Christmas. Or…anything."

He nodded. Those early years had been hard. He made a ton of stupid mistakes and poor business choices, the kinds of things he might have avoided if he'd gone to college. "I gave up a lot to claw my way to the pros, but I still haven't won the title."

She frowned. "You had top points two years ago."

The girl did her homework. "Points, yes. Money, no. I came in second place. Again."

"Why is it so important to be number one?"

He shrugged. "No doubt Dr. Freud would say it's wrapped up in my dad dying. People have told me he might have won Best All-Round Cowboy the year he died. My folks were on their way home from a rodeo when their truck rolled and went into a ditch."

In an effort to brush away the sadness in her eyes, he said, "Or, as your mother liked to say, it could be cussed orneriness. She said I inherited it from my grandfather. Bull riding is what I do."

"Even if it kills you?"

Will startled. Did she know about his doctor's report? He knew rumors had been circulating before he left, but surely Anne couldn't have heard anything. "What's that mean?"

"You're getting older. Your body isn't as malleable as a young kid's. You could land wrong and break your neck."

He released the breath he'd been holding. "Actually, I may not look it, but I'm in better shape today than I was fifteen years ago. I lift weights and run. And my timing is sharper."

She took a deep breath. "I wasn't casting aspersions on your body." The compliment seemed to loom between them and she quickly added, "So, you're planning on going back to the circuit this fall." It wasn't a question.

"Definitely."

She rose to her knees and started to gather up their mess. "And, I'm taking a new job, too—a promotion that's long overdue. It sounds like we have our futures all lined up and ready to go. To get involved on an emotional level would be terribly foolish, don't you agree?''

''When you put it like that...but—''

She didn't let him finish. ''We're adults, Will, not kids. Proximity and unresolved lust just aren't good enough reasons to risk involvement.''

Will agreed on an intellectual level, but the shimmer on her lips was speaking to him at a different level altogether. ''So, we won't get involved, but one kiss every fifteen years isn't going to kill us.''

She started to disagree, but Will knew a proven way to distract a woman. He pulled her into his arms and kissed her.

Anne gave a token resistance—a mumbled uh-uh that almost immediately turned to uh-huh. There was a small clattering sound as the colored pens scattered on the floor. Her arms encircled his shoulders, her body flattened against his as her mouth opened.

She tasted salty and sweet. Popcorn and soda, plus an intangible quality that made him groan. And as their tongues met, Will knew he'd made a serious mistake. Fifteen years hadn't been enough to make him forget, and now he had nowhere to run.

CHAPTER SEVEN

ANNE WOULD HAVE LIKED to credit her willpower for stopping the kiss, but she was honest enough to admit that she was putty in Will's hands right up to the second she heard her daughter shout, "Mommy."

As Anne's mother once told her, some subliminal connection was established at birth to inform a child when his or her mother was preoccupied. *Nothing like a passionate kiss from the wrong man to prompt a formerly occupied child to demand attention,* Anne thought.

She would have liked to breathe a sigh of relief when Will reacted to her subtle push and stepped away, but she couldn't. She wanted more of the same, more of everything promised, but that wasn't smart.

"Mommy," Zoey called again, her voice closer and more plaintive.

Anne put her hand to her mouth. Did she look freshly kissed? Would Zoey notice?

"We're just about done, honey," Anne called, willing her voice to be steady. "You can go up to bed. I'll be there in a minute."

The diversion didn't work. The door opened and Zoey walked in. "Whatcha doing? Ooh, colored pens. Can I play?"

Will had knelt to pick up the idea sheets. He was clutching the bright markers like a little boy with a bouquet. He looked at Anne for guidance.

"Not tonight, love. It's late. Did you enjoy the movie?"

Anne could tell by Zoey's petulant frown that she was overly tired. "I don't wanna go to bed. I wanna color."

Anne was still wired and edgy herself. "Tomorrow," she said sternly.

Zoey crossed her arms and looked from one adult to the other. Anne could tell she sensed something was different. To keep her from pondering too long, Anne walked to the little girl's side and laid a hand on her shoulder. "Come on, honey. If we hurry we can squeeze in a little reading time."

Zoey shrugged Anne's hand off and pointed to Will. "I want him to read to me."

Anne almost groaned aloud. "Sweetheart, it's late. Will needs to get up early. He doesn't have time…"

Fat tears welled up in her daughter's eyes. Her chin trembled, and instantly her breathing took on an ominous vibration. Anne's patience almost snapped. She was tired, too. And sexually frustrated. She longed for the luxury of a tantrum of her own, but first she needed to find the fast-acting inhaler.

"I'd love to read to you, Miss Z," Will said in a deep, calming voice. "How 'bout a piggyback ride? Is that puffer thing of yours upstairs?"

Zoey's breath chugged as she inhaled, but her smile cleared up the petulant storm clouds. She used the sleeve of her sweatshirt to brush away her tears then scrambled up Will's broad back. Her arms locked at the base of his throat.

"Leave this mess," he said, touching Anne's shoulder in a supportive way. "I'll clean up on my way out."

She would have hugged him in gratitude but she didn't think he'd appreciate a Fraser-girl sandwich. Instead, she mouthed "thank you" and turned off the lights as she followed them into the hall.

After the perfunctory teeth-brushing and face-washing,

Zoey settled down in bed with Will sitting at her side. *Children of the Earth,* the book she'd selected, was one Zoey knew by heart, but the images were so beautiful, that Anne never tired of looking at it.

Anne left them to read while she went about preparing for bed. She tried not to listen, but the low murmur of Will's voice hummed through her bones. Drawn to the French doors, she peeked in.

The tender scene twisted like a knife in her gut. Here was the image Anne had dreamed of while pregnant. A daddy who read to his little girl. Who carried her piggyback without worrying about messing up his clothes. Who didn't run in the other direction when Zoey started having difficulty breathing. Who didn't leave the mess for Anne to clean up.

Anne turned away. Right image, but wrong everything else, she thought. Wrong place. Wrong man. Wrong time.

What a shame his kiss felt so right.

"SEE THE WOLVES in the moon, Will? Mommy says the author wants to show how the earth and everything on it is connected to the universe."

The philosophic comment seemed far too wise and worldly for a child her age, but Will remembered reading somewhere that only children were adults by age eight. "What do you want to be when you grow up, Zoey?"

She ducked her head shyly. "I dunno. Maybe a veterinarian who takes care of horses." She smiled impishly. "When can I go riding with you again? That was so much fun."

He hated to put her off. He'd enjoyed their time together, too, but he knew her mother wasn't wild about the idea. "I don't know, sweetie. We're going to be pretty busy next week with all the new people coming in."

She sighed and turned the page. "Mommy's worried

that they won't be as happy as they were when Grandma ran the place.''

Was that true? Anne certainly hid her anxiety well.

Zoey went on. ''Joy said Grandma Esther was a people person, but Mommy is a businessperson. So it's harder for her to connect.''

Will cleared his throat and read from the page. He didn't feel comfortable talking about Anne behind her back. She was an astute businessperson, and there was nothing wrong with that. And while she might not appear as outwardly friendly as her mother had been, the more he observed Anne in action, the more he understood that she was naturally shy, not aloof, as he'd once believed.

And if the hormones zinging through his body were any clue, the attraction he'd felt toward her in high school never really went away. Unfortunately, warring with lust was the need to protect and cherish this bright little beauty beside him. Could he in good conscience stumble in and out of their lives with less grace than a few of the bulls he'd ridden?

Zoey was sound asleep before he reached the final page. He placed the book on the nightstand and carefully slid off the bed. His hand trembled as he tucked her special blanket under her chin.

If Anne ever remarries, Will thought, the guy will not only get to be Anne's husband but Zoey's father, as well. Will hated the man, whoever he was—or, more to the point, envied him.

Kissing Anne tonight had proved Will's worst suspicion. He was on the verge of falling in love. But that didn't mean he was giving in to his feelings. He didn't have time to be in love, especially with a woman whose life was so completely different from his. Will's biological clock was ticking—not the childbearing kind, but the old-man-on-the-bull-riding-circuit kind.

True, there were a couple of guys in their late thirties and early forties who were still riding, but given Will's medical history, his comeback was now or never. And never wasn't an option. He couldn't quit and neither could he picture Anne agreeing to a long-distance relationship while Will plunged back into the circuit this fall.

Another thought hit him. What if Doc was right? What if a bad tumble left him dead or paralyzed? Will knew Anne would feel obligated to stand by him. To nurse him or…mourn.

No, he couldn't put her through that again. She'd known enough loss.

There was the other side of the coin, too. If Will did wind up back on top, he wouldn't be able to share his successes with Anne and Zoey. He pictured the typical indoor bull-riding venue—the animals, the dust, the crowds. At outdoor events, smoke was a factor. The harsh reality was that Zoey's fragile lungs weren't compatible with the earthy world of professional bull riding.

The greatest favor he could give them both was to walk away. Unfortunately, he was stuck here for the rest of the summer.

Welcome to purgatory, he thought with a sigh.

Will turned off the light and closed the door behind him. He paused to observe Anne, who was sitting upright in her bed, eyes closed, lips parted. Her head resting on a nest of pillows, she reminded him of Zoey—innocent and vulnerable.

The covers were bunched at her waist where the book she'd been reading lay, jacket up. Although she hadn't changed out of the lounging clothes she'd worn downstairs, the intimacy of the setting made the outfit look more provocative. A glimpse of white shoulder. The elegant arch of her neck.

He closed his eyes and imagined himself crawling into

bed beside her, tenderly removing every stitch of clothing. Tasting. Touching. Making love.

"All through?"

Just getting started, he almost answered. Instead, he opened his eyes and nodded. "Yes. She's sound asleep. I noticed the humidifier on the stool beside her bed and turned it on, okay?"

She rubbed her nose in a childlike way. "That was very thoughtful of you. Now I don't have to get up."

He started toward the door, but paused. "Actually, you do. I can't set the dead bolt without a key."

She frowned. "I didn't give you a key when the locksmith was here? I meant to. You should be able to get into all the rooms if you need to." She pointed to the antique desk below the window. "There's an extra one in the top drawer."

Will didn't read anything into the offer. He knew she was being practical, business-minded. He walked to the desk and jiggled the sticky drawer to get it to open. Once he succeeded, an assortment of junk slid forward, including several photos. One caught his eye. It showed a smiling couple with a blond youngster between them. They were on a beach with an elevated dock in the background. It was Anne and a man Will had never met, although he'd seen many photos of Barry Fraser.

"When was this taken?" he asked, holding the picture up for Anne to see.

Yawning, she squinted. "About four months before he left for good. Barry had taken a position with a company in Atlanta. It was supposed to be temporary, so he stayed in company housing and Zoey and I remained in Pittsburgh. On one of our visits, we drove to Myrtle Beach."

Will leaned against the desk and studied the photo. "You look happy. The ideal young family."

Anne drew her knees to her chest, tenting the bedding.

She rested her chin on the blanket. "Looks can be deceiving. If I remember correctly, we'd just had a big fight on the patio of our hotel. We were so loud we woke Zoey up from her nap. The walk on the beach was an attempt to shake off the hard feelings and soothe her."

Curious about her marriage, he asked, "Were you happy at first?"

She nodded. "Very. Barry is as extroverted as I am introverted. I guess it was a classic case of opposites attracting." She made a wry face. "Although we were both goal-oriented overachievers."

"Do you mind me asking what went wrong?"

"I'm surprised you have to ask. Mom never talked about it? I certainly called her often enough to complain."

Will shook his head. "The most she ever said was that you weren't happy. Then she'd change the subject." *And I was too cowardly to ask more.*

Anne closed the book and set it on her bedside table. "Well, in hindsight, I guess the main issue was that I underestimated how serious Barry was about not having children. We'd talked about it before we got married, but I'd naively assumed that he'd change his mind in time. Everybody has kids, right?"

Most of the men Will knew had fathered children, but not all of them were fathers.

"I hounded him into agreeing to have one child. At first, he seemed pleased with Zoey and happy with our little family, but her illness changed the dynamic. We went from mother, father and daughter to mother, father and daughter with asthma. He just couldn't handle the trips to the doctor, the blood tests, the 24/7 responsibility of caring for a sick child."

She sighed. "Some marriages are strengthened by tests like this, some crumble. Ours did the latter."

"Do you think you'll remarry someday?"

Her smile looked tinged with regret. "Maybe later. After Zoey is grown. I can't imagine a man wanting to deal with this kind of baggage."

Will's reply came out louder and sharper than he'd intended. "Zoey is *not* baggage. She's a beautiful, smart and loving little girl."

Anne's eyes went wide. "I meant *my* emotional garbage. I don't trust easily. And I won't do anything that puts my daughter's health in jeopardy."

Will understood the implied warning. He put the photo back in the drawer and picked up the key. "Good. I wouldn't want to see either of you get hurt again."

He started to leave but paused by the foot of her bed. "I didn't mean for that kiss to get out of hand, Anne. The fact that it did tells me we could have a big problem if…" He didn't know how to word this without sounding like an egotistical fool. It was just a kiss. What if Anne hadn't felt the same impact he had?

"…we don't nip this attraction between us in the bud?" she finished, taking him off the hook.

Will nodded, grateful for her help. "Unless I'm reading more into it than…"

Her cheeks flushed and she shook her head. "No. I felt it, too. And you're right. We need to keep things businesslike between us from now on."

Will agreed. He was glad they were on the same page, but that didn't mean he was happy. "Good," he said, feeling like a fraud.

He turned to leave. As he reached the door, she said, "But, for the record, it was a nice kiss. Even better than the last one."

The hint of humor in her tone made him smile, but he didn't look back. Anne was simply too much temptation.

He locked the door behind him. His goal this summer

would be to keep his treasures safe, even if that meant keeping his distance.

Feeling deflated and tense, Will was just about to open the front door, when he remembered his promise to Anne. *"I'll straighten up before I leave."* It didn't take long to put the chairs back in place and collect their brainstorm papers, but before leaving, he paused to study Anne's interesting collection of lines and squiggles.

Sitting down behind his grandfather's desk, he let his chin rest on his palm. Her ideas were not only intelligent but intuitive. What surprised him was how little faith Anne put in her gut instinct. Granted, a couple of her ideas—like Vintage Clothing Day and a mock shoot-out at the O.K. Corral—were a bit over the top, but others were on par with her mother's "crazy" idea of blending a bed-and-breakfast with a working cattle ranch.

With a weighty sigh, he was just reaching for the switch on the desk lamp when the phone rang. Ten o'clock was a little late for business. "Hello?"

"Will? Is that you? What are you doing there? I was expecting Anne to answer."

Will let out the breath he'd been holding. "Hi, Gramps. She's in bed. Probably asleep. We had a full day. Driving lessons, cooking class, dinner and a movie." *A kiss.*

A.J.'s familiar chuckle made Will oddly homesick. He missed his grandfather's humor and wisdom.

"Sounds like you've got everything under control."

I wish. "We just put your postcard from Jackson Hole on the map. Where are you now?"

"North entrance to Yellowstone. Still got patches of snow around. Can you believe it? Rivers are gushing fast and furious. It's so pretty I decided to stay till the weekend, at least. That's when the tourists show up." A.J. never considered himself a tourist, even when visiting a new place.

"Sounds good, Gramps. Are you staying in a campground?"

"I did for a couple of nights, but it's a bit nippy and I decided I needed a good bath, so I found a nice little resort with individual cabins. Sorta reminds me of home. Speaking of home, how are your guests doing?"

Will gave him a rundown of the guests to date.

A.J. chuckled. "Can't recall the wanna-be bull riders, but the teacher from Boston is a repeat. Nice gal. Partial to dark beer as I remember. She and Esther would sneak a few on the back porch."

Will grinned. He and Esther had sipped a couple of beers in their day, too. Unlike her daughter, Esther liked the real thing. And wine. Will always brought her a vintage chardonnay when he came home by way of California.

"How's my granddaughter getting along?"

"Fine. No asthma attacks since that first day. Still bugging her mom about learning to ride."

"I was thinking about that, Will. What if you were to offer a group clinic to novice riders so Zoey could pick up the basics? You might get a couple of other kids her age to come out from town. Sorta kill two birds with one stone. A child needs playmates, you know."

Will liked the idea of Zoey making friends.

"Esther asked me to do something like that once, but I told her I was a cowboy, not a teacher."

"What makes you think I'd do any better?" Will asked, recalling Anne's praise.

"Don't sell yourself short, son. You're a good man with a heck of a lot of experience to share. And I've seen you coach young bull riders. You'd be a natural with kids."

Will doubted that, but years back he'd earned extra cash by teaching bull riders how to rope.

"Besides," A.J. said, "the adults who come to the Silver Rose aren't looking to become pro wranglers. They just need a refresher course on horse etiquette.''

Will added the idea to Anne's list. "Thanks for the suggestion, Gramps. I'll run it past Anne in the morning." Or the next time we talk. Maybe he should put a little distance between them for a week or two. Let the memory of their kiss fade.

"Gramps…" Will paused, not sure how to ask for advice. "I wasn't around much when Anne got divorced. Was it bitter?"

"No worse than most, I guess. Why do you ask?"

"At times she seems a little skittish. I wondered if it's me or if she's got reservations against men in general."

A.J. made a sound Will associated with deep thought. "You might ask her. Always seemed like the best way to handle things with her mother. If Esther was quiet for too long, I knew it was time to ask what was on her mind. Usually, she'd say 'nothing,' which every man knows means 'something.' Before long, out came a whole list of complaints."

"Anne hasn't complained about anything, but it's only been a few days since the guests started arriving." He sighed. "In all fairness, she's been a terrific sport about everything, but the longer I'm here, the more I understand how much teamwork you and Esther put into running this place."

A.J. chortled. "That's true, son, but it didn't happen overnight. Oh, Lordy, when I think back on some of the rows me and Esther had over the silliest things." Will pictured him smiling. "'Course, we had making up to look forward to. You and Anne aren't that lucky."

That was for damn sure.

"But you can be a team without being married. Give yourself a little time to get to know Anne and figure out what makes her tick. Before long, the two of you will be clicking like a finely oiled piece of machinery.''

Somehow Will doubted that. The clicking he craved was more intimate. And the mere mention of oil was enough to make his extremities tingle.

Thankfully, A.J. couldn't read his mind. His grandfather went on. ''But it goes without saying that you need to be careful of her feelings. Anne's at a delicate time in her life with her mother gone. And raising that sweet little girl all alone ain't easy. But I know you'll treat her right.''

''Thanks for the vote of confidence, Gramps. I'll do my best.'' *Even if it means a summer in hell.*

''LADIES AND GENTLEMEN, let me introduce Sophie. She's fifteen years old and one of the sweetest little mares you'll ever meet.''

Anne crossed her arms on the top rung of the gate and blocked out the peripheral ranch noise—guests talking, animals mooing, grunting, barking or whatever, cars and trucks coming and going. In the time since their kiss, the day-to-day sounds of the Silver Rose had become second nature to her, like a beloved mate's snoring. But the timbre to which she'd grown most attuned was Will's voice.

Whether working in the garden or sitting on the porch swing playing cards with Zoey, Anne could hear his laugh carried on the breeze. Ever since that night in the office, Will had kept his distance, as they'd both agreed was best for all involved. He seldom ate at the main house, unless one of Anne's special events required his presence. He handled most of their business and Silver Rose correspondence through notes. He'd even installed a wireless communication system linking the house, his cabin and the barn so she could reach him without their meeting face-to-face.

One might have thought the distance would help Anne

get her priorities straight. Unfortunately, the exact opposite was true. Anne kept busy from sunup to sundown. She mothered, nurtured, accounted, supervised, gardened, mingled and juggled WHC business from afar, but when the lights went out, Will showed up. In her head.

Determined to overcome this unhealthy addiction—after all, she'd beaten her craving for chocolate by telling herself she didn't like the taste—Anne made herself show up to watch Will give riding lessons. Besides, she thought, anything beat sitting in the office writing a marketing report for Roger, who was rapidly turning into a pest even more annoying than the mouse in the garden shed.

"Today, we're going to work on saddling your mount," Will said, gesturing toward the western saddle sitting atop a wooden stand that had been brought into the ring.

Thanks to Anne's overactive libido, the words took on a suggestive meaning and she felt her cheeks heat up. She adjusted her cowboy hat to minimize exposure to the watchful eye of the woman who joined her at the gate.

Linda Pilster had somehow become what their daughters would call Anne's "bestest" friend. The two women talked daily, and not just about business, kids or the class reunion. To Anne's amazement, she and Linda shared certain core values and some parallel experiences that made Anne wonder if they'd been sisters in another life.

As the date for the class reunion approached, Linda had turned more and more to Anne for guidance and support. The official reunion committee had splintered, leaving Linda holding the bag. Anne had found herself negotiating with caterers and hiring a deejay after someone's brother's friend bailed. The extra work added to her load, but it had brought the two women closer, too. And Anne didn't regret that.

"You like that hat, don't you?" Linda asked.

Anne looked up at the brim. "Actually, I do. I didn't

think I was a cowboy-hat kind of person, but it's functional and—according to my daughter—considerably less goofy than my gardening hat.''

The white Stetson had belonged to her mother. Anne had planned to purchase her own, but after outfitting Cowgirl Zoey at the local western-wear shop, she'd depleted her budget. Fortunately, Will wasn't charging her for her daughter's riding lessons. ''Zoey is my guinea pig,'' he'd explained when they sat down to discuss the idea of opening up group lessons to nonguests. ''If I fail, you'll be one less person I need to refund.''

Anne didn't expect him to fail. Ever since their brainstorming session, which she privately referred to as Kiss Night, Will had proven time and again that he was smart, flexible, conscientious and a team player. If the Silver Rose were a WHC property, he'd have been flagged for promotion and earned several bonuses by now. At times, his innovative ideas reminded Anne of her mother.

Like when he organized an impromptu coyote-howling contest on the night of the full moon and didn't invite her. True, she'd retired early after handling an emotionally trying situation when a single guest made a pass at one of the girls on her housekeeping staff. She'd appreciated Will's consideration, but the glowing reports the next morning from their sleepy-eyed guests had made Anne feel left out, just as she had in high school.

Get over it, she told herself. But Anne knew that some hurts never truly went away. *Once an outsider, always an outsider.*

''What do you think about our dynamic duo?'' Linda asked, drawing Anne from her self-pity. ''Are they going to be dangerous in a couple of years or what?''

Anne turned her gaze on the two youngsters in the corral. Zoey and Tressa—Linda's daughter, who was a year younger than Zoey—were as physically different as night and day but clones in attitude.

Tressa was chubby and dark, Zoey thin and fair. Tressa's long brown hair was pulled back in a ponytail that reached almost to her waist. Zoey's thin braids barely cleared her shoulders. Tressa's jeans and boots looked broken in, probably because they were hand-me-downs from an older cousin. Zoey's were fresh from the store. But both girls were beauties and, to their mothers' dismay, flirted with the instincts of courtesans.

"They already have every cowboy on the place eating out of their hands," Anne said. "I don't even want to think about the teen years."

Linda groaned. "I know. Having a preteen son is torture enough."

"Where is Logan, by the way?" Anne asked, looking around. She'd only met the eleven-year-old once.

"At a scout jamboree. His dad drove over from Sacramento to take him. They left yesterday. Tressa would have been inconsolable if it weren't for Will's class. She's been looking forward to riding lessons ever since you mentioned it."

Anne recalled the phone conversation that had started out as a discussion about desserts to be served at the reunion and ended with one of those aha moments when they realized they had daughters the same age. Will's decision to offer group riding lessons had struck a chord with both mothers. Anne had immediately invited Linda and Tressa to the ranch for *Mystic Pizza* night—pepperoni and Julia Roberts's cinematic debut.

The movie garnered mixed reviews, but the new friendship got two thumbs-up.

"He's really amazing," Linda said, nodding toward Will. "I've never met a man with such patience. For some reason, I figured a bull rider would lack finesse."

Anne didn't want to know why, but Linda elaborated anyway. "I mean, a bull rider's goal is to stick it out for eight seconds. Eight, tiny, wham-bam, thank you, ma'am seconds. Where would that leave a woman?"

Anne had no problem conjuring up an image that made her heart skip a beat and her cheeks flush. "I don't know," she said, because Linda seemed to expect an answer.

Feeling her friend's gaze turn her way, Anne tugged on the brim of her hat and leaned forward to catch Will's lecture. He stood in the middle of the hard-packed dirt corral, the pinto horse on a lead at his side. Thanks to Zoey, Anne now knew that a mixed-colored horse was either a pinto or a paint, although Anne still didn't understand the distinction. A brown horse was either a roan or a bay, depending on the color of the mane. "The hair on its neck, Mom," her daughter had added.

Zoey and Tressa stood, shoulders touching, a few feet away from Will and the horse. In addition to the girls, the disparate class included a woman in her sixties, a couple celebrating their second anniversary and a middle-aged man and woman who told Anne they came to the Silver Rose to work on their relationship. Anne wasn't sure how herding cattle would help, but she hoped it did.

Although Anne could only catch bits and pieces of Will's speech, she gathered that he was pointing out the horse's body parts. "Withers. Fetlock. Hooves." He moved to the rear of the horse and picked up one foot. The group pressed closer.

Anne's heart stuttered for a fraction of a second, then she reminded herself who was holding the beast's leg. Will. A man of patience. A man who instilled trust in woman and beast. Who generated love and admiration in small children.

Love. Anne was half-afraid to use the word in any sentence. What if what she felt for Will was love? She wanted to attribute her feelings to lust but knew that would be a lie. Maybe she'd always been in love with Will, although surely that wild boy with something to prove couldn't have moved her the way this kind, thoughtful man did.

She was certain Will had no clue that she found his selfless acts of kindness sexy. A repaired faucet—who knew the image of a man flat on his back under a sink was a turn-on? A bouquet of wildflowers left on the front porch instead of indoors where it might trigger an allergic response in her daughter. A new plug spliced to her ancient but trusted humidifier.

A hand waved back and forth in front of her face. "Yoohoo, earth to Anne. How's life on Planet Will?"

Anne cocked her head. "Sorry. I was planning next week's menu."

Linda's eyebrow rose skeptically. "Oh, really? Is Will the main course?"

Anne felt her face flush. "Pardon?"

Linda clapped her hand solidly between Anne's shoulder blades. "Woman, you are such a bad liar. Don't ever try it professionally."

Anne chuckled. "Okay. I won't."

"Then you admit that you're attracted to Will?"

"He's an attractive man."

"A very political answer. Except for the lying thing, you might have a career in government."

Anne gave up. Actually, she'd been thinking about talking to Linda about her feelings for Will. In the past, Anne had had her mother to use as a sounding board. Anne really needed a woman's perspective.

She turned her back to the arena and said, "Okay. Here's the deal. We kissed." Linda's mouth formed a huge O. "Just once. Well, twice, but there was a fifteen-year gap between times. My point is—we are attracted to each other. But since we're older and wiser, we're not getting carried away by something that isn't going anywhere.''

Linda made a rude sound. ''That sucks.''

Anne agreed, but she said, ''He plans to return to his career this fall. I have a new job waiting for me. Different worlds, different—''

Linda interrupted. ''Wait. Back up. What was that about Will returning to the pro circuit? Are you sure? I heard a rumor that his bull-riding days are over. Kaput.''

''Where'd you hear that?''

Linda shrugged. ''I don't remember. I've had so much on my mind lately I have trouble remembering my address. But if Will says he's still in the game, then—'' She turned suddenly and pointed to the corral. ''Look.''

Anne's gaze followed her finger. Zoey was no longer standing on the ground. She was perched in the saddle atop the spotted horse. A long way off the ground.

Anne took a shaky breath. Zoey waved with such gusto she almost toppled over, but Will was there. One large, sturdy hand kept her from falling.

''She's beaming like Miss America,'' Anne said. ''Confident. Proud. What a wonderful gift he's given her!''

Linda gave a funny peep. ''Ohmygod. You're in love.''

Anne ducked her head to hide the blush. ''I already told you we have feelings for each other, but given our disparate goals and agendas, we've decided not to pursue any kind of physical relationship.''

Linda made a face. ''Say that again in English. Wait. Never mind. I got the gist, and the gist stinks. You'd pass up a chance at happiness because it doesn't fit into your schedule?''

Anne's head was beginning to throb. *Maybe my hat is too tight.* Or it could be sleep deprivation. Practically every night since their kiss, Anne had awakened to a steamy dream that left her heart pounding and her extremities tingling. "Our careers aren't exactly copacetic, Linda."

"So find a new career."

The thought had crossed her mind, until yesterday's e-mail from Roger McFinney informing her that WHC had just signed the new employee health-care package that Anne had pushed for. Given her daughter's precarious—and expensive—health issues, Anne couldn't afford *not* to work for WHC.

Anne sighed. "We're doing the grown-up thing."

"Grown-ups deserve a little fun once in a while. I remember your mother telling me that her only regret in life was not visiting you and Zoey more often."

It was a regret—and guilt—that Anne shared.

In the silence that followed, Anne could hear the thud of hooves as Will led the horse in a circle. "Mommy, look at me," Zoey called. "This is so much fun. You should try it."

Anne smiled and waved. Her gaze connected with Will's for a split second—just long enough to see longing, possibly even desire. Her heart lifted and fell in a dizzying way that made her fingers grip the rusted metal gate. Maybe Linda was right. Anne and Will didn't have a future together, but they did have a summer.

Swallowing, she took a breath then said, "So, is it too late to sign up for the reunion?"

Linda's eyebrow arched suspiciously. "No, it's not too late."

Anne looked at Will. Would he go with her if she asked him? There was only one way to find out.

Linda gave a tiny yelp and threw her arms around Anne. "Your mother would be proud of you."

"What do you mean?" Anne asked, feeling awkward with the public display of affection.

Linda stepped back. "Esther and I had a couple of long

talks in the waiting room when my mom was in the hospital. I was pretty disillusioned after my divorce. I told her I'd probably never remarry.

"I don't remember her exact words, but basically she said that love without risk comes too easy and we don't appreciate it. Great love requires great risk, but when you look back at your life, it's what you'll remember best."

Anne smiled. "That sounds like Mom. Only a brave woman would leave her family and friends to travel to a ranch on the other side of the country with a man she barely knew."

"But look how great her life turned out," Linda said. "She and A.J. were the happiest couple I've ever met."

Anne started to agree but noticed two sprites racing toward them. She reached up to unhook the latch.

"So, are you going to ask Will to be your date?" Linda asked, shuffling sideways.

Will was walking toward them, too. He'd handed the horse's lead to a young cowboy. The adults followed the horse and cowboy to the barn. Anne knew that Will had scheduled a short trail ride after lunch.

"Maybe," Anne whispered, opening her arms to Zoey, who launched herself at Anne.

Anne let out a grunt. "My goodness, girl, are you growing? I swear you weigh more now than when we got here."

"Yep," Zoey said with obvious glee. "I'm growing like a potato plant in the compost pile. Will said so."

A big hand tugged down the brim of Zoey's hat. "You weren't supposed to repeat that, kiddo. You were supposed to tell her that we had to let down the stirrups a notch," he said, his tone teasing. "You're going to have long legs. Like your mother."

Zoey leaned back, her weight pulling Anne a step closer to Will. "Give me a piggyback ride, Will? Please?"

"Me, too," another high-pitched voice chirped.

"Two freeloaders?" he asked, cocking his hat back on his head. A sweat line showed on his forehead and Anne had to curl her fingers in her palm to keep from wiping it. "Well, okay."

Going to one knee, he helped the little girls climb up like twin monkeys. With a wink to Anne, he made a silly whinny and jumped up, lightly bucking. The shrill cries of glee made Anne's heart swell with tenderness. "Don't hurt him, girls," she said, lightly touching the sleeve of his western-style shirt. "I need him to be my date to the reunion dance."

Will stopped abruptly and swung around. "Say what?"

Anne was suddenly mute. She'd never asked a man out before.

Linda intervened. "I've been twisting her arm to come and she finally said yes, if you'd take her." She made a tsking sound. "It's your class, Will. You should be there."

Will looked from Linda to Anne. "Are you sure about this?"

Feeling a blush that threatened to consume her, Anne nodded. "Yes. Will you go with me? Please."

His chest rose with a deep inhalation.

Over the giggling cries of "Giddyap" and "Go, horsey" came a simple, but meaningful, "My pleasure."

CHAPTER EIGHT

"YOU LOOK BE-UUU-TIFUL, Mommy. That dress is the prettiest one in Grandma's closet."

Anne looked in the mirror of the antique vanity to see her daughter sprawled on her belly on the bed behind her. "Thank you, honey. It is lovely, isn't it?"

She studied her reflection, running her hand across the neckline of the dress. It was butter yellow, a color that Anne wouldn't have thought suited her. The sleeveless, fitted crepe bodice hinted at daring without revealing too much, and its tailored waist with a self-belt made her feel thin. The perky fullness of the chiffon skirt, which was perhaps a tad shorter than necessary, showed off the tan she'd acquired from working in the garden.

Anne loved the dress, although she had to admit, if she'd seen it at a store, she'd never have tried it on. The color was too bright, the style too girlish. But when A.J. called last night and Zoey blurted out that Anne was going to look gross because she didn't have time to shop for a new dress to wear to the reunion, he'd asked to speak to Anne.

As she finished applying her makeup, she thought about their conversation. First, he'd instructed her to check in the back of her mother's closet. "Seems to me she mentioned buying you a fancy dress at some vintage-clothing shop last fall. I believe the bag has your name on it."

Anne had been dumbfounded. "Why would she do that? I never go to parties."

"Maybe she thought you needed more fun in your life.

I know she was worried about how hard you work,'' he'd
answered.

Without intending to, Anne had blurted out her worst
fear. ''A.J., was Mom disappointed in me? I know I wasn't
the typical daughter. No boyfriends, dates or proms to get
excited about. Did she miss that?''

''Oh, honey,'' he'd answered with a sad inflection.
''None of that mattered to her. She just wanted you to be
happy.''

Anne wasn't sure she believed him. She and Esther had
argued so much when Anne had lived here, butting heads
the way mothers and teenage daughters often did. But
Anne hadn't understood then how exasperating her nega-
tive attitude must have been for her mother. Now Anne
wondered how anyone could fail to love this place. She
wondered if she'd made up her mind to hate Nevada, the
Silver Rose and all things connected to ranching life before
she moved here as a teenager, just out of spite.

Before hanging up, A.J. remarked about a postcard he'd
sent from the Black Hills of South Dakota. ''I was pretty
impressed with the Crazy Horse monument,'' he said. ''I
think Esther would have liked it, too. One of its slogans
is—Never forget your dreams. Sounds like her, doesn't
it?''

As Anne reached for a tissue to blot her lipstick, she
noticed the stack of mail that she'd forgotten to drop off
in the office. Halfway down the pile was a glossy card.
The photo showed a white marble statue that bore little
resemblance to the crude carving emerging from the side
of the mountain in the distance.

Flipping it over, she read A.J.'s shaky scrawl.

A lot of people called the fellow who started this
crazy, but he didn't listen to them. He had a vision
that was all his own. Annie, your mother used to brag

about your ability to see yourself as you were, not as everyone else thought you should be. When I looked at this mountain, I thought of you.

Anne dabbed at the moisture in the corners of her eyes. She started to set the card down but noticed a postscript winding around the outline of the rectangle.

P.S.: I bought you girls each a turtle necklace. To the Lakota, the turtle represents the heart of the soul, the keeper of life.

Anne pressed the card to her chest a moment then slipped it back into the pile. There'd be time to read it aloud tomorrow when Zoey added it to the map. That was a little ritual they'd come to enjoy.

Anne desperately wanted to believe that her mother was proud of her, but in the back of her mind, she recalled an argument they'd had over Anne's refusal to attend her senior prom. "Why on earth would I attend some provincial mating ritual when I wouldn't marry one of these local yokels if you paid me?" Anne had cried. Of course, at the time none of the local yokels had invited her to the dance, either.

Now, she was going to Will's class reunion. What if tonight's gala was prom with attitude?

"Anne," Joy called from the first floor. "Will's here."

Anne and Zoey exchanged a look. Joy's voice carried like a ringside announcer's at the circus. Two subsequent door closings told Anne her Silver Rose guests would be waiting downstairs to see them off. Somehow, this *date* had become fodder for speculation—a real-life soap opera played out before their eyes.

Anne had tried her best to downplay the romance aspect. "We're practically related," she'd said more than once.

"This is good PR for the ranch. You know, community awareness."

Will, on the other hand, seemed to find the gossip amusing. Anne admired the way he handled their guests' good-natured questions and comments, anything from, "Are you buying her flowers, Will? Women love flowers," to "Cinderella needs a special carriage, Will, not a giant yellow pumpkin like your truck."

Georgi, spokesperson for the Silver Leg-a-Cs—a female square-dancing troupe from Bakersfield—had warned Anne, "I'd wear steel-toed slippers if I were you, honey. Who knows if bull riders can dance?"

Anne pushed away from the mirror and stood up, her skirt swirling provocatively around her thighs. A pair of high-heeled sandals waited beside the bed. The shoes belonged to Linda. Anne would have preferred to wear pumps and hose, but Zoey had insisted Anne go bare-legged to display her Deliriously Delicious pink toenails, courtesy of Zoey's nail polish.

"Pretty special toes, wouldn't you say?" Anne asked, wiggling the colorful digits. While the pedicure might lack a professional edge, the hour of mother-daughter giggles had more than made up for any smudges.

Anne dropped a tube of lipstick into her purse—another loan from Linda—walked to the bed and slipped her feet into the sparkly heels.

She felt a bit wobbly. Although pumps were part of the dress code in her job, Anne had worn nothing but tennis shoes or flat sandals since she'd been at the Silver Rose. "So? Do you like it?"

Zoey rose to her knees, hands pressed together as if in prayer. "Mommy, you are f.l.a.w.l.e.s.s."

Anne walked to the bed and pulled Zoey into her arms. "And you are p.u.r.f.e.c.t."

Zoey shook her head. "No fair trying to trick me. That's not how you spell *perfect* and you know it."

Anne cupped Zoey's chin. "Old habits. Sorry. I should have known you were too smart to fall for it. But we've really been lax about your studies this summer."

Zoey made a face and tried to twist away, but Anne turned her daughter's face toward the light. Was she a tad flushed or sunburned? "Did you wear your hat during your riding lesson today, hon?"

Zoey brushed Anne's hand away and flopped onto her back. She frowned at the ceiling. "Of course. Will says a smart rider always prepares for the worst. In summer, the sun can give you heat prostitution."

Anne pressed her lips together to keep from laughing. At dinner, two of the guests had been talking about Nevada's whorehouses of old. Anne had noticed her daughter listening with rapt attention.

"I'm glad Will stresses safety," Anne said. "But you look tired. Promise you'll go to bed for Joy without any guff?"

"Yes." The word held a measure of attitude, but Anne let it go. Now wasn't the time to press the issue. Hopefully, once all the hoopla subsided, Zoey would settle down.

"Good. Then I won't have to blister your bottom." The very old and empty caveat was a favorite of Esther's—and it had held as much threat with Anne as it did with Zoey.

Her daughter giggled impudently and scrambled off the bed. "I gotta go see if Will brought you flowers. On TV, a date always brings flowers."

"This isn't a date." The disclaimer fell on empty space.

Who am I kidding? Anne thought, fetching her mother's gossamer shawl from the closet. An awkwardness had developed between her and Will that told Anne they both knew this was more than a date.

She was attracted to him beyond reason. She wanted to

rush downstairs on Zoey's heels to see if he was as gorgeous as she knew he'd be. Giving in to those whims sounded both foolish and dangerous, and totally *not* Anne.

She took a deep breath and counted to five, willing her heart rate to return to normal. After tucking her cell phone into her purse, she picked up her key and started downstairs. The murmur of voices told her their departure had drawn a crowd.

As she descended into sight of the dozen or so people crowded into the foyer, a hush fell, followed by a flurry of whispers.

"Oh, my. She's so beautiful."

"Wouldn't Esther be proud."

Anne felt the sudden prick of tears. If only her mother were here. Esther would have loved every minute. Straightening her shoulders, Anne put on a fake smile then plunged ahead, calling upon her years of working with the public to accept the kind praise and good wishes with grace. She shook hands and returned hugs.

She was less than halfway across the foyer when a deep cough parted the throng. Her gaze fell on the most handsome cowboy she had ever seen. His charcoal-gray suit was a western cut that looked made for him. The collar of his pristine white shirt was open and he wasn't wearing a tie.

"Wow, Will," she said, stepping closer. "Look at you."

His boots were glossy, hair recently trimmed. His friendly grin showcased the smooth line of his freshly shaven jaw. The tanned crinkles at the corners of his eyes were evidence of his self-deprecating humor. "Didn't expect me to clean up quite so good, huh?"

"No. I mean, yes. I…"

Everyone laughed at her flustered answer.

He stepped to her side and offered his elbow. "Shall we go, my dear?"

"He called her a dear," Zoey said with a giggle.

Will looked at Zoey, who was standing beside Joy, and winked. "Good observation, Miss Z. Have fun with Joy." He wrapped his fingers around Anne's and nodded at the others. "Good night, y'all."

Anne felt the congregation watch as they walked to the Forerunner. "I just love an audience, don't you?" she said, grateful for his support—and warmth. Had the night turned cold or was it nerves?

"This is a piece of cake," Will told her. "You should try landing flat on your face in front of ten thousand people. Then you're expected to get up and wave like you're not hurt, pissed off and feeling flatter than a cow pie."

His scent—not cologne, but something else enticing— made her lean closer and sniff. "New soap?"

"It's herbal. I found it at the grocery store when I went to buy rock salt for the ice-cream maker. Too strong?"

"No. Very nice. I like it." *I like you.*

He opened the passenger door. Before she could sit down, he leaned over and picked up a clear plastic florist's box. Inside sat a corsage of baby's breath and delicate pink roses.

"Will, you shouldn't have."

"I debated over artificial but I liked these better. I didn't bring them in because I knew Zoey would want to smell them."

She opened the box, drawing the delicate creation to her nose. "That makes you the most thoughtful man I've ever known."

He shrugged modestly. "Every once in a while I get lucky."

Anne was glad for the dark, because his innocent phrase made her blush. Getting lucky generally implied spending time in bed together. Did she intend to take this date beyond a kiss good-night?

She considered the question. It could be argued that she was an adult. Single. She had needs. She cared about Will and trusted him to tell her if there was any reason, medically speaking, that they shouldn't be together. But would such a union be wise? Anne had witnessed firsthand the devastation left behind by a workplace romance at WHC.

"May I?" he asked, plucking the corsage from its nest.

Anne dropped her purse on the seat. "Of course."

Her skin felt hypersensitive as he tentatively slid two fingers under the material above her right breast. The whole process couldn't have lasted more than six or seven seconds, but Anne was dizzy from holding her breath.

"You look absolutely gorgeous, by the way," he said, dropping a soft kiss on the top of her shoulder. "I'll be the envy of every man there."

He took her elbow and helped her into the seat, then closed the door. Her hands were trembling as she secured her lap belt. Her heart fluttered as wildly as it had the day she had walked down the aisle. Was that a good thing or bad? She decided not to overanalyze the night or her feelings. Tonight, she'd try to simply enjoy the evening. She owed that to her mother.

The drive to town sped by thanks to a couple of upbeat tunes on the radio. Will introduced several possible topics of conversation, but Anne answered with nods and murmurs.

"Are you nervous?" he asked.

She glanced sideways. "What gave me away? The wringing hands or beads of perspiration on my forehead?" She would have wiped her forehead but she didn't want to risk messing up her artfully tousled curls, the result of two hours at the local beauty parlor.

His chuckle filled the space between them like a welcome friend. "Relax. I went to the ten-year reunion and it was a big improvement over high school. People weren't hanging out in cliques, ready to stab each other in the back. We're older and our flaws are a lot more obvious."

"That's easy for you to say. You're the hometown boy done good. You're famous."

"Not very. Besides, I'd say success is relative. That's another thing you understand when you get a few years on your odometer. Someone like Linda has more to show for her efforts than I do. Making a home for two kids, taking care of her sick mother, getting through a divorce without killing her no-good ex-husband—that's pretty successful in my book."

Anne was impressed—and surprised—by his words. Like his grandfather, Will kept his opinion to himself unless pressed for it. But his praise sounded heartfelt, and Anne had to admit, Barry would have dismissed Linda in one quick glance. Divorcée. Two kids. He might have agreed to lend her money if she'd asked, but he'd have run in the opposite direction if she needed emotional succor or a shoulder to cry on.

The car slowed. Anne leaned forward to scan the crowded parking lot. Linda's SUV was parked near the front door. Good, Anne thought, at least there would be one friendly face in the crowd. Anne had met a few other women at organizational meetings and several more that morning when she'd dropped off the hay bales the Silver Rose had donated for decorations. But Anne wasn't part of their crowd. She never had been.

She took a deep breath and collected her nerve as Will got out and walked around the vehicle to open her door. "Watch your step," he said, taking her hand. "Potholes from last winter. We don't want to mess up that Deliriously Delicious pink polish."

His teasing took her mind off what was coming. "My daughter told you? It was supposed to be our little secret."

He closed his hand protectively over hers. "I'd like to say I had to torture it out of her, but frankly, Anne, your daughter blabs. Never entrust her with state secrets, okay?"

"I'll remember that. But the road runs two ways, you know. Zoey and Tressa couldn't wait to tell me about someone named Reba, who apparently is a 'mean little ball-buster.' Fortunately, they hadn't figured out what that term meant."

Will let out a hoot. "Holy c— I really do have to watch my mouth. For the record, Riva—short for Arriva Dirtshay—is a red bull with a spotted white face. He's gentle as a lamb outside the arena—I've actually seen kids feed him by hand—but open the chute and he turns on the retro-rockets."

"I assumed as much," she said honestly, but she didn't mention how much her initial twinge of jealousy had unnerved her.

When they resumed walking, he went on to explain, "A lot of bulls do a Jekyll and Hyde number. It's like they understand they're performers hired to put on a show. But you never want to forget that even the gentlest bull in the pen can kill you if you're not paying attention."

Before Anne could ask for more details, a loud voice pierced the night. "Anne and Will. 'Bout time. Sheesh. I was ready to send out Search and Rescue."

Linda stood in the doorway, beckoning them to hurry. Backlit by the bright yellow glow from inside the ugly but functional metal-sided hall, she resembled the Statue of Liberty—a flashlight in one hand and clipboard pressed to her chest. "Hurry up, you two. We're doing the program *before* dinner, remember?"

"Sorry," Anne said. "My pedicure took longer than I anticipated."

Linda looked down. "Zoey?"

Anne nodded.

Linda slipped her foot out of her shoe and wiggled her toes. "Tressa. Does this mean they're going to be cosmetologists when they grow up?"

Will shook his head. "Not a chance. They're planning to take over the Silver Rose and convert it into a girls' school where you only have to study for two hours a day and the rest of the time you ride horses."

Linda rolled her eyes. "Thank goodness A.J. plans to sell it this fall. I don't think the seven dollars in my daughter's piggy bank will get them far."

Anne felt Will's sharp look and regretted telling Linda about one of A.J.'s more melancholy postcards. He had sounded resigned to making a fresh start somewhere else, like Wyoming or Montana.

The thought of A.J. selling out broke Anne's heart, which was why she'd brought up the subject with Linda. She couldn't picture the Silver Rose Guest Ranch without A.J. Or vice versa.

"Come on," Linda said, tugging Anne across the threshold. "I had Pam save us a table."

Anne didn't know anyone named Pam. Please don't let it be someone Will dated, she silently prayed. She couldn't even think about how relieved she'd been to learn from Joy that her daughter, Judy—Will's old prom date—wasn't coming from Alaska to attend the event.

Two glasses of wine later, Anne was finally starting to relax. The music seemed to transport everyone to a time when they were more candid, optimistic and outgoing, although the eighties had been just the opposite for Anne. Her father's death, living with her dour, repressed grandparents in Maine, then moving across the country with her newly remarried mother had left Anne mixed up and angry. She honestly couldn't blame any of these friendly people for not recognizing her. She'd been a mouse hiding in the library or scurrying to class, doing her best to avoid being caught in a social situation.

Will handled every introduction with finesse. He seemed to remember everybody's name even without benefit of name tags. "This is Anne Fraser," he said time and again. "You might not remember her because she was a year behind us in school. Anne is Esther's daughter, and we're running the Silver Rose this summer for Gramps."

It struck her as curious that he let people draw their own conclusions about their living arrangements. He also seemed determined to stake a claim, giving no one else a chance to ask her to dance—not that she wanted a different partner. Will was a wonderful dancer. And fun. He kept her too busy laughing to feel self-conscious.

"You're really good," she said when they returned to their table with fresh drinks. She couldn't believe how fast her wine had disappeared. Will's can of beer, on the other hand, appeared untouched.

He leaned close and whispered, "I assume you mean dancing."

His cheek brushed hers, his lips grazed her ear. A swirl of music—the inside kind—pulsed through her. "Of course," she teased. "What else?"

He stayed in whisper range, planting one hand on the table beside her. "You're flirting with a dangerous man, Anne Fraser. I've just spent several weeks being good, and believe me, that's a new personal best. Don't tempt me unless you're prepared for the consequences."

Was she? Tonight would be the perfect opportunity to take what he was offering. The idea had crossed her mind the second she decided to sleep on the couch in the office so Joy could be near Zoey. Tonight might well be Anne's one and only chance for a little adult pleasure. Was that wrong? Possibly. Probably. But at the moment, she really didn't care.

She put her finger on the tip of his nose and let it trail downward, over his lips. "Consequences, huh? Such as?"

He nipped her finger lightly. "A night of unrepentant passion."

"Would we need to repent in the morning?"

"Only if it makes you feel better."

"How will you feel?"

"Tired. A good kind of tired," he added with a wink.

Anne made up her mind. Right or wrong, she wanted him. She needed passion, intimacy, human contact. For months after her divorce she had craved not sex, but hugs. Now she wanted concrete proof that she wasn't dried up inside. That she was a woman, desirable and alive. "How much longer do we have to stay here?"

He pulled back, his eyes questioning. A slow grin spread across his ruggedly handsome face. "Thirty seconds. I just want to tell a couple of people goodbye. Stay put, okay?"

Anne watched him walk away. She'd met her share of handsome men, but she'd never known one who moved with more command of presence—the kind of self-assurance that had nothing to do with ego and everything to do with experience. He risked life and limb for a dream. Anne had to respect his dedication even if she didn't wholly understand the sport.

"Are you going?" Linda said, drawing up a chair. "Already? Is something wrong at home?"

Home. Anne glanced at her watch. She hadn't thought about the Silver Rose in four hours. "Actually, I turned off my phone while the speaker was talking about bygone days and forgot to turn it back on. Will you hand me my purse? I'd better check my messages."

"If Zoey's not the reason you're leaving, then

what…?'' Linda's question trailed off. ''Ohmygosh. You and Will? You're going to…to…''

''Stargaze,'' a deep voice provided.

Linda shot to her feet. ''Oh. Hi, Will. Stars, huh? Cool. Very cool. Count a few for me.'' She swallowed a giggle. ''I'm particularly fond of the Missionary constellation, myself. Some call it boring, but I say it all comes down to whom you're stargazing with, if you know what…''

''Damn,'' Anne said, turning sharply. Her hand knocked over her plastic glass full of wine.

Linda grabbed a wad of napkins. ''What's wrong?''

''Joy called an hour ago. She was concerned about Zoey's breathing.''

Linda stopped blotting. ''Did you call her back?''

''I tried. The machine picked up.''

Will didn't ask what to do. He walked to the hatcheck counter and returned a moment later with his Stetson and Anne's shawl. ''Let's go home. We'll both feel better if we check this out. She's probably fine, but why take any chances?''

Anne blinked back tears as she gave Linda a hug. She'd never known a man who put Zoey's health and her own feelings first. She couldn't count all the times that Barry had pretended to be asleep while his daughter struggled for each and every breath.

Perhaps out of habit, or because she didn't trust any man to stick by her, Anne paused at the doorway. ''I can drive back alone,'' she said. ''You don't need to miss the rest of the party. If she's sick, I'll be up with her the rest of the night. No time for…um, stargazing.''

He looked at her as if she'd suggested they blow up the capitol dome in Carson City. He put both hands on her upper arms and gently squeezed. ''Listen, Anne, I'm not some hedonist who only cares about having a good time.

I adore that little girl and I would never forgive myself if something happened and I wasn't there to help.''

"But…''

He shook his head sternly, his frown harsh. "Don't use Zoey's illness as a wedge between us. If you don't want to be with me, just tell me. But don't look at me like I'm you're ex-husband. I'm here for you both. Now, get in the car.''

WILL WAS PRETTY SURE he'd blown it. One minute he and Anne were flirting like teens, the next they were silent strangers. Normally, he wouldn't have come on so strong to her suggestion that he stay at the party, but the inference—that he only wanted one thing from her—had wounded him deeply. Did Anne really think so lowly of him? Or did she expect the worst from men, in general?

He wanted to ask but could tell by the way she twisted the beaded bag in her lap that now wasn't the time for an in-depth analysis of their relationship. Besides, his gut was in knots, too. Emergency rooms, scalpels, needles and sutures were such a common part of rodeo life that Will didn't give them a second thought—where his body was concerned. But picturing Zoey in respiratory distress, like that first morning when A.J. left, was enough to make his knees weak.

He stepped on the gas. "A couple of the younger cowboys carry cell phones. I wish I'd thought to write down their numbers,'' he said.

"How would that help? Only a trained paramedic knows what to do when her airway is blocked.''

Her voice sounded surprisingly strong and calm. "I meant that I could have one of them run up to the house to check on things. If Joy called an ambulance, we're going miles out of our way when we should be headed to the hospital.''

Anne let out a sigh. "I could be wrong, but I'm hoping that this is a false alarm. I tend to panic where Zoey is concerned, but Joy is very capable. Did you know one of her grandchildren had asthma as a child? He's in his twenties now and very healthy."

Will didn't know that. The only member of Joy's family he'd ever met was Judy, who, from what he'd heard at the party tonight, was happily married and living in Alaska.

Anne added, "If this had been a real emergency, I'm sure Joy would have asked one of the guests to come and get us. Don't you think?"

He eased off the gas. What she said made sense, but he couldn't let go of the tension that gripped his insides. He wasn't used to *caring* about someone else. And this little episode tonight proved to Will that his feelings for Anne and her daughter ran deeper than mere caring.

The fact was he loved them.

There, he thought, slowing to make the turn into the Silver Rose driveway. *I said it.*

He loved Zoey and he was pretty sure he was in love with Anne. There'd always been something between them—familial, sexual or whatever—but what he felt now was too intense to be anything but love.

Not that he intended to tell her. She had enough on her plate without fretting over his declaration of love.

"I'm coming in," he told her, pulling to a stop in front of the house. A cloud of dust enveloped them. "If we need to go to the hospital, I'll call ahead to alert the emergency room."

"Okay," she said, leaping out before the dust had settled. She left her purse and shawl on the seat. He turned off the engine and picked them up. As he walked to the house, he lifted the bundle to his face and inhaled her scent. Not perfume, but some indefinable quality so Anne that he could have picked her out of a lineup with his eyes closed.

He was at the foot of the stairs before he realized something was wrong. The house was dark. No bluish stutter of television from the parlor windows. No lights in the kitchen or dining room. If this were a crisis, he would have expected a bustle of volunteers.

Inside the foyer, he paused to listen. The creak of footsteps overhead told him Anne was in her room or Zoey's, but apparently everyone else was asleep. He set Anne's purse on the hall table, then hung her shawl and his hat on the coatrack before heading upstairs.

He was concentrating on being quiet and didn't realize Anne was standing at the top of the stairs until he bumped into her. She put her finger to her lips and motioned for him to go back downstairs.

Was she shutting him out? He hesitated for a second then turned around. To his surprise, she followed.

"Let's talk in the office," she said softly when they reached the foyer.

Will's curiosity mingled with relief. Whatever had happened, at least Zoey wasn't in danger.

Anne flipped on the overhead light and closed the door behind him. She leaned against it with a long sigh. "Turns out Joy overreacted. It must have been a minor attack. Joy said by the time she read through my emergency list, Zoey was already doing every step. She used her inhaler and went into the bathroom and ran the hot water so she could breathe the steam. She's fine. Sleeping like a baby."

Will felt his tension dissipate. He let out a bark of relief. "That's great. Why didn't she call you back and tell you?"

Anne looked down sheepishly. "Apparently, she did. I just listened to the first message and went ballistic. I'm sorry."

Will stepped to her and pulled her into a hug. "Don't

apologize. Your reaction was completely understandable. It was a big night and Zoey was excited. Frankly, it crossed my mind when we left that she seemed a bit wired. I'm just glad it didn't turn into something more serious.''

Anne gave him a peculiar look then slowly relaxed against him. "You never cease to amaze me."

"Oh, yeah? That's what everybody says. Everybody who doesn't know me."

She punched him lightly on the shoulder. "I know you, and I think you're wonderful. Empathetic and kind. Pushy when needed. If you hadn't driven me home, I probably would have had a wreck along the way. I kept seeing visions of Zoey choking and passing out."

Me, too. He squeezed her tighter. "But that didn't happen. So, let it go. How 'bout a nightcap?"

"Like what?"

Will stepped back and looked around. "I don't know, but I'm sure Gramps has some kind of liquor in the house. Esther was rather fond of a little toddy by the fire on a cold winter's night."

He crossed the room to a cabinet near the fireplace. As he did, he noticed the pile of bedding at the foot of the big leather sofa. He'd forgotten about the arrangement— Joy was sleeping in Anne's bed while Anne took the sofa. His mouth went dry.

He misjudged the force necessary to open the sticky doors of the hutch. The bang made his heart jump. His hand was trembling when he reached inside for a bottle. Cognac. Did he like cognac? Did he care?

He poured an inch of amber liquid into two glasses then turned around. Anne was standing in front of the map where A.J.'s trail of postcards was making progress across America's heartland. "Try this," he said. "Should be well aged if nothing else."

Her nose crinkled like a rabbit's when she lifted the

glass to her lips, but she closed her eyes and took a sip. Her wince wasn't as prominent as he'd expected. "Not bad. My ex used to drink cognac. He thought it made him look classy."

Will polished his off in one gulp. The burn felt good. "I used to drink on a regular basis till I found out I don't have the head for it. In my job, you need all the balance you can get. Alcohol messes with that."

Anne took another ladylike sip. She looked like a princess in her pretty yellow dress and sexy shoes, so beautiful it almost hurt him not to draw her into his arms and kiss her. But this was her call. He would make no moves until she gave him some kind of signal.

"I'm seeing progress in your grandfather's cards," she said, turning toward the wall again. "Wouldn't you agree?"

We're going to talk about A.J.? "He seems to make pretty good time each day."

"Not mileage—emotional healing. Each card seems a bit lighter in tone. And he says he misses us. That's good."

"Why is that good? He still has a long way to go. Do you want him to be unhappy all the way to Maine?"

She set the glass on the corner of the desk and walked to the wall. "No, of course, not, but it shows that he's healing. Listen to this…" She plucked a card from central South Dakota. The photo was of a giant buffalo statue. She flipped it over and read aloud: "'Dear family, Had breakfast at Al's Oasis in Chamberlain this morning. Coffee was a nickel. Do you remember suggesting we raise buffalo on the Silver Rose, Will? Can't recall now why we didn't give it a try. They seem like an interesting animal. Bought you a book of Sioux legends, Miss Zoey. Maybe you can read me one when I get home.'"

Looking up, she gave Will a satisfied smile. "See? He's

looking ahead. That's a good sign. And he obviously misses us. Especially you.''

"*Especially* me?"

"Yes. He mentioned your name. That means he's thinking about you. Men aren't always real obvious with their feelings."

Will took a step closer. "There you go again making rash generalizations. It should be pretty *obvious* what my feelings are. You're the one sending mixed signals. Do you want to clear those up for me?"

She stood her ground, but Will could tell she was debating how to reply. After a pause—eight seconds, to be exact—she said, "What are the chances that we have a key for that door?"

Will's heart flipped and twisted. "As a matter of fact, I ran across one the other day. I meant to give it to you this morning when you mentioned that you planned to sleep in here. Guess I forgot."

"Do you still have it?"

He gave her a slow grin. "Oh, yeah. I've got it."

Anne reached out and put her hand on his shoulder. "Show me."

CHAPTER NINE

ANNE FELT EIGHTEEN again. Nervous. Insecure about her body, her looks. But something was slightly different this time, and she was pretty sure it had to do with the way Will was looking at her. As if she were a genie who'd just granted him three wishes.

While flattered and excited, she was also scared. What if she wasn't good enough?

"Um, I think it only fair to warn you that I'm not very accomplished in the art of making love," she said, stumbling over her choice of words.

She expected him to laugh. Instead, he rested his butt on the edge of the desk and crossed his arms. "Is that a standard disclaimer? Or do you think I'm some kind of cowboy gigolo?"

She wondered if she'd somehow hurt his feelings. She walked to the grouping of chairs and sat down, her skirt making a poofy puddle around her. "I'm just being honest. I haven't had a lot of experience in man-woman things, especially when it comes to sex."

"You were married. You have a child. Both are things I can't claim."

"True, but my relationship with Barry was sort of…perfunctory. Even from the beginning when I told myself we were in love. I think for both of us marriage was a means to an end. We'd graduated from college. Had good jobs. Time to marry, right? Settle down?"

"Perfunctory. What's that mean? Businesslike?"

Anne smiled. "Actually, that's a good description. We were never an in-each-other's-pocket kind of couple. We were independent, with separate agendas, and when our paths crossed we sometimes made love."

Will didn't say anything but Anne could tell he didn't approve. And she knew instinctively he would never settle for that kind of relationship. Just being his date for one night had proven that he took his connection to a woman seriously. From the minute they walked into the hall, Will had made it clear to everyone present that Anne was with him. And she'd liked the feeling. But in defense of her former life, she added, "Believe it or not, that kind of relationship worked for us. We took great trips. Ate at marvelous restaurants. Seldom argued...until Zoey was born."

"Barry was an idiot."

Anne suddenly had a clear image of the last party she and Barry had attended. He'd left her at the door to "work the room." Their paths never crossed until she sought him out to leave because their baby-sitter needed to get home. Anne remembered hearing someone ask, "They're a couple? I never would have put the two of them together."

Will rolled his shoulders. "Was Barry the only guy you ever dated?"

Anne looked at her hands clenched in her lap. "No."

"Was he the best?"

She assumed he meant in bed. "No." That title belonged to Eduardo, her impetuous fling in Spain.

"I take it you were involved with someone before Barry," Will said. "Was he married?"

"Of course not." *I don't think so.* Although he was mysterious, and their meetings had been on the secretive side. She would go to his studio at a specified time. He'd paint. They'd eat bread and cheese and drink wine. Make love.

"He was my winter break fling during my junior year of college. I spent a three-week internship in Spain."

Will nodded. "I remember hearing about that trip when I came home for Christmas. A.J. was afraid you'd fall in love with some 'furinur.'"

She did fall in love, almost from the moment Eduardo approached her in the small café and showed her the sketch he'd done of her face. The pencil drawing made her more beautiful than she was, but he swore that was how he saw her.

"In retrospect, it was impossibly romantic and doomed from the start," she said, picturing the cluttered loft where they overcame a language barrier and laughed and made love on the floor. She never met his friends or family. He told her they would have disapproved, and while this had hurt her feelings, Anne still agreed to pose for him in the nude.

"He was my attempt to be cosmopolitan. I failed miserably. Instead of being glad that he didn't ask me to rearrange my life and stay with him in Spain, I returned home with a broken heart and an oil painting I eventually gave to Goodwill."

That was a lie. An odd, impressionistic wash of body parts, the painting was in her closet at home. The only aspect that resembled her was the heart-shaped mole on her left breast.

She looked down at her chest. Will's very interested, very male response this evening was flattering, but what if it was due to the dress? And her excellent bra? Childbirth and a grueling schedule that precluded time at the gym had taken a toll on her muscle tone. Nerves and a demanding job kept her thin, but was she too thin for Will's taste? So far this summer, her most revealing outfit had been shorts and a crop top.

Marshaling her courage, she looked at him. "I want to do this, Will, but I have to admit that I'm really nervous."

His lazy grin sent a shot of something far more potent than cognac through her veins. "And I'm not?"

"It's not the same. You're a guy."

"And guys don't get nervous when faced with the possibility of making love with a beautiful woman? Anne, it's time to burn your outdated guy manual. This is a new millennium. Men are just as insecure as women."

His lighthearted banter helped her relax. She crossed her legs, and her hemline exposed a few more inches of leg.

Maybe the cognac was doing its job, she thought, replenishing her drink from the bottle Will had left on the lamp table.

"Hoping to relax your inhibitions or do you need a shot of courage?" he asked, a teasing quality in his tone.

"Both," she admitted. "I haven't been with a man since Barry left."

"Five years ago?" He sounded shocked.

"Hey, I've been busy. You try climbing the corporate ladder while taking care of a sick kid. See how much time you have left for a social life."

He pushed off from the desk and walked to her. Lowering to a squat, he balanced on the balls of his feet and touched her cheek. "That wasn't meant to sound critical. I'm just amazed that any woman as beautiful as you wouldn't have to turn down a hundred propositions a day."

"Eighty, minimum," she said lightly. "But I'm not big on having sex with someone who sees me as a way to advance his career or some guy who's in town for the week and decides I meet some highly refined criteria. I don't have time for meaningless friendships, much less meaningless sex."

"So you're saying what happens between us will mean something?" he asked.

Of course it would, but Anne didn't want to think about that right now. "Yes, it means we like each other. But let's be honest, Will. Even though we're drawn to each other and we have this slight unrequited history between us, what's happening here is more about proximity and opportunity than long-term possibilities."

Will's eyes narrowed. He started to say something but Anne took advantage of his slight hesitation. She pressed her lips to his.

She'd tasted him before, but this was different. Her cognac added an exotic element that fired an intense reaction in her belly. "You taste minty," she murmured, shifting her mouth to explore another angle.

His tongue was dexterous and playful. His nice white teeth nipped her upper lip before he drew back slightly. "Gramps left a supply of breath mints in the drawer," he said. "I'd offer you one, but I happen to like the way you taste. Rare. Perfectly aged."

She tossed back her head in laughter. "Never use the A word when you're seducing a woman."

"Who's seducing whom?" he growled, pressing his lips to her throat. When he licked the pulse point in the hollow under her jaw, Anne nearly melted.

"Maybe you should give me some pointers," he murmured, running his fingers across her bare shoulder. "It's been a while for me, too. What should I talk about? How fair your skin is?"

Anne felt her face heat up. Not fair now.

"The texture is smoother than a polished agate buckle your mother once gave me."

His tongue traced a pattern downward to the plane of her collarbone. "And I love its color—sort of a gold and bronze mixed together." He slipped the strap of her dress aside. Anne was glad her bra was strapless. "But I can't wait to see more of this color." He nuzzled the outline where her tan stopped. "It reminds me of the pinkish white inside a seashell."

Anne put her hands on his shoulders and pushed back. "My artist friend used to describe my attributes as he...um, painted me."

Will rocked back and rose in one fluid motion, pulling her to her feet. "Paint you? Now, there's an erotic idea. What color do you want to be? Where can I start? Belly button and work out or toes and work in?"

She knew he'd deliberately misinterpreted her remark and she was reminded once again not to underestimate his sharp wit. "Not this time, thanks. Passionate-pink toe nails are quite enough for me."

"Aw, shucks," he said with a roguish wink. "I'm not half-bad with a brush."

She ran her fingers across the solid expanse of his chest, pausing at the buttons. "Somehow, I have the feeling you couldn't be *half*-bad at anything you tried." When he made a contrary sound, she scolded him. "Don't give me that humble-cowboy look. You dance like a dream. You're smart and funny and, at times, you speak like a poet."

He shrugged. "A friend of mine, Hayward Haimes, was the poet. He used to hitch a ride with me once in a while, and he'd read his stuff aloud to pass the time."

"Is he published?"

"Not that I know of. He passed away the summer before last."

Anne held her breath, afraid to ask the cause.

"Train wreck," Will supplied as if reading her mind. "Somewhere in the Southwest." His forehead knit and he looked away. "Strange, isn't it? Hay rode bulls for ten years and never even broke his little finger. Then he boards a train to visit his kids back in Tennessee and boom."

Anne could tell Will had been moved by his friend's death. She responded without conscious decision, offering comfort by pressing her body to his. The big metal buckle at his waist rubbed against her belly in a strange but provocative way. She ran her fingers upward into his hair. "I'm sorry." They'd both known loss. Her mother, his friend. Maybe they were meant to comfort each other.

"Nothing to be sorry about. He had a good life. One of his choosing. How many people can claim that?" he said, cutting off her reply with a kiss.

And what could she say anyway? Was hotel management the career she would have chosen if she'd known the kind of hours that were required to succeed at the corporate level? Maybe before Zoey was born, but not now. Unfortunately, she was caught in a vortex of her own making, and the shore of second chances looked too far away to reach without drowning.

But Will was offering her a lifeline. Was she brave enough to reach out and take it? Not without making certain they were on the same page about what this meant. One night. Nothing more.

What if you're in love? a voice asked.

She refused to think about that. Love was not an option.

"You'd better lock the door," she said.

He walked to the desk and opened the middle drawer. When he bent over to search for the key, Anne's gaze was drawn to the framed photograph on the desk, one she'd looked at a dozen times since she started working in A.J.'s office. Esther and A.J.'s anniversary two years earlier. They'd traveled to New York to see Anne. As usual, her work had interfered. She'd barely made it to Tavern on the Green in time for Esther's toast.

"I'll never forget the day I took the biggest gamble of my life. I called a stranger," her mother had begun. "By the time we hung up, I knew he was the man I was going to marry."

Anne had heard various renditions of her mother's story over the years. She'd always marveled at Esther's bravery, her ability to trust her gut.

"Having a change of heart?" Will asked, watching her from across the distance of the desk.

"Not at all," she said. "We have the perfect window of opportunity. I don't want to look back someday and think, 'I wish I would have…'"

He put one hand flat on the calendar blotter and leaned across the distance to kiss her. "How could someone who was quiet as a mouse in high school learn to talk so much?" he asked, his tone laced with humor. He held up the old-fashioned key. "Me lock door. You go sofa."

Anne rolled her eyes at the caveman talk, but complied, using the time to watch him move across the room. She'd already decided Will epitomized the ideal behind in a pair of Wranglers, but that was before she saw the way his tailored slacks defined his derriere. He'd tossed his suit coat on a chair, and his white shirt—slightly rumpled and partially untucked—begged to be removed.

When he joined her on the couch a moment later, her hands flew to work unbuttoning his shirt.

Will wasn't particularly shy. He was used to dressing in locker rooms. He once split his pants in front of a packed house and still managed a bow. But his panic level rose when Anne started to push his shirt over his shoulders.

Would she be turned off by his scars? The matching pair above his pecs was just the beginning. His entire history was spelled out all too clearly on his body's road map of scar tissue.

As if sensing his disquiet, she scooted down and tenderly brushed her lips across the right scar. "Did it hurt?" she asked.

"Not the surgery. I was out cold."

"What about what necessitated the surgery?"

A bad draw in Columbus, Ohio. Demon Juice. A bull that turned out left when everyone said he'd turn out right. Will had gotten hung up and never got his feet under him. He'd felt something tear deep inside his right shoulder, and when the bull fighters finally got him free, Will was too stunned to move. The bull stepped on his left shoulder, adding insult to injury.

Will's body tensed as if reliving the moment. "Yeah. That one hurt."

Her hand traveled down his chest, her fingers lingering on an inch-long raised silver line across his ribs. "Only horn gouge I ever took and it wasn't in competition. I was helping a friend move some cows on his place outside of Houston and I got between a mama longhorn and her baby. Not a good idea."

She chuckled softly. "If I point to a mark, can you tell me which bull and how many points you made riding him?"

"Probably not. But some you never forget."

"Like women?"

Will tensed again. She'd been honest with him, but her record was a pittance compared to his. Honor compelled him to say, "In the early years, when I was just starting out, there were a lot of girls. Most never lasted more than a weekend. Once or twice I spent the night with a woman just so I wouldn't have to pay for a motel room."

Instead of repulsion, Will thought he read compassion in her eyes. "That couldn't have been easy."

He didn't deserve her sympathy. "Wasn't so bad. Soft bed, warm arms. Sometimes even a free breakfast."

She pushed back and gave him a stern look—the kind he'd seen her give Zoey. "Don't pull that macho act with me, Will Cavanaugh. You're way too kindhearted to be able to spend the night with a woman you barely know without feeling guilty.''

She had him there. He hated feeling like he was using people, and he'd always done his best to make sure the women he slept with understood the rules—no strings, no commitment. ''Well, I don't know about that, but luckily, I started winning. As long as the money was coming in, I could be a little more discriminating.''

''Wasn't there ever someone serious?''

He nodded. ''A couple, actually. I even brought one home to meet Esther and A.J. Didn't your mother tell you?''

She shook her head. ''I'm sure I would have remembered. What was her name?''

Why were they talking about other people when the heat was rising between them? ''Does it matter? We both knew we didn't have a future together. She wanted the white picket fence. I wanted the championship. We split up. She's now married and has three kids.''

Anne ran her nails up the sides of his ribs, producing an unbearably pleasant shiver. ''How come you don't have any kids? You're wonderful with Zoey and Tressa.''

''Old-fashioned,'' he murmured, kissing her neck. ''Need a wife first. Wanna get married and have a couple more?''

She laughed. ''Quit joking.''

''What if I'm serious?'' *Am I?*

She shook her head. ''You can't be. Tonight is just a one-shot deal.''

Is this what they call karma? he wondered. ''It is?''

Her hands stopped moving. ''Isn't it?''

Will couldn't keep from snugging his obviously aroused body into the V provided by her welcoming legs. She was hot, half-dressed and gorgeous. Since when did he need the promise of tomorrow to make love to a woman?

He eased his hands behind her back and reversed their positions so Anne was lying on top of him. He unzipped her dress. As the material fell from her shoulders, he had a clear view of her lovely white breasts cupped by some scrap of lace. He hurt with wanting her, but something made him say, "You don't think making love will change things between us?"

"I guess I was hoping we'd be mature enough to handle what comes next with aplomb," she said, watching him.

Normally, he liked her vocabulary, her precise way of talking, but just now it pissed him off. He felt his desire start to fade. "If I wanted to take what comes next to a more serious level, you'd say…?"

A look of pure bafflement crossed her face. "What level?"

Did he really have to spell it out for her? "A relationship. You and me. Together."

"For the rest of the summer?"

For the rest of our lives. "Or longer."

"But what we feel for each other won't work beyond this room, Will."

"Come again?"

She blushed as if he'd said something risqué.

Will loved her blushes. She hadn't come yet, but he was willing to bet that her face would be flushed with passion if they continued on their present course.

"We can't be lovers on a casual basis, Will. Zoey sleeps in the room right next to mine. I couldn't leave her alone while I went to your cabin and you couldn't stay with me. It's not the right image to give to an impressionable young girl."

Will agreed, and her analysis told him she'd already given this some thought, but her eagerness to accept that no alternative existed made him angry. "So, we'd be careful. We could pretend she's your spouse and you're cheating on him.''

"That's not funny, Will. I'm not a sneak-around kind of girl.''

"What kind settles for one night of sex?''

She pushed off him and sat up. She reached behind to zip up her dress. ''I thought you wanted me, too.''

"Jesus, Anne, what do you think I'm upset about? I want you so badly my teeth are aroused.''

"Well, I'm sorry, but this is the way it has to be.''

"Why?''

She faced him, her color high. ''Because at the end of the summer, you're going back to your life and Zoey and I will return to the city. Do you honestly think it would be fair to any of us to try to maintain a long-distance relationship? Imagine what that would do to Zoey's perception of love. You'd come for the occasional visit. You'd want to stay with me. 'Don't mind Will, Zoey, he's my sleepover friend.'''

Will winced. He had to admit she had a valid point. He'd been in that kind of relationship once and it had nearly killed him to say goodbye to the child who was caught in the middle.

Anne moved to the end of the couch and drew her knees to her chest. Only the passionate-pink tips of her toes showed from beneath her dress. ''And what do I tell her if you get hurt again? If you're laid up in a hospital on the other side of the country?'' She shook her head. ''I tried taking care of my mother that way, Will, and it nearly killed me.''

He sat up with care and started buttoning his shirt. ''Those are worst-case scenarios, and you're getting ahead of yourself. I just want us to spend time together this summer. You, me and Zoey. You won't even give us a chance.''

She heaved a sigh of defeat. "Why bother, Will? When the summer is over, you're going your way and I'm going mine. Except for A.J., what do we have in common?"

No guts, no glory. "Love?"

She blanched. "You're basing that on a couple of kisses and one near miss of hot sex?"

His anger percolated, but he tried to understand her fear. She was right about the disparity in their goals, but whatever happened to love conquers all? "I based that on how I feel. But it's pretty obvious you're too afraid to let yourself risk that kind of involvement."

Her mouth opened and closed but no words came out.

He stood up. "I'd better turn in. Big day tomorrow. Our first Silver Rose trail ride and picnic. Are you still planning on letting Zoey join us?"

She nodded. "If she feels up to it," she said quietly. He could tell she was just as frustrated as he was.

Will walked to the door. He turned the handle then stopped and sighed. "I'm sorry, Anne. This sure as heck isn't how I saw the night turning out."

She gave a soft snicker. "Me neither."

Unable to help himself, he retraced his steps, hauled her up against him and kissed her with everything he felt, with everything he'd hoped to share with her the whole night long. When he lifted his head, Anne's eyes were closed. She felt practically boneless in his arms. He let go carefully, watching as she sank back down. He leaned over and touched his lips to her nose. "See ya in the morning, partner."

He closed the door with care. He hoped she'd think to lock it, to remove his temptation to go back inside. What the hell was wrong with him? Ten minutes earlier, he'd admitted that he readily slept with women he didn't intend to stay with. So she wanted to keep it simple. A quick roll in the hay. What was wrong with that?

Shaking his head, he snatched his hat off the coat tree and headed for his cabin. What a hell of a time in his life to develop principles.

ZOEY WOKE UP so excited she felt as if her body might jump outside her skin and run away. But the echo of warnings from nurses and doctors and her mother cautioned her to take deep belly breaths and move slowly. Well, as slowly as possible. Today was going to be her first ever trail ride. How could a person not get a little breathless over that?

She quickly put on her favorite Britney Spears T-shirt and a long-sleeved shirt for layers and sun protection, along with her boots, jeans and hat. Although, knowing her mother, she'd probably have to wear the dorky riding helmet instead. Her toothbrush touched a couple of teeth and she swallowed the mint-flavored gritty toothpaste to save a step. No need to comb her hair. It was going to get messed up anyway.

As she passed through her mother's room, she paused to look around. Joy's overnight bag was gone and the bed was made, but there was no indication her mother had been back to hang up her dress and change. That was odd. Was she sleeping in?

Naw, Zoey thought. Her mother never overslept.

She unlocked the door and dashed to the stairs. The smell of coffee and cinnamon rolls filled the air. She was glad she wasn't allergic to cinnamon. It was one of her favorite smells, second only to horse.

She trotted down the steps, pretending she was a high-stepping prancer, like the Tennessee Walkers that Will had pointed out in a book on horse breeds in her grandfather's library. Zoey thought they were too elegant for words, but a bit too prissy to live in the mountains. For pure love of life, she favored Arabians. Like Tulip, the horse she would be riding today.

Giving a whinny, Zoey tossed her pretend mane and galloped toward the kitchen.

"Hi, Will," she cried, delighted to see her favorite cowboy perched on a stool near the phone. "How was the party?"

He'd apparently been searching for something in the phone book, but it must not have been important because he closed the cover and held out his arms. "Good morning, Miss Z," he said, giving her a wonderful squeeze that left her happy and sad at the same time. This whole summer had been like that. It was the best one of her whole life, but it was going to end. She couldn't think about September without her chest hurting, so she asked, "When are we leaving on our trail ride?"

"Right after lunch."

"What?" She jumped back. "But what about our picnic?"

"Sorry, sweetness, we're going to have to postpone it. One of our incoming guests missed his connection and won't be arriving until ten. I need to go to the airport to pick him up. That won't leave us enough time to do both, but we can still take a short ride after lunch."

"Couldn't somebody else get him? What about Mommy?" Zoey looked around, but the only other person in the room was Joy, who was measuring flour into a big bowl. Where was her mother? She was always around at this time of day, pouring coffee, chatting with guests and making sure everyone was happy.

From the volume of voices in the adjoining room, their guests were enjoying their breakfast, but Zoey had yet to hear her mother's distinctive accent.

Will made a funny face, as if he had a stitch in his side, and stood up. He put the phone book back under the counter then stuffed his hands in his pockets and said, "I haven't seen your mom this morning. We had a late night. Maybe she's still sleeping."

Something wasn't right. First of all, her mother didn't sleep in. Ever. Second, Will was acting weird. Like maybe he didn't want to see Mom. Oh, no, Zoey thought. Did that mean they had a fight? She could remember some of her parents' fights. No loud voices to upset her, but cold looks and mean-sounding words.

"Are you mad at her for something?" she asked Will.

His mouth opened and closed twice before he said, "No, sweetheart, I'm just trying to juggle business stuff and I'm used to having your mom here to do it. She's good at it. I'm not."

That sounded truthful. Zoey rushed to him and threw her arms around his waist. "Sure you are, Will. You're the best. And don't feel bad about the trail ride. We can try a longer ride another time. Maybe for my birthday."

It never hurt to lay the groundwork for presents far in advance.

"When is—"

Before he could ask his question, a person stumbled into the kitchen. Zoey had to look twice to make sure it was her mother. Mom wore her usual cotton pajamas, but they were rumpled and one leg was hiked up at the knee. Barefoot, no robe, and hair as messy as some of the big kids' at Zoey's school, she stood frozen, her eyes blinking at the brightness.

"Mommy?"

Mom looked from Zoey to the clock to Will. Her cheeks got red and she turned so fast her heel made a squeaking sound on the floor. "I overslept," she shouted. "I'll be right back down. Don't leave without me. I'm going on that trail ride, too."

"What?" Will and Zoey both squawked in shock.

There was no answer because Mom had disappeared. Joy left the room, returning a few seconds later with a travel mug that she handed to Will. "You'd better hit the road. Sooner you pick up our guest, the sooner you can lead Annie Oakley and the others on their trail ride."

Annie Oakley. That was a good one, Zoey thought, covering her mouth to hide a snicker. She couldn't wait to tell it to Tressa. Not that there was any chance Mom actually intended to *ride* a horse. "Maybe Mommy plans on driving the truck alongside us or something," she said.

The look Will gave her said he was as baffled as anyone. For some reason, that made Zoey nervous all over again.

He took the cup from Joy but stared at it almost a minute before turning to leave. "Would you please remind Anne that cabins three and six are checking out, and the new people are due in this afternoon by car." Then he left.

Zoey was about to go find her mom when the back door burst open and Tressa charged in. Linda, Tressa's mother, followed—a lot more slowly. Linda didn't take her sunglasses off and she moved as if her head hurt.

"Coffee?" she asked, making a weak wave at Joy.

"There's a new batch brewing. If you don't want to wait, you'll have to get it from the thermos in there," Joy said, pointing toward the dining room. Her voice sounded even louder than usual, and Linda made a funny face before disappearing into the next room.

Tressa ran to Zoey. "Hey. We just saw Will at the mailboxes and he told us the ride was pos'poned. Can we go upstairs and play Barbies?"

"Not till you get some food in your tummies, girls," Joy said sternly.

Zoey liked Joy. Not only did their names sorta rhyme, but she was good at giving orders in a way that didn't make Zoey huffy. When her mom asked Zoey to do something, Zoey's first inclination was to argue. She never argued with Joy. "Got any oatmeal?"

"Yep. With raisins and cinnamon. Just the way you like it."

Before this summer, Zoey had believed that oatmeal only came in little packages that you mixed with water and heated in the microwave. Joy bought big bags of oats that kinda looked like horse food then cooked it on the stove with warm milk and plump, chewy raisins.

"Yuck," Tressa said. "I hate oatmeal. We had jelly rolls from the bakery. I'm full."

"Tress, don't be impolite," her mother scolded, returning with a big, steaming mug. "If you don't want something that's offered to you, simply say, 'No, thank you.'"

"No, thank you," Tressa said with a heavy sigh.

Joy set a bowl on the counter. The smell of cinnamon made Zoey's mouth water. "No problem," Joy said with a wink in Zoey's direction. "But I'll bet Oatmeal Girl lasts longer on her horse than Jelly Roll Girl."

Feeling smug and hungry, Zoey climbed up on the stool that Will had vacated and picked up her spoon. "Thank you, Joy," she said before digging into the fragrant concoction.

Linda and Joy stood together drinking coffee and talking about the party the night before. Zoey pretty much blocked it out because Tressa sat down beside her and launched into a story about her older brother, who was a stupid toad because he stole the remote to the television and wouldn't give it back even when their mother threatened to ship him to Siberia.

Normally, Zoey would have paid close attention to anything about Logan, because despite what his sister thought, he was killer cute. But this morning, she tuned that out, too. The sound she needed to hear was her mother's footsteps.

Something was wrong with Mom. Zoey knew that for sure. She had never appeared in public without combing her hair. That was crazy.

Anne walked in just as Zoey was chasing the last two raisins around the bottom of the bowl with her spoon. Her hair was combed but her cheeks were a strange shade of pink and she was breathing fast, like Zoey did just before an asthma attack.

To Zoey's immense surprise, Anne was dressed in jeans and a black Silver Rose T-shirt like the ones for sale in the office. Zoey wanted one real bad, but her mother said she hadn't expected such a huge response to her idea and had ordered only adult sizes.

Mom dashed to the coffeepot, elbowing Linda out of the way. "Hi, Linda. Joy. Fill me up. I need caffeine."

Zoey's grip on her spoon loosened. *Coffee?* Her mother only drank tea.

Joy obliged. Her mother took a sip then looked around. "Zoey, how come you and Tressa aren't at the barn?" she asked.

"Uh…we're waiting till Will gets back," Tressa answered when Zoey failed to make her voice work.

"Is he running behind schedule?"

"We all are," Joy said. "Got a late arrival coming in. Will just left for the airport to pick him up." Before Zoey's mom could say anything, Joy added, "Means a shorter ride this afternoon, but nobody's complaining. A couple of the folks wanted to go to church *and* take part in the trail ride. Now they can do both."

Mom looked a little confused, like she didn't even know today was Sunday. "O…kay, then. I'll say hi to our guests, then be right back. If we're not packing a picnic lunch, maybe we can eat under the big tree."

As she hurried into the dining room, Zoey and Tressa

exchanged a look. "Is your mom wearing boots?" Tressa asked.

Zoey nodded. Her stomach didn't feel right and she didn't think it was from eating too much oatmeal. "They're my grandma's old pair. Mommy said they pinch her toes. She let me wear them for fun until I got my own." She kicked the heels of her very cool aqua-blue leather boots together.

"What's she got 'em on for now?"

"I don't know." An unpleasant thought struck her. Was her mother planning to join the ride because she was afraid Zoey might have an attack? Had Joy told her about what happened last night?

Tressa leaned closer and whispered, "I heard my mom tell somebody on the phone this morning that your mom and Will are in love." The way she said it told Zoey how repulsive her friend found the idea.

Zoey dropped her spoon. It clattered to the floor, launching the last two raisins airborne. *Love?* she mouthed in disbelief.

Tressa nodded, making a face.

"No way," Zoey said, slipping off the stool. She dropped to her knees and stretched for the spoon to give herself time to think. *Is it possible?*

A tingle started in her chest. Instead of a scary tightening, a warm glow spread through her insides. This could be the coolest thing ever, she thought. If Will and her mom *were* in love, Zoey might never have to leave the Silver Rose. What could be better than that?

CHAPTER TEN

ANNE PAUSED at the parlor window, her gaze attracted to the colorful scene unfolding beneath the giant cottonwood. Given the heat of late July, they'd decided to hold Zoey's birthday party outside, where an inflatable swimming pool had been erected. Will and two of his young ranch hands had secured the swing to the tree and were now attempting to suspend a festive, horse-shaped piñata in its place. Dappled shade cast roving shadows on the nearby picnic tables, which, as per Zoey's request, were adorned with bright pink tablecloths. Balloons and a "Happy Birthday, Zoey" banner fluttered in the arid breeze. A barbecue grill and three large coolers completed the setting.

In an hour, six children would be arriving for the kind of party her daughter had always dreamed of—games, swimming, hot dogs and cake. The kind of party Anne's demanding schedule had prevented her from throwing for her daughter. Now, thanks to Will and Joy, Zoey was going to have the best birthday of her life.

Anne wished she could claim more of the credit. But she'd been busy—avoiding Will. In the weeks since their romantic near miss, Anne had devoted herself to improving the Silver Rose, overseeing everything from an immaculate, weed-free garden to newly painted bathrooms in every cabin. Her campaign had procured the physical distance she needed to convince herself she'd made the right choice. But emotionally, Anne was still a long way from admitting she hadn't made the worst mistake of her life.

Will's outwardly benign attitude toward her would have driven Anne mad, if not for the occasional glimpse at the turmoil beneath the facade. He might act as though he'd put their sexual attraction behind him, but every so often, when he thought she wasn't looking, she'd catch a hint of longing in his eyes. That look would make her recall the all-too-vivid details of their encounter.

Anne told herself she'd made the only decision possible given their circumstances. But practicality didn't make the nights any easier to take. Or the days, either, she decided, leaning closer to the window so she could watch Will at work. Shirtless.

Her grip on the Hello Kitty napkins tightened as she scanned his broad shoulders. The waistband of his jeans was almost black from sweat. When he leaned over to pick up the gaily adorned papier-mâché pony, she caught a glimpse of white at his waist. Pale skin or underwear? God help her, she really wanted to know.

Throat dry, she closed her eyes and sighed. *Fool.*

The trill of the phone interrupted her mental castigation.

Please, let it be Barry, Anne prayed as she hurried toward the office. She'd e-mailed him and left two messages on his service to remind him of Zoey's big day. Would he make the effort to call his daughter? Probably not. Which meant Anne would have to call him before Zoey left for Tressa's sleepover; Barry would pretend he'd been poised to call and Zoey would be thrilled to talk to him. Then a few days later a nice big check would arrive in the mail. Such was Barry's idea of fatherhood.

"I got it," Zoey cried, charging into the room past her mother.

She launched herself into A.J.'s chair. "Hello? I...I mean, Good morning, Silver Rose Ranch." Anne listened for any telltale rattle in her daughter's breathing, but all she heard was expectation in the little girl's voice.

"Grandpa," Zoey shrieked with delight. "You remembered."

Anne paused in the doorway. Tears clouded her eyes. Thank heavens for the Cavanaugh men, she thought—A.J. for remembering, Will for teaching Zoey how to ride.

Just look at her, Anne thought, observing Zoey with as impartial an eye as possible. She'd grown two inches, at least. Her lanky legs were as brown as walnuts. Her hair had grown, too. It brushed her midback and was almost ash blond from the sun. The wavy locks looked full and lustrous thanks to Joy's mysterious mayonnaise beauty treatment.

Zoey had blossomed in other ways, too. No longer shy and tentative, she'd become the Silver Rose mascot— adored by guests, confident in social settings.

What Anne found even more thrilling was that, despite the ranch's abundant supply of dust, pollen and animals, Zoey hadn't experienced another critical respiratory episode.

She's happy here and healthy. What that might mean when they returned to New York was anybody's guess.

"Mommy," Zoey shrieked, motioning Anne to come closer. "You'll never guess what Grandpa bought me." Into the phone, she cried, "Oh, Grandpa, thank you so much. I love you. I love you."

Hearing her daughter's effortless declaration touched Anne deeply. Why couldn't love be that simple? Why, when Anne knew she was in love with Will, couldn't she come out and tell him? Why did she have to make everything so complicated?

Anne had agonized over the matter enough in the past five weeks to know there was no simple answer. Was she a spineless coward who hid behind her job and her daughter to avoid involvement with a man who made her want things she couldn't have? Or was she a woman with defined goals and dreams that could only be met in a larger arena than the Silver Rose could provide?

"Mommy," Zoey cried, "Grandpa bought me a car."

"A what?" The napkins slipped from Anne's hand, spilling pink kittens in French berets across the floor.

"A car. It's my size. Runs on a batt'ry. And it's pink. My favorite color," she added on a last whisper of breath.

"Do you have your inha…?"

Before Anne could finish the word, Zoey pulled the plastic medicine dispenser out of the pocket of her shorts. She took a measured puff and inhaled deeply. Within moments, she was breathing freely, but the dark look she gave Anne said Zoey hadn't appreciated her mother's interference.

"Grandpa wants to tell you about it."

Anne's step faltered as she walked to the desk. To think she'd been afraid A.J. or Will would try to give Zoey a horse.

Zoey started to pass Anne the receiver then jerked it back. "Come home soon, Grandpa. So I can kiss you. And drive my car."

Anne took the phone and stepped out of the way so Zoey could race past. Her joyous cry filled the house. "Grandpa bought me a car."

Muffled applause came from the kitchen, where Joy was holding her weekly cooking class.

"What have you done, A. J. Cavanaugh?" Anne said, her voice not nearly as stern as she wanted it to be.

"Don't fret, Annie. It's harmless. A miniature pink convertible. Cutest thing you ever saw. I spotted it in some farmer's yard. His granddaughter was grown up and he was getting rid of the thing. Only cost twenty bucks. He wanted forty, but when it wouldn't start, he came down."

"A car that doesn't run. Okay. I like that."

He chuckled. "I figure it needs a new battery. Heck, that'll probably cost more than the car."

All sorts of practical responses chased through Anne's mind. Zoey was too young to operate a motorized vehicle. Too reckless. What if she drove it through a fence or flipped over or got in the way of a truck? And they couldn't take it home with them. What would happen when they left?

Instead, Anne said, "I'm sure she'll be over the moon when she sees it. How were you able to fit it in the motor home?"

His laugh almost sounded like the A.J. she remembered from years past. "Strapped it to the back of the RV. You should see the looks I get."

Anne wondered if the idea of seeing Zoey behind the wheel had lifted his spirits—given him something to look forward to. Only an ogre would ruin that. "Well, you shouldn't have, but if you could see the bright smile on my little girl's face, you'd be glad you did."

"Got enough regrets without passing up a chance to please my only granddaughter." He cleared his throat. "Speaking of regrets, what's going on with that grandson of mine?"

Anne put her hand to her chest. Only years of working with the public kept her voice steady. "What do you mean?"

"The last time I talked to him, he was surly as a bobcat with a sore foot. I got thinking he might be getting antsy. Will's never been one to stick in one place too long." The truth of that statement hit Anne harder than the impact of a pink convertible. "His daddy was like that, too. I offered to set Johnny up with a hundred-acre parcel. Help him build a place. But he said he wasn't going to put down roots till he was too old to follow his dream."

Anne's heart went out to A.J. It must have hurt when

his son turned his back on the legacy his father had offered.

A.J. cleared his throat. "Anyways, I thought that since you have things under control guestwise, we might be able to cut Will loose a little early." His voice faltered when he added, "I'm heading to Maine in the morning."

Anne's gaze went to the map. The density of postcards in the Pennsylvania, Maryland and Virginia area dramatized A.J.'s arrested forward motion. Civil War sites. Revolutionary War sites. Jamestown. Manassas. He'd been stalling for weeks.

She couldn't blame him, of course. Just thinking about him casting her mother's ashes into the ocean made her cry. "Does this mean you might come home earlier?" Anne asked.

"Mebbe. Once my job is done, not much sense in fooling around out here. No real family to visit, since Esther's parents have passed on."

Anne knew that her grandparents had never completely embraced A.J. as their son-in-law. For the first couple of years after Esther and A.J.'s marriage, there had been no communication with Maine whatsoever. But Anne had helped open those channels while in college.

Esther and Anne had been at the hospital when Grandmother Jensen passed away. Two months later, after the neighbors found Grandfather at the foot of the stairs, Esther, A.J. and Anne had attended the funeral.

Anne consulted the calendar on the desk, then her gaze fell upon the Roger-related tower of papers on the corner of the desk. What she wouldn't give for some extra time to prepare for the big summit meeting Roger had scheduled for early September. Why was Will the one being given the break, not her?

As if hearing her complaint, A.J. said, "I know you're anxious to get back to your life, too, Annie, but I was hoping you'd stick around a bit longer so I can spend time with Zoey."

Anne immediately regretted her selfish thoughts. Zoey would be devastated if she didn't get to see her grandfather. And she'd want to drive her car, too. "I'm here for the duration, A.J. You can count on me. And I'll give Will the word, unless you want to stay on the line. He's outside by the big tree hanging up a piñata for the party this afternoon."

"I heard you've got some kids coming."

"Yes. My friend Linda's son and daughter will be here and a couple of children Zoey met at Linda's house. Joy is preparing a feast—hot dogs and her famous spicy calico beans. All of the Silver Rose guests are coming, too. It should be great fun.

"You know, A.J., Will's riding clinics have been a big hit, and I've had several people tell me they'd like to bring their children or grandchildren with them next year. Isn't that exciting?"

He didn't answer right away. "Somethin' to chew on, I guess."

His lack of enthusiasm made her frown. Anne knew it was unrealistic to think he'd just snap out of his grief and return to Nevada ready to resume his life. That life was forever altered. Besides, she could attest to the fact that it took two people to run this place. What would he do next summer?

Without pausing to think it over, she said, "You know, A.J., Zoey and I have really enjoyed our time here. Maybe there's some way we could come next year, too."

A.J. was silent for so long Anne thought they'd been disconnected. But a sniffle told her he was there. "I'm mighty touched by the offer, Annie. And I'll give it some thought on the way home. Got a nice long drive with some big stretches of empty road where a man can't do nothing but think.''

She squeezed the phone between her shoulder and ear and wiped her sweaty palms on her shorts. Had she really volunteered for another tour of duty? Was she out of her mind?

Before she could withdraw the offer, a shadow fell across the floor. She looked over her shoulder and nearly dropped the phone. Will was in the doorway—shirt on, unfortunately—picking up spilled napkins. ''Well, speak of the devil, A.J., Will's here.'' Her voice sounded almost as high-pitched as Zoey's. ''I'll give you to him. But before I go, I want to thank you for calling. Zoey's father has been known to forget her birthday, so this call was extra special. You're a wonderful man and we...love you.''

I said it. She silently congratulated herself, passing the phone to Will. He offered her the napkins in exchange, and her smugness evaporated the instant their fingers touched. The tingle that shot through her body nearly took her breath away.

She hurried out of the room and walked briskly to the kitchen. Joy's cooking class that morning involved baking and decorating a special birthday cake. The room was too crowded and the mood was too chipper to suit Anne's unsettled emotional state. She slipped outside to the garden.

Anne was proud of her novice gardening efforts. Her tomatoes were growing. Her basil was fragrant. Her snap peas *made* Joy's stir-fry. But something was eating her beans, and the culprit wasn't human.

She walked to the shed. Sunlight filtered through the cobwebbed curtains framing the corners of the room's single window. Anne upended an empty five-gallon plastic pail and sat down to study the laminated cheat sheet her mother had left. What was she missing? The fledgling plants came up with vigor. They sent out wiry feelers to attach to the strings she and Zoey had laced between the upright poles. Green leaves back-filled the gaping holes. Baby beans formed. Then, just prior to harvest, the beans disappeared.

Anne hunched forward, resting her chin in her palm. Was this a metaphor for her life? Carefully nurtured plans that never fully matured? Her marriage. Her career.

A pain radiated outward from behind her eyes and she rubbed her knuckle between her eyebrows. "Crap," she muttered.

"Professional gardeners prefer the term *manure,*" a voice said.

Anne's chin came up. "Will," she exclaimed. "That was a short chat."

"We're men. We manage to say almost everything in five sentences or less." His jest was one of the few she'd heard him utter in her presence since their close encounter of the sexual kind.

She made a tsking sound. "Update your handbook, mister. Men are talking more and saying less than ever before. Pretty soon you'll all be politicians."

He laughed. The sound poured over her like warm honey. She suddenly realized just how much she'd missed him. Their repartee. Their end-of-the-day chat, when they shared both triumphs and failures. Had she been totally off base to turn him down? Sitting in her mother's potting shed, Anne had no doubt what choice Esther would have made.

"A.J. wanted me to give you a message," Will said. "Apparently, your mother left Zoey a present. It's on the top shelf of the closet in her sewing room. It might not have her name on it because Esther usually bought a special card closer to the actual day."

Anne rose. "Mom was one amazing lady, wasn't she?"

Will nodded. Even though he hadn't entered the shed—just stood casually in the threshold, one shoulder resting on the jamb—his presence made the place too crowded. Or maybe it was the elephant-size awkwardness between them that made the room seem so small.

Anne pitched the garden guide to the bench. "I think mice are eating my beans."

"Little furry mice or little mice girls?"

Zoey? Intentionally eating green vegetables? Not likely. Even Anne's cherished creamed peas and potatoes recipe had received a mixed response—the child loved the creamy potatoes but built a Mayan temple out of the perfect green globes. "The former, I'm sure. Most eight-year-olds aren't big on crudités, and Zoey is no exception."

Will's mirthful grin said he might know something about her daughter that Anne didn't. "Well, if the critters are to blame, I suggest you set a trap. They're creatures of habit. They travel the same path over and over to get what they want. You should catch one without much effort."

"What would I do with it if I caught one?"

"Slow, methodical torture?"

Before she could protest, he laughed to show he was joking. "If you use a humane trap, which I happen to know is the only kind your mother would allow, you set him free in the field the next morning. He gets a vacation with his rural cousins, you get the satisfaction of seeing your beans develop into dinner."

He stepped forward. Anne braced against his touch, but Will made sure that didn't happen. He reached overhead and plucked a matchbox-like container from the rafters. "Here you go," he said, offering it to her.

The printing on the sides had faded, but she could make

out the words Mouse Jail. ''Bait it with a little cheese. Or peanut butter,'' he suggested.

She took it with both hands. ''Okay.''

An almost visible sizzle arced between them. One careless spark could have burnt down the whole place. Anne started to speak, but Will beat her to the punch. ''Look, Anne, I'm sorry. I've been an ass these past few weeks. When Gramps mentioned he might be coming back early, I realized that I didn't want to spend what time we have left being mad at each other. Can we put that night behind us?''

She released a hesitant breath. ''I'd like that, too.''

He offered his hand to seal the deal.

Anne took his proverbial olive branch. Unfortunately, the contact went deeper, much deeper, and Will felt it, too. She could tell by the way his eyes narrowed and his grip tightened. He reached out to touch her cheek. From the frown on his lips, she knew the movement went against his better judgment.

She could sympathize. She had no intention of looping her arms around his shoulders, but somehow they did just that. She absolutely, positively wasn't going to kiss him, but she did, with a need that blocked every other thought.

She tossed the Mouse Jail onto a shelf. Hands groped. Lips slanted for more access. Noises of mutual need filled the dusty quiet.

They stumbled backward into a thigh-high stack of fertilizer sacks and bags of potting soil. Will lifted her slightly so she was seated. Her legs locked around him and she found the perfect place for their bodies to meet.

Will allowed it—facilitated it—for a few seconds, then he lifted his head. Eyes closed, he said on an outward expulsion of air, ''Joy's calling.''

Anne groaned. ''I knew this was a bad idea.''

She tried to push him away, but he stubbornly peppered

kisses along her forehead, her nose and, finally, her lips. "Even married couples have trouble squeezing in sex in the afternoon."

"How would you know?" she asked crossly.

"I have married friends. Men have been known to gossip from time to time." He stepped back and held out his hand to help her off her perch. "Besides, this isn't exactly the most romantic place on the ranch."

Anne looked around. *The potting shed?* Heat filled her cheeks and she dropped her chin so Will wouldn't see her mortification. The sound of Joy's bullhorn-like paging penetrated the walls of the shack as clearly as Will's chuckle, now that the roar of passion had dissipated.

Will moved aside to give Anne access to the door. She hurried to the threshold and leaned out. "I'm here."

Joy waved from the porch. "That guy from your office is on the phone. Says he *has* to talk to you. Right now."

Anne let out a defeated sigh. "I told Roger I was going to be busy with Zoey's party today," she muttered. The current political wrangling at WHC had Roger edgy and nervous, and he was making darn sure Anne knew it. "Tell him I'll be right there," she called.

She turned to look at Will, who'd picked up the mousetrap and was sitting where she'd been a moment earlier. "Duty calls," she said, striving for a lightness she didn't feel.

"Don't top executives ever get a day off?"

"Well, maybe after you *become* a top executive. For those of us on the road up, we jump when our names are called. I may have mentioned that Roger wasn't very happy about my request for family leave, but he couldn't turn it down, either. This is payback for the inconvenience I've caused him."

She expected to hear, "So, quit." Instead, he rose and

walked toward her. "Here," he said, placing the humane trap in her hands. "But I should warn you. It won't work."

Her heart stuttered. "What do you mean?"

"The garden mouse will enjoy his visit with his cousin in the country, but eventually he'll return to where he's most comfortable."

She straightened her shoulders. "What if he discovers he likes the country better?"

"By the time he figures that out, you'll have removed the trap because you think your problem is solved, and he'll be stuck."

Was he telling her she could be missing an opportunity that might never come again?

He started to leave.

Anne cleared her throat. "Did I mention that Zoey is spending the night at Linda's? Her first official sleepover. It's…um, part of her birthday present from me," she admitted, knowing he'd understand how difficult it was for her to let her daughter go.

He hesitated. "I mighta heard a rumor to that effect."

"I gave Joy the night off, too. The guests are on their own."

A hint of a smile twitched in one corner of his mouth, but his eyes gave away nothing. "And how are you planning to spend your free time?"

Anne reached deep for courage. "A glass of wine. Maybe a soak in the tub." She looked at the mousetrap in her hand. "Do you want to join me?"

He didn't answer until she lifted her chin and their gazes met. "Will there be bubbles?"

"Probably." In negotiations, it paid to keep your options open.

"Then you've got yourself a date, ma'am. I'm a sucker for bubbles." He started to leave, but stopped abruptly. "I almost forgot. Gramps would like you to take a video of the party, so he can see it when he gets home.''

Anne was touched. Those Cavanaugh men really did seem to have a line on her heart. "No problem."

He gave a nod. Such a cowboy thing, she thought. What was it about the gesture that made her pulse race?

WILL STOOD at the window of his cabin and squinted toward the main house. Anne was waiting. And he was almost as nervous as he'd been the last time he'd ridden a bull. Some kind of intuition had warned Will not to get into that chute that night. He'd ignored the precognition and had wound up unconscious on a gurney. For months afterward, he'd asked himself how different his life might have been if he'd listened to that voice.

Now, his gut instinct told him to stay put. Let it go. Let her go. But he couldn't. Wrong or right, being with Anne seemed fated.

At one point in the afternoon, Will had been certain Anne was going to change her mind about letting Zoey go home with Linda. Who knew a piñata could bring out such a fierce competitive spirit in little girls? But after a short mother-daughter talk in private, Zoey settled down and the afternoon progressed without loss of life or limb. At four o'clock, all the children had piled into Linda's minivan, Zoey waving with glee.

Anne had looked momentarily stricken, but before he could offer a comforting hug, a phone call from New York had had her racing to the office.

He glanced at the clock beside his bed, then at the open doors of his closet. Will couldn't decide whether to wear what he had on—shorts and flip-flops—or jeans and boots.

With a sigh, he walked to the bathroom. His open shaving kit reminded him of one other possible necessity. They hadn't discussed birth control. Since his shorts lacked pockets and he didn't want to be clutching a handful of condoms if he bumped into any of their guests, Will opted for jeans.

When he sat down on the bed to pull on his boots, he landed on the leftover paper he'd used to wrap Zoey's gift. Not the pony she'd hinted at but a fancy belt with her name tooled into the leather and an ornate buckle of silver with a golden horse rearing.

She'd seemed genuinely pleased by the gift, hugging Will so fiercely his crotchety rib started to ache. But he hadn't minded. Will knew then that he loved Anne's daughter more than he'd dreamed possible. The thought of telling her goodbye in September made his knees weak.

He left his cabin before he could change his mind. He didn't bother turning off the outside light. Maybe one of them would come to their senses.

"Nice night, isn't it?" the couple from Dallas said as Will passed by cabin number three.

Will took a deep breath. "Beautiful. Look at those stars."

"You want to see stars, you need to come to Texas," the man said. A moment later he laughed. "Oh, hell, you've been to our state hundreds of times, haven't you? Why, Lucille and I saw you ride in Abilene. That was one ballistic bull you drew. Missed out on the money, didn't you?"

Will snickered softly. "Yep. Devil's Advocate. Tough and tricky. I don't think he's been ridden yet."

The man cleared his throat. "Well, as a matter of fact, we caught a PBR event in Odessa on our way here. One of the new fellows rode that bad boy for a 94.5, I believe."

Will felt a punch in his gut—the kind he got every time he picked up a copy of *ProBullRider* magazine and read the latest stats. Life went on in the bull-riding arena. Either you were in the money or you were history. "That's good to hear," he said with fake enthusiasm. "Means I can try for a bigger score next time around."

After a little more chitchat, Will continued toward the house. A silvery-blue light flickered in the windows of Anne's room. Was she watching television?

He paused outside her door to wipe a bead of sweat from his forehead. It was a warm night, but not that hot. He'd ridden with a cracked wrist and had felt less trepidation than he did at this moment. *What's the big deal?* he asked himself. *We're adults. Single. Responsible.*

He rapped softly. The chatter from the television went silent. A second later, the door opened. Anne was dressed in lounging shorts and a loose yellow tank top. She looked cool and relaxed; he felt overdressed and uptight.

Her gaze dropped to his boots. "You're all dressed up."

"Cowboy uniform. Force of habit."

She smiled. "I know what you mean. It's taken me two months to wean myself from panty hose." She stepped back to welcome him. "Come in. I was just watching you on television."

He froze. "Pardon?"

"This afternoon when I was looking for the video camera, I ran across some tapes marked Will Bull Riding." She held up the remote control. "It took me a couple of tries to figure out the chronology. Mom was never very good about labeling things."

Will chuckled. "Like Zoey's present?"

Anne groaned. "Don't remind me. I should have peeked under the wrapping paper before I brought that gift downstairs."

Zoey had pounced on the gaily wrapped gift from her grandmother, but the whole party had gone silent when she pulled a sexy black negligee out of the box. Anne had turned three shades of red and immediately raced back upstairs to find the real present.

Will couldn't resist teasing Anne, who looked mortified just recalling the incident. "I was kinda hoping that negligee might reappear tonight."

Anne cocked her head and said, "Well, we'll have to see about that. First, I need you to narrate this video. Tell me who the other people are and what's going on, and—most importantly—why the heck anyone would start riding bulls in the first place."

Will rolled his eyes. "People ask me that all the time. I usually turn the question back on them and ask how they got involved in their job. Why did you pick a job that doesn't even give you a day off to enjoy your daughter's birthday?"

She took a breath, which made him all too aware of the fact that she wasn't wearing a bra beneath her loose shirt. Her shorts were the kind that could be worn to bed—extra short, with an elastic waist. Way too easy to take off.

"You know what? You're right. There was no excuse for what happened today. And I plan to make that clear to my boss the next time he calls." She pretended to consult her nonexistent wristwatch. "Which, knowing Roger, will probably be in six hours. He seems to have no concept of the time difference between here and the East Coast."

Will liked her best when she lost her defensive posture. He closed the door, listening for the satisfying click of the lock. "Why do you put up with it?"

Anne shrugged. "Why do you put up with broken bones?"

"Because it comes with the territory?"

She nodded. "Exactly. Roger is like a rank bull—see how I picked up the lingo? But if you ever tell him I said that I'll have to hurt you."

He chuckled as he walked to the foot of the bed. "I'll remember that." Facing the television, he asked, "So, where are you? My early, early years, huh? Your mother and I watched this video last November when I was here for Thanksgiving. She was feeling nostalgic, she said.''

''Do you think she knew she was sick?'' Anne asked. She sat cross-legged on the mattress, leaving ample space for him to sit beside her.

Will did so, but his accidental glance at the inviting gap in her shorts made him swallow hard and look back at the screen. ''No,'' he said, shaking his head with more force than necessary. ''She seemed fine. Not quite as peppy as usual, but she blamed the weather. They'd had several storms.''

''I know. That's why Zoey and I didn't come. I was afraid we'd get snowbound. Things were piling up at work and I couldn't afford to lose any time…''

The regret in her voice made him put his arm around her shoulders. ''You made the right decision. I was stuck here two extra days and missed an important event in Laughlin. I was trying to make up for it when I drew the bull that gave me the concussion, which is the reason I'm not riding this summer.''

Her smile said thank-you, and something else. Something inviting, but he couldn't accept until he was clear about what this meant to her. Was this casual sex between two consenting adults or were they taking the first step toward something meaningful? If the latter was the case, Will had to make certain Anne understood who he was and what he did for a living, because that wasn't going to change.

''Anne, do you want to know the real reason I ride bulls?''

When she nodded, Will took the remote from her hands and fast-forwarded until he spotted a familiar face. ''Him. John Albert Cavanaugh.''

''Your dad?''

''He was twenty-nine when he died. He left some unfinished business and it's up to me to get the job done. I started participating in rodeos almost as soon as I could walk. Mutton busting, greased-pig chase, calf riding.''

"Seriously? Those are events?''

He grinned. "Yes, ma'am. I've been told that I was very good. Not fast enough to catch my little oinker, but close.''

He hit play. Six little boys in boots and hats stood in line, their fathers behind them. Each child had a big black number pinned to his shirt. "That's me,'' Will said, pointing to a scrawny runt wearing the number six.

Anne let out a whoop. "Look how little you were. I can't wait to show this to Zoey,'' she exclaimed. "She's been bugging me about attending a rodeo before we leave. If she sees this she'll want to participate.'' She frowned. "They don't let girls, do they?''

"Nowadays it would be dangerous to tell a girl she can't do something.''

A.J.'s infrequent commentary clued them into what was happening. Will pointed out his father, mother and grand-mother when they came into range of the camera. The view panned to the wooden chutes across from the bleachers. An announcer's voice could be heard. "Okay, folks, give a big round of applause for Mr. William Cavanaugh, who's riding his very first bucking bull…calf. This young man has some pretty big boots to fill since his pappy is rodeo favorite John Cavanaugh.''

Will glanced sideways. Anne had scooted to her knees on the mattress and was leaning forward, her body language fraught with tension. "Anne, relax. I survived.''

She gave him a quick smile but returned to her scrutiny. "Your father looks upset about something.''

Will eyed the screen. He didn't remember this part. Had Esther fast-forwarded the tape for some reason?

He turned up the volume to catch what his father was saying. His was a voice he couldn't remember hearing in real life. "Pay attention to me when I'm talking to you, son. Do you want to win or not?"

"Johnny, let it go," a woman said off camera. "He's just a little boy. He did his best."

"Stay out of this, woman. This is between me and my son. If he wants to represent the Cavanaugh name in rodeo, he needs to do it right so he wins. We don't have room for losers in the family. Ain't that right, Will?"

The screen went to blue, but not before Will saw the child's face barely visible beneath the brim of his big black hat. Cheeks streaked with tears, lips trembling, but chin set stubbornly. Obviously trying hard not to show his pain. *No room for losers.*

"That seemed a bit harsh. Do you remember it?" Anne asked.

"Nope," Will answered truthfully. "I barely remember either one of my folks. They were on the road a lot of the time and I stayed with A.J. and Grandma or my mom's aunt in Chico. I was here when the call came from the state troopers."

Thank goodness, he thought he heard her whisper.

"I remember the funeral, though. Grandma told me I couldn't swing on the tire because that would insult their memory." So Will had hidden under the porch. That was how he had overheard a man say something about John's "problem." Will had listened closely, thinking they were talking about him, but another man had argued that "John Cavanaugh drove better drunk than most men drive sober."

Will frowned. Was that true? he wondered. He'd have to ask A.J. when he got home.

Anne touched his shoulder. "How soon after that did you start riding bulls?"

"Most of that winter, Grandma was sick. A.J. rigged up a bucking barrel for me in the barn. Gave me something to do and kept us both out of the house. I think he needed it as much as I did.''

''Was he hoping you'd follow in your father's footsteps?''

Will shook his head. ''No. I don't think he wanted that. In fact, he tried to get me interested in helping with the ranch, but I had my mind set. I was going to be a rodeo cowboy, like my dad.''

She took a breath and let it out. ''I guess I can understand why you'd want to follow in his footsteps, but why bulls? It's so dangerous.''

''Danger is relative. When you're young, eight seconds on the back of a bull sounds like a breeze. Unfortunately, by the time you get some sense knocked into you, you're hooked.''

''On what? The rush?''

''I guess you could call it that.''

''You're going back to it, aren't you?''

He nodded.

''As soon as A.J. gets home?''

''If I can get my doctor to sign off on my medical release. He'll probably want to run a few tests, take some X rays.''

''Of your head?''

Had she heard something? ''What do you mean?''

She made a funny face and shook her head. Her silky hair bounced about her jaw in a provocative way. ''Anyone would have to have a screw loose to ride bulls. Just think about it.''

Will let go of the breath he'd been holding. ''Never said I wasn't crazy.''

She went still, then lifted her hand and touched his lips. ''Are you crazy enough to get involved with me?''

''Of all the risky, insane things I've done in my life,

Anne, making love with you feels pretty rational by comparison. Is that what you're asking me to do?''

Will waited until she nodded before pulling her into his arms. ''Then the answer is yes.''

CHAPTER ELEVEN

A THOUSAND THOUGHTS crashed through Anne's head the moment he kissed her. *I love him.*

This was my mother's bed.

Are the windows open?

What if I cry out his name?

He's even more handsome than he was in high school.

Are my teeth brushed?

The question she hadn't meant to ask popped out. "Is this wrong?"

Will moved off the bed to face her. He tilted his head and gave her a smile she'd only seen once or twice—a little-boy grin that almost broke her heart. "Probably. Do you want me to leave?"

The smart answer was yes, but Anne was sick of making the so-called *smart* choice. She wanted to feel. To experience. Ride horseback like her daughter, splash in the pool, try the spicy salsa instead of the mild. Make love with Will—her most enduring dream.

"I want you to stay."

He stepped close enough for Anne to feel a connection so tangible she could almost see it shimmering in the silvery cast of the television. His gaze caressed her face, her body. "Please," she added.

One corner of his mouth curved upward but he remained a step away. "Are you always so polite?"

His tone implied a challenge. Anne had to smile. He

knew her well. "Sometimes, I ask. Sometimes, I take. Which do you prefer?"

The serious look in his eyes lightened. He wet his lips and gave her that cowboy nod she adored. "Can't say without giving both ways a try."

Anne closed the distance between them. "Then I guess it's up to me to make an executive decision." She grabbed a fistful of shirt and pulled him to her. Nose-to-nose, she told him, "Take off your clothes and get in bed."

"Yes, ma'am. Soon as you let go of my buttons." Humor twinkled in his eyes, which had taken on a smoky gray-blue hue.

Anne released her grip and stepped back to watch the slow, sexy process of a man's hand working each small white button free. When he reached his waist, he yanked the fabric from his jeans and completed the process.

No undershirt. Just bare, tanned flesh and an inviting thatch of dark curls nestled between his well-molded pecs. Was his body hair silky or springy? Her fingers itched to find out.

"Speaking of buttons, where's that remote?" Anne spotted it on the bed. She reached for it, but Will was faster. He pushed the Off button on the television, plunging the room into momentary darkness.

Anne blinked, trying to focus. A soft pinkish glow from the adjoining bathroom gave them enough light to navigate by. It was a gentle light that might hide various imperfections. And while there were many on the man who shrugged off his shirt and let it fall to the floor, Anne knew they were all superficial.

His big, strong-looking hands worked his leather belt free of its impressive buckle. He laid it across the footstool of the nearby chair, then undid the button at the waistband of his jeans.

Anne's throat dried up with anticipation.

He tugged on the zipper, making an accommodating wiggle to avoid the bulge pressing against the fabric.

White cotton briefs, she thought with a secret smile. She'd wondered.

He moved to the side of the bed and sat down to remove his boots. Anne couldn't resist touching the broad expanse of back when he leaned over. Warm as the soil in her garden at noon. She ran her fingers along the curve of his spine.

"I like this light," he said. "Maybe you won't be distracted by my scars."

Her sensitive fingertips paused on a raised notch. She leaned over to kiss it. "We both have scars," she murmured. "Yours are just easier to spot."

His boots hit the floor in quick succession then he half turned to face her. Quick as lightning, he pulled her across his lap so her shoulders were resting in the curve of his left arm. As her brain registered the fact that she was safe, that he wouldn't let her fall, she relaxed.

He lowered his head to kiss her exposed shoulder, setting off a shiver of exquisite anticipation. "Will you show me yours?"

Anne's heart stuttered. No one had ever asked her that. Could she talk about her past? Her failed marriage? Her missed opportunities to be a better daughter and mother? *Yes,* she thought. But now wasn't the time. This was about feeling. "Show and tell comes later. This is about taking." She looped her arms around his neck and pulled him closer. "And giving." Her tongue tickled the corner of his mouth. "Satisfaction."

He snickered softly. "I love the way your mind works." He teased her lips with tiny kisses that made her hungry for more. "Almost as much as I love the way your body feels in my arms." His free hand trailed down the outside of her rib cage to her hip.

When he flexed his arm to pull her closer, Anne felt the sinewy strength controlled for her benefit. And she couldn't wait to push the boundaries of that control.

She wiggled off his lap. With what she hoped was a provocative smile, she walked to the other side of the bed and knelt on the mattress across from him. Will turned to face her.

She beckoned him with a sultry "come here" motion. "Minus the pants, please."

Will stood, jeans riding low on his hip, the discernible outline of his arousal visible. "I don't want to seem picky, but why are you fully dressed while I'm naked?"

No guts, no glory. Anne gripped the hem of her tank top, closed her eyes and yanked the shirt off. She kept it clutched in her right hand as she sank back on her calves. She'd never felt more naked, even when posing nude for Eduardo.

Then she opened her eyes and saw Will's face. His lips were parted as if in wonder. When his gaze met hers, he smiled. Broadly. "You are a woman of many surprises. And breathless beauty."

The hunger in his eyes gave Anne permission to let go. Sex was a complication she'd told herself she didn't need. She was wrong. The desire she read in his look made her feel more alive than she had in years.

His pants hit the floor and he leaned down to remove his socks. When he straightened, Anne looked at him. Her breath lodged in her throat when she realized he'd removed his shorts at the same time. "I'll second that," she said in a strangled voice. A spike of heat hit her cheeks, when she realized that hadn't come out right. "I mean, you. You're full of surprises, too. Wonderful…big surprises."

Will's low hoot was the release she needed to move. Shorts flew. Underwear followed. Covers were drawn back. "Hurry," she urged, surprised to find him still standing in the same spot.

"Why?" He peeled back his half of the bedding then knelt on the edge of the mattress in a predatory fashion. "Please, don't tell me we're on the clock."

Anne brushed her bangs out of her eyes and sank into the foam pillows. She modestly pulled the corner of the sheet over her breasts. "No. No clocks," she said, her voice going higher as he stalked toward her. Lion to lioness. Predator to prey. "In fact, you'd better last longer than eight seconds or…"

His bark of laughter cut off her threat. Anne wasn't worried. If she lasted eight seconds she'd be lucky. She felt very close to burning up just looking into the fathomless depths of his eyes. She'd never wanted a man more, needed his touch with the kind of intense desire that threatened to consume her.

Now she wanted to shout. *Touch me. Make me feel all the things that have been missing from my life.*

When he was over her—one hand on the headboard behind her head, the other beside her hip—he paused to stare into her eyes. "I want you, Anne. More than I've ever wanted any woman."

Her heart did a little flip. Her throat was too tight to talk so she let her lips send the message. *I feel the same way about you.* She put her arms around his neck and pulled him to her. She closed her eyes to experience every single nuance. His wonderful, masculine smell. His amazingly taut muscles. His hands, roughened from work, but hot and tender.

Will's touch made her feel centered and focused in a way her career never did. At this moment, Anne was in control of her destiny. And, for the first time ever, she felt brave enough to share that power with the man she loved.

Eight seconds or eight hours? Will wasn't sure he could

tell the difference. Time ceased to become relevant the moment their lips met. This kiss was different from earlier kisses. Naked bodies. Crisp cotton sheets. Honest desire without any of the defensive posturing of the past few weeks.

This wasn't a kiss to seduce. It was a kiss of the seduced. Will understood that he and Anne were giving in to their mutual needs. But he hoped—no, he believed—their feelings ran deeper than mere lust. He wanted to bring Anne satisfaction, to make this experience good for her. She'd told him she hadn't made love in a long time. He planned to make up for that. He'd start by tasting every part of her—toes first.

He swept aside the sheet that hid her loveliness.

"What are you doing?"

"Taking."

"Taking what?"

"My time."

She groaned and reached out as if to draw him back. Her hand accidentally brushed against his arousal and Will flinched. *Maybe the toes will have to wait.*

He placed his hand on her belly. A darker image superimposed on a perfect white background. "No bikini for you, I see," he said, making a slow, provocative circle with his thumb stroking the underside of her breasts.

"Left it home. In the drawer. Wasn't expecting a pool. Or a man."

Her honesty touched him. She hadn't planned for this to happen any more than he had. "If we had a real pool," he said, watching with satisfaction as her nipples tightened. "We could be skinny-dipping."

"We might get caught."

"That's half the fun."

Resting his left hand on the mattress beside her waist, he used his right to cup her breasts—first one, then the

other. Perfect globes—firm, slightly upturned. "Beautiful," he murmured, his thumb and finger tweaking the nipple to a point. "I picture you floating on your back. Arms
outstretched above your head. Your breasts would rise and
fall with each intake. Giving me time to kiss them." Her
lungs filled and he lowered his head to fondle her with his
lips. "Lick them," he whispered on her next inhale, his
tongue bathing the erect nipple until she squirmed with
pleasure. "Taste them." He suckled until she let out a soft
moan.

"Yes. Gotta get a pool," she said, writhing with pleasure. "Next year."

Will looked up. Her eyes were closed, head back, one
hand gripping the metal headboard. Was that passion talking or had her plans changed? He'd overheard her mention
returning to the Silver Rose next year when she was talking to A.J., but surely she wasn't seriously considering a
repeat stay. And why did it matter? He'd be back on the
circuit in full swing by then, hopefully closing in on the
title. He couldn't think that far ahead, nor did he want to.
Right now, all he wanted to focus on was pleasing Anne.

He leaned down to bury his face in the soft, feminine
valley between her hips. Childbirth changed a woman, his
experience had taught him. For the better, in Will's opinion. He loved the arc of a woman's hip, the hollow between pelvic bone and hipbone. He explored her belly button with his tongue then nuzzled her rib cage with his nose.
No scars here.

When his hand cupped her feminine mound, Anne went
still and opened her eyes. In the shadowy light, he could
read both her desire and her nervousness. "I won't hurt
you, Anne."

She sucked in her bottom lip. A Zoey look. It reminded
him that there were all kinds of hurt. Then she tilted her
pelvis and moved against his hand. "I know, Will. We

both have things to lose, but we're not going to think about that right now, okay?''

An echo of the voice he'd heard on the video chimed in his head: "You're not a loser, are you, boy?''

As if sensing something was wrong, Anne reached out and closed her hand around him. Heat shot through his veins on a burst of yearning. Their gazes met as she manipulated her wrist in a provocative dance that overrode the hurtful voices. Here and now, he told himself. Anne. Now. Love.

He closed his eyes, reveling in the sensation. And the truth.

And even though neither had said the words aloud, Will knew she loved him, too. That made him a winner. For the night, at least.

A.J. DIDN'T KNOW what he'd expected, but the Atlantic Ocean didn't impress him. He and Esther had visited California's Big Sur on their honeymoon. Now, *that* was an ocean. Rocky coast, rugged spires sticking up to send foaming white waves crashing skyward.

The part of the coast closest to Esther's old hometown was anything but dramatic. The terrain was flat. There were marshes that he'd had to circle to find the proper outcropping on a point—a place that appealed to him for its distance from houses and people and boats.

He'd made an obligatory stop at her parents' resting place early that morning. In truth he'd never forgiven the bitter old couple for voicing such fervent opposition to their daughter's marriage. Not that he blamed them for being upset that she planned to move so far away. He could understand that. But little birds left the nest. That was the way Nature planned it. Their harsh prediction that Esther would fall into a den of iniquity with a bunch of gamblers was so far from the truth it had bordered on the ludicrous.

Through Esther's persistent efforts, the gulf between them had been repaired, with Anne's help. But A.J. had never felt comfortable around the older couple.

That was in the past, he told himself. Now, he was here to give their daughter back to them. And, God help him, A.J. wasn't sure he could do it. The bronze box on the rock beside him was still sealed. His face and fingers felt numb, even though sunrise had brought a modicum of warmth with it. Low, gray clouds—fog, he presumed—remained poised on the horizon, ready to sweep in and whisk him out to sea.

Gulls cried as they careened overhead, perhaps wondering if his shiny box held something of interest. In the distance, the high-pitched squeals of children taking a morning walk with their parents mingled with the persistent crash of waves against the odd-colored rocks on the point.

"I suppose this is it, old girl," he said, drawing the bronze box onto his lap. "Time to you-know-what or get off the pot."

He smiled as he patted the top of the box. Esther had always hated that phrase. She claimed it was her first husband's favorite saying. A.J. had never resented the man who'd shared Esther's youth, and he knew Esther felt the same way about Peg. As a couple, their life together was a combination of who they were before they met and who they became after they married. A.J. was a better man for having known Esther. A happier man. He'd laughed more in her company than he'd believed possible.

"I will miss you something fierce, honey girl," he whispered hugging the box tightly. Tears clustered in his eyes and his nose started to run. He had to loosen his grip to reach into his shirt pocket for his handkerchief.

I know, old man, he thought he heard Esther say. *I miss you, too, but it won't be long till we're together again.*

A.J. had had this conversation with his imagination for the past thousand miles. Once he crossed the Mississippi, he'd felt a heavy weight settle into his bones. He'd stalled for weeks in the mid-Atlantic states, pretending it was what Esther would have wanted. More than once, he'd started to turn back so he could bury her ashes at the Silver Rose.

But somehow he'd found the strength to keep going. And now he couldn't do it.

"Nope. I can't."

A.J. started to stand up but he felt a powerful hand on his shoulder. It forced him to sit abruptly. When he looked around, no one was there. A shiver raced from his head to the tip of his toes.

Do this for me, my love.

He blew his nose then rested his chin on the box.

And for the kids.

A.J. had sensed for some time that something was wrong at the ranch. He could feel it in the way Anne sounded—too perky to be real. And the way Will seemed to be avoiding his calls. When they did talk, Will only answered questions about the ranch or the stock. He never mentioned Anne or the future.

Only Zoey was completely honest. When A.J. called last week, Zoey told him, "They don't argue like Mommy and Daddy did when he still lived with us, but, Grandpa, they don't talk much, either. This morning after riding lessons, I asked Will if he and Mommy were mad at each other and he said, 'Adults don't always agree on everything, but that doesn't mean they don't like each other and r'spect each other.' Does that mean they're still friends, or not?"

"I'm sure they're friends, honey. Did you ask your mother how she feels about Will?"

"She said, 'Not now, Zoey, I have a headache.' You don't think she's sick, do you? Like Gramma Esther?"

A.J. had reassured the little girl that her mother wasn't going to die anytime soon. "They're probably just anxious to get back to their real jobs."

"Either that or they're in love," Zoey said with such frank simplicity A.J almost laughed.

"What makes you say that?"

"My friend Tressa said her mother told somebody that on the phone. Tressa says people in love do stupid things and are sad all the time except right at first when they laugh a lot and buy new clothes."

A.J. was struck dumb by the child's observation.

"That's why I don't think Mommy's in love." Zoey continued. "She hasn't been to the store in weeks."

A.J.'s heart nearly burst with affection. "How 'bout Will? Has he been shoppin'?"

She was silent a few moments, apparently giving his question due thought. "I don't think so, but he's been talking about getting a new truck. Does that count?"

Unable to repress a chuckle, A.J. had answered as truthfully as he dared. "It just might, sweetness. We'll have to keep an eye on them and see what happens."

A.J. sighed and put the conversation out of his head. He had no business fretting about Will's and Anne's problems. They were adults. They would do what was best for them without his interference. He shouldn't have to rush through this very important step in his mourning because they couldn't fall in love and live happily ever after, like him and Esther. "Dang kids have to make everything so complicated," he muttered. "Won't they ever grow up?"

We never did.

A.J. lifted his head and saw Esther standing before him, as healthy, robust and beautiful as she'd been before her illness. A rush of tenderness overwhelmed him. Memories of their life together flashed through his mind. He wondered if he was having a heart attack.

You're not going to die, my love. Not yet. You still have work to do. Do you want more grandchildren or not?

"I can't do it, Esther. I can't let you go."

Those are just ashes, my love. This is the reason you came. To honor my parents and live up to your promise. Let Maine have my ashes. I'm still right here beside you, in spirit.

Suddenly, A.J. felt an abiding sense of peace. He knew why he'd come all this way. *His promise.* "I'll bring her back," he'd vowed so many years ago. "And a Cavanaugh never goes back on his word."

He set the bronze urn on the rock and clumsily rose, his knees catching from sitting still too long. After brushing his hands on the seat of his pants, he picked up the metal box and walked to the water's edge. Best get this done, he thought. I gotta get home. Darned kids can't even manage to work together a couple of months without doing something foolish.

As the gray ash mingled with the dark, frothy water, he heard Esther's distinctive laugh. *Falling in love is never foolish, you old goat. Love is life eternal. Now, get home and fix things.*

It wasn't until he was in the motor home headed west that he recalled Esther's words. *Do you want more grandchildren or not?* A.J.'s heart lifted and he reached over to turn up the volume on the radio.

Smiling, he turned to the empty passenger seat and said aloud, "So, tell me this, Miss Smarty-pants, if my grandson and my stepdaughter have a child, will it be my grandchild or my great-grandchild?"

There wasn't an answer, but then he wasn't expecting one. Instead, A.J. felt a wonderful, life-affirming laugh bubble up from a place deep inside his chest. An Esther kind of laugh.

He had to pull off the road to wipe the tears from his eyes, but they were good tears. Healing tears.

CHAPTER TWELVE

ANNE AWOKE to a low, placid sound. She recognized it as breathing. A man's breathing. *Will.*

Turning her head on the pillow, she opened her eyes. What a gift! A handsome man beside her. Tendrils of pale yellow light slipped past the slits in the miniblinds that rattled with the morning breeze. The window, she noticed, was open. Had she cried out his name?

She smiled. Oh, yeah. She'd lost count of how many times.

Lifting herself up on her elbows, she looked around the room. Boots upended. Jeans in a heap. Will had stashed the telltale condom wrappers, though.

What a sweet and thoughtful man, she thought. *And virile.* Three times in one night. Four if you counted the shower. And, boy, did she.

She'd never in her life made love four times in one night. The wonder of it made her grin. Eduardo paled by comparison. Exotic Spanish artists be damned, she thought with a rueful grin. Give me a cowboy any day—or night.

Moving with care, she slipped out of bed. Her good humor paled slightly when she spotted the alarm clock. She'd forgotten to set it, for the second time since she'd moved here. She had a good excuse, though. Her partner had kept her too occupied to think about anything other than mad, passionate sex.

She tiptoed into the adjoining bathroom and nearly landed on her bare rump when her foot connected with a puddle of water. Her grin returned. Fact: two people in a tub of bubbles equals spillage.

She used a damp towel to mop up the moisture as she waited for the shower to warm up. The shower. "We need to rinse off these bubbles, don't we?" he'd asked with such an innocent smile. She closed her eyes and pictured their squeaky-clean bodies rubbing up against each other like otters in kelp, Will's tongue introducing her to an aspect of her personality she hadn't known she possessed.

Possessed. Good word. Perhaps the only explanation for her behavior. Never, not even during her earliest days of marriage, had Anne responded to a lover with such inhibition. She'd liked the feeling. Too bad she couldn't...

Anne pushed away the thought. Reality loomed, but she preferred to face it after a cup of coffee. Today was definitely not a day for tea.

Fifteen minutes later, Anne walked into the kitchen. Most Sunday mornings were low-key. People who were leaving used the time to pack. New guests wouldn't be arriving until much later in the day. Two-week guests liked to sleep in or sip coffee on their porches so they could say goodbye to the people they'd met.

As Anne expected, Joy was bustling about her domain, preparing for the ten o'clock brunch, humming along with a hymn on the radio.

"'Morning," Anne said, making a beeline for the coffeepot. "How was your night off?"

"Well, good morning, sleepyhead," Joy called out, her back to Anne. She was intently scrubbing a pan at the sink. "The grandkids and I rented a Disney movie." She glanced over her shoulder. "Kinda cute. About a bunch of dogs in Alaska." Her eyes narrowed. "What's happened here that I don't know about?"

Anne tried to hide her blush behind the steam from her coffee mug. "Um...not much."

Joy gave a little yip. She looked out the window toward
Will's cabin then back at Anne. The question was obvious.

Anne gave up the bluff. She couldn't hide what they'd
done. Besides, she wasn't ashamed. Worried, maybe, but
not ashamed. "He's upstairs."

"Oh my gosh," Joy exclaimed. The skillet in her hand
dropped into the water, sending suds flying. Joy grabbed
a towel and dried her hands as she scuttled across the room
to give Anne a rib-cracking hug. "Well, good for
you…both."

Anne's coffee sloshed over the rim of the cup. "Spilling," she peeped.

Joy quickly knelt to wipe up the mess. "All I can say
is it's about time," she said, giving Anne a good-natured
wink. "And A.J. is going to be tickled pink that new blood
is taking over the Silver Rose. And family, no less."

Anne's sip of coffee lodged in her throat. She swallowed
with difficulty. "Joy, I hope I didn't give you the wrong
impression. Will and I care for each other but we don't
have any plans for the future. Nothing…long-term, I
mean," she said, stumbling over the word as a wave of
regret washed over her.

"Oh, pshaw," Joy said, returning to the sink. "A plan
is like a recipe. It gives you the guidelines to go by, but
you add your own quantities and spices to make it fit your
life and taste buds."

She rinsed a pan and placed it on the drying rack before
turning to face Anne. "Everybody raves about my calico
bean recipe, but I never thought it was anything special
until I tossed in a few of those chipotle peppers. I'd heard
of 'em on the cooking channel but didn't know how they'd
taste. One day, I saw a can in the store and, on impulse,
bought it. When I got home, I called your mother up and
asked her what she thought. And being Esther, she said,
'Go for it. What's livin' without change?'"

Anne smiled, but before she could reply, Joy added, "Didn't you tell me you had a plan in mind when you married Zoey's daddy?"

Her point was obvious. Barry had fit into Anne's plan until the introduction of a new ingredient. But loving Will and being in love with Will were two different things. One meant a respite from loneliness, the other meant drastic changes for one of them. Anne knew only too well what happened when you tried to force change. She and Will both had lives waiting for them in September. Totally incompatible lives.

"Joy, this thing between me and Will is supposed to be a harmless, little summer fling. He has his life. I have mine. There is no middle ground."

Joy made a clucking sound. "Sure there is, honey. It's called the Silver Rose. You two belong here. A.J. can't run this place alone. What you and Will need to do is cut loose the old and focus on the new."

The coffee in Anne's stomach churned. "That's easier said than done. I've signed a contract with my company. I'm inches away from the promotion I've been breaking my back to get. I can't just drop out of the game."

"Why not?"

A tingle pulsed through her. The question sounded familiar. How long had it been zinging about in her head, whispered in silence? Weeks? Months? Since the first time she saw Will Cavanaugh step out of his foolish yellow truck? "Because this is my career. It's what I do best. The same way Will is a bull rider. He's going back to that, too, you know," she added defensively.

Joy took a deep breath and let it out. She dried her hands and turned to face Anne. "Not according to what I heard."

Anne moved closer. "What do you mean?"

Joy frowned. Her candy-apple cheeks deepened in hue. "This is just hearsay, Anne, so you'd best take it for what it's worth. My friend's son-in-law is a stock handler with one of the companies that provides bucking bulls to the PBR. This is a small world. Everybody knows everybody.''

Anne froze. ''So?''

''People talk. Especially when one of their own gets hurt.''

Anne nodded to encourage her to keep talking.

''Remember hearing about Will's last ride? He landed wrong on his head. He was knocked unconscious and had to be taken off on a stretcher.''

Anne hadn't heard that but she didn't say so to Joy. ''He was okay, though. He seems fine now.''

Joy nodded. ''True. But there was talk at the time that he wouldn't ride again. Some went so far as to say that if Will risked another ride, he might wind up dead or paralyzed.''

Anne swallowed hard to keep her coffee in her stomach. Hadn't Linda mentioned a similar rumor? Could it be true? She understood Will's need to prove himself, but surely he wouldn't risk his life for his dead father's approval? But what else could drive him to take such a foolhardy risk? The money? She knew riches held little allure for Will. He owned land he didn't ranch. His single possession was a truck he didn't like. Was he in it for the fame? She doubted it. He always reacted modestly when guests asked about his career. The glory? No, Anne couldn't see it. What she *could* see was Will in a hospital bed with tubes and machines keeping him alive.

She set down her cup and dashed for the door. She'd just reached the foyer when she spotted Will on the stairs. A wide smile lit up his face when he saw her. She recognized the look in his eyes. Love. He loved her as she loved him—even if neither of them had been brave enough to say the words aloud.

"Good morning, beautiful," he said, walking straight to Anne. His arms rose as if to hug her, but stalled when she put out a hand to stop him. "Anne? Are you okay?"

A tornado of emotions whirled inside her brain: fear, bafflement, anger, love, defeat, remorse.

"No," she said, her voice choking on tears. "No, Will, I'm not okay. I'm furious. With you."

His freshly shaved jaw dropped. "Why?"

"Because I just found out that I love you, you stupid idiot."

His initial smile faded when she added, "It happened by accident. I thought I could do the sex thing and be okay with it, but then I woke up and saw you there. Damn it, Will, you snore. A nice, happy snore, like a contented dog. I could get used to that.

"And when I was in the shower, I toyed with the idea of trying to make this work. But then I found out that you're insane. I fell in love with a madman. And I hate you."

The look on his face went from surprise to joy to confusion. "Crazy how? Because I love you, too?"

She stabbed her finger on his chest, dead center above his heart. "No. Don't even say that word unless you can tell me that you're never going to ride another bull."

He stepped back. "What are you talking about?"

Suddenly, her mind was filled with the image she'd seen on television last night before Will came to her room. A gate opened. A huge, powerful bull leaped into the air, snorting and twisting. The man on his back fell off, but his hand was caught in the rope. His body flapped and slapped like a rag doll until the moment the rope released and he dropped lifelessly to the ground. After a few seconds, the cowboy—Will—had stumbled to his feet. He'd waved to the crowd and picked up his hat, then faltered, his pain obvious. Two men had helped him from the arena.

If what Joy said was true, the next time might hold a totally different outcome.

She drew back, being careful not to touch him. "Were you advised to stop riding because your next fall could be fatal?"

He looked toward the ceiling and let out a soft groan. "Where'd you hear that?"

"Is it true, Will?"

He looked her squarely in the eye. "More or less, but…"

Anne turned away. She couldn't listen to excuses, to justifications. Barry had given her plenty when he'd explained why it was best for Anne and Zoey that he leave. She paused at the foot of the stairs. "Please tell Joy that Zoey and I are going to spend the day in Reno. We need to shop for school clothes. We might be late."

"Anne, wait." He put his hand on her shoulder. His touch went all the way to her toes. "Let me go with you. We can talk in the car. Before we pick up Zoey."

She wanted more than anything to crawl into his arms and forget what she'd heard, what she knew for a fact. Will cared for her, deeply. But he wouldn't—or maybe he couldn't—give up bull riding. Even if it killed him.

"No. She'll pick up on the tension between us. She's very sensitive to my moods. It wouldn't be good for her."

"Is it Zoey you're worried about, or yourself?"

She lifted her chin. "Both. I'm a mother first. Just like you're a bull rider first, lover second. Now, if you don't mind, I need some time." *To think. To plan. To put the most wonderful night of my life behind me.*

TWO HOURS DISAPPEARED beneath the burden of figuring out how to turn on the computer and print receipts for guests who were checking out, and how to settle a squabble between members of the housekeeping staff. Will closed the office door. He would have hung a Do Not Disturb sign on the handle, but he didn't know where Anne kept them.

Even though the circumstances were different, Will thought he understood how overwhelmed his grandfather must have felt after Esther died. A.J. didn't just lose his wife, he lost his partner. Anne had made herself such an integral part of the Silver Rose's makeup that Will couldn't picture the place succeeding without her.

Will sat down heavily in his grandfather's chair. He rolled his neck to loosen the tension that had been building since Anne left. This wasn't how he'd pictured the day unfolding. Mildly disappointed that he didn't get to kiss Anne awake, he guessed that he'd find her in the kitchen, helping Joy. Anne was driven—not just in her city job, but in everything she did. He appreciated that goal-oriented attitude because he shared it.

That was one of the reasons he was so ticked off. Apparently what was okay for Anne—dreams and ambition—wasn't acceptable for Will.

Joy had apologetically explained about the rumor she'd shared with Anne. Will wasn't surprised to learn that people had heard of his diagnosis. Will could have denied the allegation, but that would have been a lie. What angered him was the way Anne left without giving him a chance to explain.

That time in high school when he got too close to her, she'd clammed up and hidden behind her plans for college. Apparently this time, she was going to use his job and her daughter to keep them apart.

He was tempted to cut his losses and throw in the towel. *We had a good time last night,* he thought. *Hell, the best damn time of his life.* But was that enough to make him give up bull riding?

The question hung in the air as if Esther's ghost had

spoken it aloud. It sounded like an Esther question. Blunt. To the point.

"I don't know," he said, shaking his head.

Yes, you do.

The phone rang. He snatched up the receiver. "Anne?"

"No, it's me. Gramps. You expectin' her call? Where is she?"

Will rocked back in the chair and put his feet on the desk. "She took Zoey to town. She has her cell phone, though. I thought she might be checking in."

Will was pretty sure his voice hadn't betrayed his feelings.

A.J. didn't say anything for a full minute. Just enough time for Will to start sweating. "Might as well tell me what's going on, son. I'll find out soon enough. I'm on my way home."

Will sat up sharply. The soles of his boots made a slapping sound when they hit the floor. "You did it? Esther?"

"Yep," A.J. answered, his voice somber. "Just after dawn. It was gray and misty. I think she would have liked that better than sunny and bright."

Will's eyes misted, too. "I'm sorry, Gramps. I bet it was tough."

A.J. sniffed twice. "Not as bad as I thought it was going to be. She and I had a little talk first. She told me I was an old fool for hanging on to ashes when I should be home with my family."

Will rubbed his hand across his eyes. "That sounds like Esther. I was just thinking about her. In fact, I thought I heard her call me a few names."

"Oh, Lordy, what did you do now?"

"It's complicated."

"Love usually is."

"Who said anything about love?"

A.J.'s laugh was reminiscent of the old A.J. "Son, I've

been fortunate enough to have had two wonderful women in my life. I'm not so old and decrepit I can't remember what it's all about.''

"Gramps, Anne and I care about each other. But, face it, we're from different worlds. And we're going back to those worlds in a month. How the heck is love supposed to survive that kind of situation?''

A.J. sighed. "I figured you were going to hit that wall sooner or later.''

"Perfect image. Kinda how I feel right this minute.''

"Well, if you're suffering whiplash, you can be dang sure Annie is in even worse shape. Women feel things harder than men. Of course, they're stronger, so it all works out, but she'll be hurting just the same.''

Will frowned. He'd been so busy stewing in his own juices he hadn't considered how Anne might be feeling. What if she was too upset to drive? She might accidentally drive too fast, miss a turn, overcorrect, and swerve out of control… "Gramps, I gotta hang up. I want to call Anne's cell phone and make sure she's okay.''

"I understand. But, grandson, you'd better take a minute and think about how you're going to apologize. Most times, sorry don't cut soft bananas, as your grandmother used to say.''

"Gramps, she wants me to quit bull riding.''

"She ain't the only one.''

Will's mouth dropped open. "You, too? Since when? I thought you were proud of me. You've always been supportive.''

"And I always will be, because this is your choice. But if you'd ever asked for my opinion, I'd have told you what I thought.''

Will swallowed the lump in his throat. "I'm asking now.''

"A man's dream and a boy's dream ain't the same.

When you were fired up to buy that dang yellow truck, I thought you were out of your gourd, but I kept my mouth shut. I figured it showed the world what a success you were. But next time you go car shopping, you'll pick with your head, not your ego.''

Will smiled. Gramps had that right.

''You went into rodeo, Will, partly because it's what your daddy did, partly because you're damn good at it. But bull riding is a demanding life and even the best—and I'm including you in that list—know when to get out.''

''Are you saying I'm too old for this?''

''Nope. I'm saying it's time you sold that yellow truck.''

''And hang up my spurs.''

A.J. was quiet a moment. ''Not necessarily. You can wear those spurs around the Silver Rose. Might impress the guests.''

''Are you asking me to stay here and work for you?''

''No. I don't think that would work. You're your own man, always have been. What I'm asking is that you move home and take over for me. Permanent.''

Will leaned forward and put his elbows on the desk. He rested his head in his hand. ''Where would you—?''

''We got eight cabins. I think I'd be happy in one of 'em.''

Relief flooded over him—Gramps was thinking about retiring, not selling out. ''You don't think we'd butt heads if we tried to run this place together?'' he asked, wondering why the idea didn't strike him as ridiculous.

''You got a hard head. Don't suppose running the Silver Rose will be any more dangerous than doing a Humpty-Dumpty off a bull.''

Will smiled. ''Good point.'' He'd enjoyed his summer, but was he ready to give up life on the circuit? His friends? His career? Although he had to admit fewer and fewer of his contemporaries were still riding professionally.

His income was another issue. The lure of million-dollar "shoot-outs" and bonuses from corporate sponsors wasn't something to shake a stick at, but Will hadn't added much to the bank lately. And if he got hurt again, his savings might go for long-term treatment.

But what about your dream? a stubborn voice asked. At the edge of his consciousness, Will heard an answer. *What good is winning if Anne isn't there?*

"Gramps, I'll admit the thought has crossed my mind, especially since Anne came into the picture. But I've been a nomad so long I'm not sure I can settle down. Maybe I'm too much like my dad. Footloose and—"

"Now, hold it right there, boy. I don't want to make you feel bad, but the truth is you don't know squat about your daddy. You were just a little tyke when he passed away. And it's pretty clear to me that you got certain things mixed up in your mind." He coughed. "It hurts me to say this about my own son, but John wasn't the hero you've always made him out to be. He was a troubled young man who made rash decisions, ran away from responsibility, and…hid from his troubles in a bottle."

That old memory of the funeral came back to him. "Was he drunk when he died?"

"It's possible. We'll never know for sure. There were a few beer cans in the wreckage, but the sheriff was a friend of mine. He didn't ask for an autopsy. We both agreed your grandmother couldn't have handled the results if it showed Johnny was drunk when the crash happened." He cleared his throat again. "Doesn't much matter, anyway. He was driving too fast—they could tell that from the skid marks. He wasn't thinking about what might come from it if something happened to him. How much his mother would suffer. How much his little boy would miss him. That his son might grow up thinking he had to fill his daddy's shoes. Follow his daddy's dream. Even if it killed him.''

Tears burned behind Will's eyes. ''Is that what you think I've been doing, Gramps? Living my father's life?''

A.J. didn't answer right away. ''I don't know, son. I'm an old man. You and Annie and Zoey are the only kin I've got left. All I know for sure is that I'd be a lot happier about coming home if I thought there was a chance we might be more of a family.''

Will felt as if he was being torn in two. Anne and A.J. on one side of the tug-of-war rope, his lifelong dream on the other. ''I'll give your offer some thought, Gramps, but I can't promise anything. Especially where Anne is concerned. She's got her life pretty well planned out.''

''That's our Annie,'' A.J. said with a chuckle. ''Like I said, I'm starting for home, but I got a whole country to cross, so you all can use the time to think about what you want to do. If you decide to give bull riding one more shot, you'll have my support. Just like always. If you decide to stay at the Silver Rose, then we'll make it official and put your name on the deed. Same goes for Anne.''

''Thank you, Gramps. For everything.''

There was a funny, muffled sound, like a man using a handkerchief while juggling a receiver. A few seconds later, his grandfather mumbled goodbye, then the connection ended.

Will hung up then quickly called Anne's cellular number. There was no answer. He didn't leave a message.

He rose. He needed to ride. Clear his head. Do a little soul-searching. He was almost to the foyer when the phone rang. He paused and listened to the answering machine. If it was A.J. again… ''Will? Are you there? This is Anne. It's Zoey…''

Will raced back to pick it up. ''Anne,'' he cried. ''What happened?''

"Zoey had an asthma attack. A bad one."

He closed his eyes, remembering all too vividly Zoey's desperate breathing that first morning. "What caused it?"

"A…a combination of things," she said, her voice strained and whispery. "Not enough sleep. I'm not completely clear on whether or not she took her pills. She might have used a feather pillow, even though her regular pillow was in her backpack. Plus, there was something about a dog."

Will sensed she wasn't telling him everything. "Where are you? I'll be right there."

"That's not necessary. I just wanted to tell you—"

"Anne," Will snapped. "Where are you?"

She gave him the name of an urgent-care clinic he'd noticed on his drive to the airport.

"I'll be there in twenty minutes."

ANNE BLAMED HERSELF. If she'd been paying attention instead of thinking about her own problems—her feelings for Will—this wouldn't have happened.

She bit down on the end of the pen she was using to fill out the insurance papers for the treatment center Linda had recommended. "My kids are regulars there," her friend had said. She'd followed Anne to the car with Zoey's overnight bag and Anne's purse. Anne's arms had been occupied with her limp, whimpering daughter.

Linda had tried to apologize, but Anne hadn't had time to listen. Nor was any apology necessary. None of this would have happened if Anne had been more observant and less self-absorbed.

This attack was her wake-up call. For as long as Zoey was living under Anne's roof, Anne needed to make her daughter's health and well-being her top priority. Two months of relative calm had lulled her into a false sense of security. Today proved how fast an asthma attack could demolish their fragile harmony.

She needed to get Zoey home to their apartment where Anne could monitor the little girl's meds, diet and rest more closely. Anne had let her guard down for one night and look what had happened.

"Anne?"

Her heart jumped against her rib cage.

Will hurried across the institutional carpeting. Why would anyone put carpeting in a medical facility? Anne thought irrelevantly. Don't they know about allergies?

"Anne. Oh, God, I was afraid I'd go out of my head before I got here." He reached down and pulled her out of her chair and into his arms before she could react. "How is she? Can I see her?"

Anne's senses warred. One part of her wanted to crawl into the comfort he offered; the other wanted to run out of the building screaming. She shook her head. "She's with the respiratory therapist."

He held her at arm's length and studied her. "You look like a strong wind could blow you to Canada. Let's sit down."

She didn't have the energy to protest—to do the right thing and send him away.

He took the chair beside her. He was still in the clothes he'd worn to her room last night. She couldn't look at his buttons without remembering, so she stared blankly at the papers in her lap.

"Sweetheart, are you okay?" he asked. "Can I get you something? Water? Coffee? A stiff drink?"

She almost smiled. It occurred to her that she hadn't eaten all day. And after an energetic night like last night... Anne took a deep breath, drawing on her reserves. She wasn't needy or pathetic. "I'll be fine. Something like this always takes the wind out of your sails. It's so difficult to see your child blue and limp.''

He wrapped his arm around her shoulders and hugged her again. "I heard about it from Linda. She called a minute after you hung up. Wanted to know if I had any news."

Linda was a good friend. Anne was going to miss her.

"She feels terrible. Blames herself for not checking to make sure Zoey took her medication this morning. And for letting the kids play tag. She said she should have—"

"It wasn't her fault," Anne said. "It was mine."

He gave her a questioning look. "If Zoey didn't take her medicine, I'd say some of the responsibility falls on her shoulders, wouldn't you?"

Anne looked at him sharply. "She's only eight."

"Nine," he corrected. "She's nine. And she's lived with this condition all her life. She knows what's good for her and what isn't, doesn't she?"

He had a point, but that didn't absolve Anne of her blame. "The meds are important, and she should have had her fast-acting inhaler close by, but the real reason we're here is me."

"How so?"

Anne sank back into the chair and sighed. "I was distracted. When I got to Linda's, my mind was on—well, you. I wasn't listening to Zoey."

"To her breathing?"

"To what she was telling me. Apparently Linda's son stole her hat and Zoey had to chase him through the neighbor's backyard where this black Lab puppy lives. She stopped to pet the dog and…"

Anne took a deep breath. She hoped that what her mother had always told her about confession being good for the soul was true. "I blew it, Will. When I heard the part about the dog, I looked at her and saw that her cheeks were flushed and her breath was raspy. I grabbed her by the shoulders and said, 'You chased after a boy instead of thinking about your health?'"

Will winced.

"See? Stupid, huh? I embarrassed her in front of her friends. This never would have happened in New York."

"Why? There aren't boys in New York?"

Tears filled her eyes. "She doesn't have any friends there."

"Oh, Anne," he said, his voice softened with sympathy. "That isn't true and you know it. Zoey has a good life because you're a wonderful mother, but even the best mom snaps once in a while. Nobody's perfect."

She wished she deserved his support.

"Besides, Linda told me to tell you that the other kids didn't hear a thing. They were arguing over something else by then." He squeezed her shoulders. "Sweetheart, they're kids. They have the attention span of gnats. Nobody is going to remember this."

"Except Zoey."

"She's the most resilient child I've ever met. She'll be fine."

Anne wanted to believe him, but she didn't.

"Hey," he said, giving her a smile. "A.J. called. He's on his way back." His voice dropped. "He said everything went fine. It wasn't easy, but Gramps said it was just the way Esther would have wanted it."

Anne touched his arm. She knew Will had loved her mother, too.

"Maybe this isn't the right time to bring it up, Anne, but Gramps wants us to think about taking over the Silver Rose permanently."

"Us? Will, there is no us."

"There could be."

Anne jumped to her feet. "How? Even if I could get

out of my contract and abandon my career, my dreams, I have Zoey to consider. Her future, her health—"

"Which has been excellent," he interjected. "Except for this one time, which you just admitted was caused by extenuating circumstances. Zoey's been doing great. You can't use her health as an excuse."

"Is that what you think I'm doing? Well, you're wrong. Allergies aside, there are still emotional precursors like stress and worry that come into play with certain types of asthma. Zoey is especially sensitive to emotional trauma."

She didn't know how to say what she feared without sounding morbid. "Will, I'm not the only one who loves you. Zoey hangs on your every word. She follows you around like a lamb. What happens to her when you go back to bull riding? What if the next time you hit the ground wrong you don't get up?"

He wove his fingers together in his lap and looked down. "A.J. wants me to quit, too. Maybe I should."

Anne closed her eyes. Was that what she was waiting to hear? If so, why did she feel so empty inside?

Neither spoke for a minute, then Anne said, "Will, this is one of those proverbial no-win situations. I figured that out while I was driving to Linda's. It's why I was so upset that I missed all the signs leading up to Zoey's attack."

"What do you mean?"

"To put it bluntly, if you continue to ride, there is no us—for all the reasons we already talked about. If you give up bull riding and move to the Silver Rose, there'll come a time when you look at me and Zoey and realize that we're the reason you gave up your dream."

He snorted, but she put her hand on his shoulder and said, "Believe me, Will, I know what I'm talking about. People don't just change because you want them to. They don't give up their dreams without suffering major consequences down the road."

"You're talking about your ex-husband, not me."

"I remember my mother telling me once that if you learned anything from your mistakes, it was not to make the same mistake twice. I didn't listen to Barry when he said he didn't want children. I thought my dream was big enough to sweep him into the picture. I was wrong and we all paid a price."

The flatness in Anne's voice broke Will's heart. Not for the first time, he wished her bastard ex-husband would drop by for a little ass-wupping. "Anne, I promise you, if I—"

A woman in a nurse's uniform approached them. "Mrs. Fraser?"

Anne lifted her head. Will kept his arm around her shoulders when she turned to face the nurse. "Yes?"

"Zoey is all done. She's tired and a bit cranky but breathing well. Her blood/oxygen level is back to the normal range. The doctor wants her to spend forty minutes on oxygen then you can take her home." She pointed toward the hall. "You can sit with her, if you want, but she's watching *Scooby Doo* and resting if you want to wait. It's better if she doesn't talk."

"Yes, I know. We've been through this before. Thank you."

Anne's knees seemed to buckle and he used the excuse to pull her closer. "Have you eaten?"

It took a minute before she shook her head.

Will cursed softly. "There's a deli across the street. Come on. You heard the woman. Zoey is fine, but you're a basket case. And I won't let you near the steering wheel if you don't eat something first."

She ate half a bowl of soup while Will polished off a Reuben sandwich. They didn't talk. He could tell the letdown from the intensely emotional drama—and their intensely amorous night—was taking a toll. He knew Anne was capable of handling this crisis just fine without him, but he felt good sharing her load. He couldn't imagine *not* being here.

He pointed through the fake greenery in the café's window to the dozen or so cars lined up beyond the stucco wall. "See that parking lot?"

Anne craned her head. "Uh-huh. What about it?"

"When I drove past, I noticed all those cars have For Sale signs in their windows. What do you say I park the truck there, then I drive you and Zoey home?"

"Park it? To sell?"

He nodded. "While you're getting Zoey discharged, I'll run into the hardware store and buy a sign. There's lots of traffic on this road. I bet the truck goes in a snap."

She looked dumbfounded. "Why are you selling it?"

He scooted out of the booth, suddenly energized. "Because it's a kid's truck. I've been wanting to get rid of it for a long time—just needed the right push."

Her eyes narrowed. "Not because—"

He offered her his hand. "It's time, Anne. I've outgrown this truck. It happens, you know. Same with dreams."

She looked doubtful but obviously didn't have the energy to argue.

That was how he wound up driving her mother's Forerunner with Zoey asleep in the back seat and Anne out cold in the passenger seat. He felt like a family man and, Will had to admit, the feeling reminded him of that millisecond before the chute opens—a mix of fear and possibility.

His right hand—his riding hand—caressed Anne's hair. He knew that regardless of what decisions he made this relationship wasn't a done deal. Even if he were prepared to quit riding, what right did he have to expect Anne to give up her dream job? That dire prediction she'd mentioned earlier worked both ways. Will remembered all too well how anxious Anne had been to leave Nevada—a state she'd hated in high school and didn't seem all that sorry to leave now. If she decided to stay—for him, for Zoey, out of some sense of loyalty to A.J.—would she someday regret it? He'd witnessed firsthand how hard she worked. For her sake, Will wanted Anne to realize the sweet taste of victory.

Before she'd dozed off, Anne had asked Will to give her the time and space she needed to make an "informed" decision. He'd agreed to back off—how could he not? Besides, he had some thinking of his own to do.

CHAPTER THIRTEEN

"I THINK SOMETHING is wrong with my mom."

Will eased his horse a bit closer to Zoey, who was riding at his side. She had claimed the right to be his partner before anyone else was done saddling. "Since Tressa can't come, I get to ride with Will," she'd announced with a challenging look toward her mother.

Sixteen other riders, including Anne and Linda, were strung out in tandem along the trail behind them. Linda's son was somewhere near the end of the line, but her daughter had missed out on the long-promised trail ride and picnic thanks to an ear infection, which explained why Will and Zoey could talk in private.

"Well, Miss Z, your mom's been working extra hard to get the place ready for Gramps's return," Will suggested. "She's probably tired."

"It's more than that," Zoey insisted. "She always works hard."

Will couldn't deny that. Since their tumultuous night together and Zoey's asthma attack, Anne seldom left the office before midnight. Will knew because he spent most nights watching the office window until the light went out.

Zoey glanced over her shoulder before adding in a low voice, "I hear her at night, Will. She paces around and I think she cries sometimes."

Will's stomach clenched. He didn't want to hear that, although it confirmed what he suspected. It didn't surprise him that Anne was suffering—so was Will, but he didn't know what to do about the situation. She'd made it clear she wanted him to keep his distance.

"It's my fault," Zoey said flatly. "Because I told her I want to stay here to go to school. I know we can't. I know her job is back East, but I love it here, Will. I don't want to leave."

Tears welled up in her eyes. He reached across the distance and squeezed her shoulder. "I know you're worried about what's been happening, honey, but you can't let it upset you. Not here, not now," he said, tilting her chin so he could make eye contact. "An asthma attack would scare your horse."

The distraction seemed to work. Zoey made a visible effort to control her breathing. She took a hit on her inhaler then glanced over her shoulder to see if her mother had noticed.

Will looked, too. Fortunately, Anne seemed engrossed in her conversation with Linda.

He gave Zoey a nod of support. "Good job, sweetie. Now, let's talk about this problem. We both know your mom has a lot on her mind, including the fact that you're obviously very happy living on the ranch and more than anything she wants to make you happy. But her job is a big factor. It's what pays the bills and puts food on the table. A good mother takes those things very seriously."

She gave him a sad smile. "Mommy and Joy were arguing again this morning. Mommy wants to train Joy to take over the office after we're gone, but Joy says she likes the kitchen better."

Gone. The word sucker punched him in the gut.

"Hey, cowboy," a voice called from behind them. "When's lunch?"

Will shifted in the saddle to gauge the condition of the horses and riders behind him. A few of the city folk looked ready to nod off from the slow pace and warm temperature. "Lunch in five minutes," he hollered.

Anne tucked a stray lock of hair behind her ear. The ball cap she'd borrowed from one of the guests sat slightly askew, lending her a tomboy appeal that made Will want to kiss her. Totally unlike her usual calm, organized self, the Anne of late was frazzled and absentminded. She'd seemed close to tears this morning when she couldn't find her mother's old cowboy hat.

Even after two hours in the saddle, she still managed to look sexy as hell. Her faded denim shirt was tied at her waist. A faint shimmer of sweat glistened on the skin exposed by her black tank top. Is she getting sunburned? he wondered. Or is it just a reflection?

Will hadn't expected Anne to participate in this outing, but she'd been adamant. "If my daughter can do this, so can I. I took a riding class in college. I think I can handle it."

He'd insisted on giving Anne, Linda and the newest guests a quick refresher before heading out on the trail. He wasn't surprised that Anne found her seat after only a few trips around the arena.

"There's a clearing up ahead," Will said, raising his voice so the whole party could hear him. "If anyone feels up to it, a hiking trail leads to the ridge where you can see Lake Tahoe. I'm told this is a favorite spot for cross-country skiers in the winter."

Half an hour later, members of the group were scattered to various spots enjoying their hoagie sandwiches and the amazing vistas. Some clustered in the shade of the Jeffrey pines, napping or discussing the wonderful weather—a rare August cool spell. Will knew the pleasant temperature was beguiling but dangerous, given their altitude and exposure to the sun. He insisted each person carry and drink bottled water.

"Be back in half an hour for dessert," he told those heading off for a hike. "We'll need to be off the mountain by sunset or Joy will track us down with a frying pan."

Returning to the rock formation that had served as an impromptu table, Will looked around for Zoey. Seated in Linda's lap getting her hair braided, Zoey held a fruit drink in one hand and a half-eaten sandwich in the other. Her gaze seemed fixed on the lanky boy who was helping Will's wranglers water the horses.

Will emptied the ice from a mostly empty cooler into a second then offered the plastic shell as a seat to Anne. She finished folding the insulated bag that had held the sandwiches before eyeing the stool warily. "Thanks, but I'm afraid if I sit down, I might not be able to get up again."

Will smiled. "You'll get your land legs back in a minute."

She made a face. "It's my land butt that I'm worried about."

His hoot made people stop eating to look at them. Quickly, he grabbed two drinks from the slushy water and dropped to a squat a foot or so away from her. She gingerly lowered herself to the cooler and heaved a sigh. "Maybe this trail ride wasn't such a good idea, after all."

Will handed her the cold fruit drink. "Don't say that. Zoey's glad you're here." *And so am I.*

Anne's left eyebrow cocked in question. "What makes you so sure? As far as I can tell, she only has eyes for you-know-who."

Will followed her slight nod. The boy. Linda's son. Will had noticed Zoey's repeated looks over her shoulder, but he'd assumed she was checking on her mother. "You mean she has a crush—"

Anne shushed him. "She'd never forgive me if she thought I told you about this. First crushes are…special."

Will heard a funny, almost wistful note in her tone.

"But she's too young to like boys. Do you want me to drop him over the cliff? I know he's your best friend's son, but…"

Anne's smile—the first he'd seen in nearly a week—made his heart dance. "I don't think that will be necessary since it's totally one-sided. Zoey is two whole years younger than Logan. She's a pesky child to him."

Will pretended to wipe sweat from his forehead. "Whew. Good thing I don't have to do away with him. I kinda like the kid."

Anne sipped her drink. Her gaze stayed on Will. "You'd be that kind of dad, wouldn't you?"

"What do you mean?"

"Involved. Proactive. The kind who would grill his daughter's dates, enforce curfews, check up on her friends."

"Hell, yes," Will said without stopping to think. The idea of some guy messing with Zoey made him growl. "I was the kind of guy every teenage girl's father dreads. Who better to know what evil lurks in a teenage boy's itty-bitty pea brain?"

Anne's smile looked forced. He realized they'd wandered into dangerous territory—What-If Land. What if Will was Zoey's father? What if Anne and Zoey lived where Will could look after her, stand up for her, help enforce the rules?

He jumped to his feet. He wasn't ready to go there. First, he needed to talk to his grandfather. A person didn't tangle with bulls for a living without developing fairly acute survival instincts, and Will knew he was going to need help if he had any chance at all of talking Anne into some sort of compromise.

ANNE MOVED WITH CARE. She didn't hurt at the moment. Well, there was a definite tingle in her thighs and the muscles in her butt felt twingy, but something told her the real pain would arrive tomorrow.

"Oh, God, I'm never going to be able to get out of bed," Linda said, hobbling to a stop beside her. "What on earth was I thinking? I sit at a desk for a living. I'm no cowgirl."

Anne gave Linda a supportive hug. "It's okay. I have a foam pillow I'll lend you. You'll live. And it was worth it, wasn't it?"

The two started across the compound toward the house, where the tantalizing aroma of pork and spices beckoned. Anne's mouth watered. She couldn't remember the last time she had been this hungry.

Linda snuffled. "I guess. But Logan and I didn't quite get that touchy-feely bonding time I'd hoped for."

Anne chuckled. "I think that time fell by the wayside when he was four, pal. He's a guy now. You're a mom." Linda made a sad face, so Anne added, "But a very cool, hip, cowgirl kind of mom."

Linda took off her dusty hat and wiped her forehead. Her pleasant face was streaked with sweat and dirt. Her blond hair lay flattened in places and her shoulders were definitely burned, but she looked happier than Anne had seen her in weeks. That might be because she'd bumped into an old friend at the reunion and he'd called to ask her out. Linda swore she wasn't getting her hopes up, but Anne knew for a fact that love—or the possibility of love—could make you hope for things that weren't ever going to happen.

"Hey," Linda said, stopping abruptly. "Where'd that RV come from?"

Anne spun around. Her heart leaped at the sight of a boxy old motor home with a bizarre pink appendage attached to the back. "A.J. is home," she cried, running— well, limping—across the compound. "Thank God."

"WHAT DO YOU MEAN you won't be a party to it?" Will cried, striding to the fireplace in his grandfather's office just as the gong on the clock struck midnight.

The last of the forty or so revelers—a combination of guests, Silver Rose employees and a few neighbors who had found out about A.J.'s return—had finally dispersed a few minutes earlier. Spurred by Joy's chili verde, burritos and icy margaritas, the impromptu fiesta had lasted way too long.

Will was exhausted and he was sure his grandfather was ready to drop from his long drive, but Will knew he wouldn't be able to sleep without ironing out a few details of his plan with A.J.

"I said I won't try to talk Annie into doing something she doesn't want to do," the older man repeated. "She's a grown woman. She knows what's best for her." Before Will could protest, A.J. added, "Just like you know what you gotta do."

Will frowned. But did he know?

They'd all heard the message Joy had blurted to the crowd when she first spotted Will. Even before he'd had a chance to greet his grandfather, Joy had announced, "The rodeo doc called, Will. He'll be in Reno on Tuesday and he said to tell you he's prepared to give you a green light if you pass the physical."

Will would happily have strangled the gregarious woman for sharing his private business in public, but there hadn't been time. Anne had rushed their guests into a serving line and ordered him to start mixing margaritas. After dinner, they'd gathered around the cottonwood to listen to A.J.'s travelogue.

"Just because Doc said he *might* let me ride doesn't mean I'm going back on the circuit full bore," Will said. "I thought maybe I'd give part-time a try. So I could spend more time here."

A.J. coughed deliberately. "Now, hold up a second. That sounds pretty lukewarm to me. How many times have you told me the key to bull riding comes from inside? If your heart ain't in the game, you got no business being in that chute. Ain't that so?"

The truth left a bitter taste in Will's mouth. He nodded.

"So, where's your heart?"

With Anne. But would Will's declaration of love and vow to give up bull riding be a strong enough incentive for her to quit her job and stay at the Silver Rose permanently? Was he brave enough to ask?

"What if I retire from riding and Anne decides to go back to New York anyway?"

His grandfather turned his chair and gazed at the map with his many postcards dotting the path of his trek. There weren't any from his trip home. "Sounds to me like you want your cake and Anne's piece, too. Life don't come with any guarantees. But one thing I do know is that love is worth taking the gamble."

A.J. shifted in his chair and leaned forward, resting his elbows on the desk so he could study Will. "You know, boy, for a person who's ridden some of the meanest, orneriest bulls in the territory, you sure seem skittish about asking Anne to marry you."

Marry. The word had been stalking Will for weeks but he'd hidden behind his and Anne's agendas to avoid thinking about it.

"Well, that's the thing, Gramps. This isn't about eight seconds. It's about the rest of my life."

ANNE WALKED downstairs gingerly. Each step produced a quivering pain in her butt and thighs. The pulsating jets of the tub last night and this morning had eased some of the stiffness from yesterday's ride, but Anne had a feeling she was going to be sore for days.

The house seemed quieter than usual, even for a Sunday. Dust motes flickered in the yellowish light of morning. She'd arranged to meet A.J. for coffee. The chaos surrounding his arrival last night had precluded any chance for a private chat. The ravenous trail riders had welcomed him home like a long-lost pilgrim and had insisted A.J. regale them with stories of his travels while they stuffed themselves on Joy's chili verde, fresh flour tortillas, rice and beans.

Anne had been delighted to see him safely home, but she'd had her hands full with tired guests, an exhausted and wheezing daughter and her own tumultuous emotions. When he'd climbed down from the cab of the motor home to give her a hug, Anne had nearly succumbed to tears.

"It's gonna be too hectic to talk right tonight," he'd said, as if reading her mind. "How 'bout we have coffee in the morning?"

"It will have to be early, before Zoey wakes up. She's going to want to drive that…thing you brought home."

Anne picked her way down the last few steps. She wasn't looking forward to telling A.J. that she couldn't stay beyond her three-month agreement—in fact, if he and Will would agree to it, she needed to leave sooner. After this morning's predawn wake-up call from Roger, what choice did she have?

A.J. met her at the foot of the stairs. "Good morning, beautiful girl."

She gave him a hug to hide her blush. "You're good for my ego."

He brushed back her hair clumsily. "The Silver Rose agrees with you, I'd say. My, my, look how fresh and pretty you are. Except for the sunburn on your nose."

Anne touched the skin that still felt hot and tight even though she'd treated it with cream. "Can you believe it? I was the one walking around squirting sunscreen on peo-

ple yesterday and I forgot to put any on me.'' Thank goodness Will had noticed and mentioned the fact or she'd be
peeling when she met with the WHC board.

"Doesn't surprise me. Your mother was the same
way—always looking out for others first.''

Anne sighed. She truly wished she were more like her
mother, but if nothing else, this summer had proven that
Anne was no Esther.

"What's that sigh for?'' A.J. asked, his eyes narrowing.

"Let's grab a cup of coffee and I'll show you,'' Anne
said, leading the way to the kitchen.

Joy was intently measuring flour into a crockery bowl.
"Blueberry pancakes this morning,'' she told them. "In
honor of our returned hero.''

Now it was A.J.'s turn to blush. Anne chuckled as she
led him out the back door and down the steps to the garden. "Welcome to Disasterville,'' she said, opening the
gate. "Home to mildew, mice and giant, horned green dev-
ils that devour everything in sight.''

A.J. followed her to the center of the garden and turned
in quarterly increments to assess the damage. "Yep, tomato worms. Those pesky critters used to drive your
mother crazy.

"One time she patrolled the garden at midnight with a
flashlight. A guest happened to look out his window and
saw a woman in a long white gown flashing a light and
pacing back and forth. Nothing we said could convince
him he hadn't seen a ghost.'' A.J. chuckled. "Your mother
got a big kick out of that. I'm surprised she didn't write
you about it.''

Anne vaguely remembered hearing something about a
"haunting,'' but she hadn't realized the story was garden-
related. "Are you serious or just being nice?'' she asked.
"Mom had problems like this?''

Anne took his elbow and ushered him to the box where

her decimated tomato plants stood. The leafless stalks reminded her of something she'd seen in photos of forest fires. "I mean, look here, A.J. I didn't even have enough tomatoes for dinner last night. I know Mother's tomatoes were more plentiful than this. She used to send me jars of her homemade salsa."

He reached out and plucked a two-inch-long green worm from the plant. The beast reared back and glared at him. A.J. dropped it to the ground and crushed it under his heel, nodding with satisfaction when it exploded, sending green goo in every direction.

Anne jumped sideways with a squawk. "That's gross," she said, knowing she sounded exactly like her daughter.

"True, but your mother seemed to get tremendous satisfaction from squishing them." He winked. "I think the worms were a challenge to her. She could have bought chemicals to kill them, but she liked her garden organic— even if it meant losing a few tomatoes."

"How'd she get enough vegetables to can salsa?"

"Bought 'em."

Anne nearly dropped her cup. "What?" she cried. "I've been busting my behind out here trying to be as good a gardener as my mother and you're telling me she *bought* tomatoes?"

A.J. appeared to be trying not to smile. "Who said Esther was a great gardener?"

Anne pointed to the shed. "I found her laminated gardening tips in there. And all the seeds and fertilizer and stuff. Her tip sheet looks professional."

He nodded. "It is. She copied it from some television program. Truth is, every year she ended up so mad she swore she wasn't going to have a garden ever again. But then the seed catalogs would arrive and she'd start planning. Last fall, before she fell ill, she said this summer was going to be her glory year." His eyes misted. "That's why she made that how-to page and took it into town to have it laminated.''

Anne couldn't decide whether to laugh or cry. ''I wish I'd known.''

''Why?'' he asked. ''What would you have done differently?''

Anne thought a minute, remembering Will eating the winter carrots, planting peas with Zoey, plotting to exterminate the mouse that had made off with her beans. ''Nothing, I guess. 'Cept maybe fumigate for tomato worms.''

A.J. put his arm around her shoulder and led her to the gate. ''There's always next year.''

Anne's heart felt as though A.J. had lanced it with a tine of the pitchfork she'd left by the shed. How could she tell him she'd made up her mind to return to New York? And she wouldn't be back next year, either. Any dream she had of spending her summers in Nevada was pure fantasy. Anne knew the realities of her job. Once she was back in the groove, she'd be lucky to find two weeks free, let alone three months.

Instead of walking to the porch, A.J. led her to the shade of what Anne had come to think of as the piñata tree. She would never forget her daughter's joy—and Will's look of surprise—when Zoey swung with wild abandon at the colorful papier-mâché pony.

A.J. lowered himself stiffly to the bench of the picnic table. Anne sat down across from him, not bothering to hide her wince.

''Will said you were quite the cowgirl. Born to the saddle, I believe were the exact words he used.''

Anne couldn't prevent a small trill of pleasure. She'd worked hard to stay seated on her frisky mare. It pleased her that Will had noticed. She hadn't been able to take her eyes off him, either. She'd watched his muscles play under his white shirt. His lean butt molded to the saddle. His hands on the reins and, later, dripping with icy water when he handed her a drink.

God, she was going to miss his touch. His smile. His presence.

"I have to go, A.J.," Anne said before thoughts of Will could make her change her mind. "My boss called me this morning on my cell phone. He said he needs me in the office as soon as possible."

A.J. didn't say anything for a minute. He drank his coffee and let the awakening sounds of the ranch flow between them. This was Anne's favorite time of day. The dew made everything sparkly—even the fresh cow pies that provided fodder for the little birds that seemed to inhabit every tree and bush.

"I can't say as I'm surprised, Annie," he said, catching her daydreaming. "I was thinking about what to say to you all the way across Colorado, and I finally came to the conclusion that you're a grown woman. You oughta know your own mind."

Yeah, well, maybe. Or maybe not.

"I imagine you're anxious to get back to the city, but I have a favor to ask." He shrugged. "I know I used up a lot of favors this summer, but this one would mean a lot to me."

Anne swallowed noisily. "What is it?"

"I was hoping you might let Zoey stay a bit longer. I promise to get her back to you before school starts, but one thing I discovered on my trip was how much I miss being a grandpa. That little girl was always on my mind—she reminds me a lot of Esther."

"She does?"

A.J. nodded, his eyes misty. "Although I hope she doesn't drive like her grandma. Esther had a bit of a lead foot, you know."

"That's right," Anne said, stifling a few tears of her own. "She knew all the local highway patrol officers by their first names, didn't she?"

Anne's mind raced. Did she dare leave Zoey here? Joy was going to have her hands full combining office duties with the kitchen chores. Would Will be here to help or was he returning to bull riding, as she'd understood from his phone message last night?

A.J. winked. "Three or four of 'em came to her funeral. She'd have been so pleased."

Anne took a deep breath. They hadn't talked about what happened in Maine. He spoke before she could ask.

"It was peaceful, Annie."

Anne reached out and covered his wrist with her hand. "It must have been really difficult. I'm not sure I could have done it."

He sniffled and pulled a handkerchief out of his pocket. "Now, that's where I disagree. From what I've heard and seen since I got back, I'd have to say there isn't much of anything that you can't accomplish once you set your mind to it."

In business, maybe. Too bad her personal life wasn't that simple. "A.J., I don't know how to say this. Will and I have grown close this summer. We care for each other but our worlds aren't mutually compatible."

As if on cue, Will crossed the compound toward the barn, apparently unaware of their presence. Anne tried to picture her life without him in it. To her dismay, she couldn't even bring to mind an image of her apartment. Her building. Her street.

A.J.'s lack of surprise made her ask, "Will told you about us, didn't he?"

"Didn't have to. His feelings for you are pretty easy to spot, but he did ask me for advice," A.J. answered.

"What did...? No, that's between you and Will. It

doesn't matter, anyway. I heard the message Joy took from the team doctor,'' she said, picturing Will's initial look of surprise—and she was certain *glee*—when Joy said the words *back on the circuit.* Remembering that look helped strengthen Anne's resolve. "If I do leave Zoey here, A.J., you have to promise not to take her to the bull riding. I hate to think what would happen if Will got hurt right in front of her.''

"You have my word that if my grandson rides in the Labor Day Buck-Off, me and Zoey will be right there.''

"Thank you,'' she said, starting to rise. "Now, I guess I'd better tell Zoey the good news. I know she'll be thrilled. And, in all honesty, this will be better for her. August in the city is particularly bad for allergies. The smog, the heat—''

Anne's words were drowned out by a loud, high-pitched squeal. "Grandpa,'' Zoey cried, bursting out the door and down the steps. "Did you get a new battery for my car? Can I drive it now?''

A.J. gave Anne a wry smile as he rose. "A promise is a promise.''

Anne agreed. She'd promised her boss to return at the end of the summer, and she was going to fulfill her vow. Even if it meant saying goodbye to everything—and every-one—she loved.

WILL COULD HONESTLY say he'd never seen a person as happy as Zoey was the minute she got behind the wheel of her miniature car. Her mother was understandably not quite as pleased.

"Now, take it slow, Miss Z,'' Will said sternly. It was hard to be strict when Zoey was beaming like a hundred-watt bulb.

"I will. I promise. And thank you again for fixing the batt'ry.''

To A.J.'s delight, the battery hadn't been faulty, just in need of a charge. Will solved the problem last night after he washed and waxed the little pink vehicle. Following his talk with his grandfather, Will had been far too keyed up to sleep.

He squatted beside the car to give Zoey one last check. "Brake with this foot," he said, tickling her right knee.

She giggled. "I know. I know."

"Did you take a hit on your puffer thing?" Her cheeks were twice as florid as her car.

Zoey looked up at her mother, who was standing a foot away. "I did. Really. And I took my medicine this morning. I didn't like those doctors at the clinic. I'm going to stay healthy so I don't have to go back."

"Good," Anne said. "That means no broken bones, either."

Will had seen Anne talking with A.J. under the tree a short while earlier and guessed they were discussing her plans. So far, nothing had been said about her intentions, probably to keep Zoey from getting upset.

"All right, then. Let's get this show on the road." He stood up and waved his hat back and forth, a signal to the men stationed at the far end of the circle. No traffic would be allowed in when Zoey was behind the wheel.

"Okay, sweetness, let 'er rip."

Zoey adjusted the chin strap of her riding helmet. It wasn't as safe as the crash helmet he planned to buy, but it would work for today.

"Don't hit any homeless people or wine bottles," Anne said, giving Zoey a quick hug.

Will gave Anne a questioning look, but her explanation was muffled by the high-pitched whine of the tiny engine, which was so loud, it nearly muffled Zoey's shriek of delight. "Whee…"

Anne stepped to Will's side and grabbed his arm with a death grip. "What if she crashes?"

"We've got hay bales anywhere even remotely dangerous."

"I'm neurotic, aren't I?"

"You're her mother. It's allowed."

The car shot past going a whopping ten miles an hour. Will knew that was fast enough to cause injuries if the car crashed or rolled over, but with each revolution, Zoey seemed to acquire more control.

The adults all moved to the porch to watch from comfortable chairs.

"Are you going to forgive me for buying it, Annie?" A.J. asked.

"Of course," she said, giving him a hug. "But I want your promise you won't her let drive it without this kind of supervision when I'm gone."

"Gone?" Will asked, looking from A.J. to Anne.

A.J. gave Anne a light peck on the cheek. "Joy and I will keep an eye on things here. You two had best take your talk inside."

Will suddenly knew what this "talk" was going to be about. No way was it going to be on Anne's turf, he decided. He grabbed her hand. "Nope. It's too nice a day to be inside. Gramps, I'll have my cell phone if you need to reach either of us."

Anne balked momentarily then sighed. "Okay."

She followed him to the garage and climbed into the Forerunner without a word. As Will had predicted, his truck had sold in less than forty-eight hours, to a nineteen-year-old motocross biker who loved the color. "It's a statement, man," he'd proclaimed.

Will agreed. A statement that no longer represented his life.

"Where are we going?" she asked when they reached the highway.

"To the top of the ridge."

"Is it bumpy?"

"Some. Why?"

She moved gingerly in the seat. "I can still feel my horseback ride."

Will bit back a grin. "If you rode more often, that wouldn't be a problem. Once every ten years or so won't cut it."

"Thank you. I'll keep that in mind when I'm back in New York," she said, effectively wiping the smile off Will's face.

Neither spoke again until he turned onto the little-used fire trail.

"Are you sure you know where you're going?"

"Absolutely. How 'bout you?"

She huffed and grabbed the overhead handgrip to keep from getting jostled about by the rutted road. When they reached a clearing, Will parked under the scanty shade of a pine. He got out and hurried around to open Anne's door.

"There's a lookout just beyond those trees," he said, helping her down. In such proximity, her scent was unavoidable. It filled his senses and triggered a need so great it took every bit of willpower he had not to haul her into his arms and beg her to stay, to marry him, to grow old with him on the Silver Rose. But his sense of self-preservation was stronger. He couldn't put his heart on the line until he knew for certain whether or not he stood a chance.

The wind was hot and gritty. While not the prettiest vista in the state, it was the panorama he wanted. He pointed to a little group of buildings nestled in a clearing midway between them and the flat, silvery imprint of the valley. "There's the Silver Rose."

"It looks like a small village."

"That's what it is. And you know that saying about needing a village to help raise a child, right?"

She sighed. "Is that why you brought me here? To talk about Zoey?"

"Partly," he admitted.

Her green eyes narrowed and she crossed her arms in a defensive posture. "Well, don't bother. I know what a difference this summer has made in my daughter's life. She's stronger, more self-assured, braver, happier—even healthier—than she was at the beginning of the summer. And I have you, A.J., Joy and all the people she's met this summer to thank for this transformation. But, the fact remains that my life is in New York, Will. My job is there. My future."

The words cut with surgical precision. "When are you leaving?"

"Tomorrow, if I can get a flight. Tuesday at the latest."

"I have a doctor's appointment in Reno on Tuesday."

"I know. Ironic, isn't it? You get a call from the person who holds your future in his hands, and the next morning my boss calls to say it's crunch time. Either I get back ASAP or he gives the position to someone else."

Will heard the underlying edge in her voice. He knew what she was feeling. Fear. Panic. The unnerving sense that everything you had worked for was sliding further and further out of reach. He felt the same thing this very moment.

She reached out to touch his arm. "Will, I did a lot of soul-searching this past week, and I know myself well enough to understand that I need the validation this promotion will give me. It's my payoff. After everything I've sacrificed to get here, I can't just walk away. And I apologize for acting so smug and judgmental. You have every right to follow your dream, no matter how great the risk."

What if the dream has changed?

"Thanks," he said. Three months ago he'd felt exactly the same. Now he knew there was more than one kind of winning. But he wasn't a chauvinistic hypocrite. If Anne needed to play the game to the end, he'd cheer her on, even if his heart was shattered.

"So, you and Zoey are flying back to the big city, huh?"

"Actually," she said, her gaze following a red-tailed hawk soaring on the warm updrafts, "A.J. asked if Zoey could stay a while longer. Her return ticket is for the sixth of September. I thought I might let her stay." She blinked suddenly and looked at him. "Is that okay? Do you mind? I'm going to be busy playing catch-up, and the smog is so bad in the city."

Mind? His heart took flight with the hawk and a shiver of hope coursed through him. Anne didn't seem to understand that she'd just given him the greatest gift of all. Her trust. "Hell, no, I don't mind. I was afraid she might try to drive back in that little pink car if you didn't give her some time to get tired of it."

Her smile was the one he loved best—unguarded and playful. He took her in his arms and kissed her. Anne was leaving, but she'd entrusted her precious daughter into his care. That had to mean something, didn't it?

CHAPTER FOURTEEN

THREE WEEKS in Manhattan had done nothing to improve Anne's outlook on life. Each morning she awoke with a voracious craving in the pit of her stomach, the kind of hunger food couldn't appease. By the end of the first week, the bags under her eyes were a clear indicator that she'd made a mistake in returning to the city.

Sheer stubbornness and a sense of loyalty to Roger made her get up each morning, shower, pick a suit from the wide array that clogged her closet, then leave for work, swiping her Metro card through the metal turnstile, jostling among impatient strangers, dodging fume-spewing buses and honking taxis. Each cough triggered by a woman's perfume or some harsh-smelling emission reminded her of what Zoey would soon be facing.

In the WHC office, Roger seemed to be the only person who even remembered who she was. Several young junior executives who hadn't been around when Anne left seemed openly hostile and threatened by her return. In the rest room, she'd overheard one woman refer to Anne as "Roger's precious cowgirl."

Heaving a long, weary sigh, Anne rocked forward in her desk chair and dialed a number. Tucking the receiver between her shoulder and her ear, Anne undid the button of her DKNY jacket so she could reach the waistband of her suit. *Too many of Joy's cinnamon rolls.* The thought made her mouth water.

Her slight groan of relief when the zipper gave coincided with a distinctly accented "Hello?"

Maria. Their former housekeeper/nanny. Anne had put off calling her. "Maria, it's Anne Fraser. I'm back in town and lining up child care for Zoey. Are you available?"

While Maria explained that she had decided to take a permanent position with her new employer, Anne took a sip of lukewarm Earl Grey Tea from her "I Love My Mommy" mug. The queasiness that had accompanied her the whole flight back returned. *What am I going to do now?*

Anne wished Maria all the best and hung up. Zoey was scheduled to return in a little over a week, and Anne hadn't even started looking for a nanny—maybe because she had discovered this summer that *she* was the best child-care provider for her daughter.

One thing this time apart had proven was how much Anne missed Zoey. They talked every day at lunch—midmorning Zoey's time. The fifteen or so minutes were by far the bright spot in Anne's day. And if Will or A.J. happened to pick up when Anne called, she considered it a bonus. She missed them all.

Additionally, e-mails had become her life source. Will had purchased a digital camera, and he'd taught Zoey how to send photos over the Internet. The most recent image had been waiting for Anne when she arrived at her desk an hour earlier.

Although it probably conflicted with her ultraprofessional image, Anne had saved the photo to serve as her desktop's wallpaper, so every time she looked at her computer screen she saw Zoey and Tressa hanging upside down like happy monkeys from side-by-side trapeze bars. The e-mail message that came with it read:

Will took us to the park. We had fun. I love you, Zoey. P.S.: Tressa's school starts on Monday. Can I go with her?

School. The word had sent a jolt of panic through Anne. What kind of mother forgot to register her nine-year-old daughter for school?

One whose corporation was undergoing a major overhaul. From the moment Anne had walked through the door of her office, she'd been besieged with files, reports, correspondence and complaints. Normally, her attention-to-detail mind thrived on this kind of challenge, but now she found it boring, redundant and inane.

She rested her head on her hand and sighed. She wasn't the type who gave up easily. She'd fought Barry about the divorce, insisting they could fix the problems between them with counseling. She'd pushed her mother to hang on well past the point where Esther's body had given up the fight.

Is that what I'm doing here? Anne asked herself. *Holding on to an outdated goal?*

Maybe it was time to admit that she wasn't the same person who once sat at this desk. The new and improved Anne Fraser belonged in Nevada—where her family was. Where her life was.

But there was still the issue of health care insurance.

Where's that new employee benefit package? She found the folder and started reading. Half an hour later she was smiling. She and Zoey were entitled to extended coverage for eighteen months. Enough time to find a new policy.

She opened her word processing program and started typing.

Attention: Roger
Regarding: Resignation
Dear Roger, please accept my resignation effective immediately. I regret any inconvenience this might cause, but family commitments require my presence

in Nevada permanently. Thank you for your support
and friendship over the past years.

Most sincerely,
Anne

She had her finger on her mouse button ready to hit
send, when the door of her office opened. "Anne," Roger
McFinney said, charging into the room without waiting for
an invitation. "Thank God you're here. Come quick. You
won't believe what's just happened."

Anne rose. "Rog, I was just—"

He cut her off. "Whatever it is can wait. The board just
met and it looks like WHC is undergoing a complete overhaul. I've been named CEO, Anne. That means you're
going to be my VP."

"Vice president?" she croaked.

"You earned it, my friend. All that long-distance work
this summer is paying off royally. You know what kind of
salary we're talking, right? And with the two of us at the
helm, we'll be pulling in bonuses that ought to buy you
that house in the country you always wanted."

Anne couldn't move.

Roger laughed at her apparent shock. He hurried to her
desk and took her arm. "Come on. The press is gathering
for the announcement. Do you need to powder your nose?
It looks like it's peeling."

She put her hand to her face as Roger pulled her with
him. Her last glance was over her shoulder at her computer
screen where her grinning daughter was hanging upside
down, like a monkey.

WILL SANK into a comfortable chair in the lobby of one
of Reno's most popular hotels. He was a few minutes early
for his appointment with Walt Crain. Since this was a ca-

sual meeting to go over the results of the tests the doctor had run on Will the day after Anne left, both men agreed a less formal setting was fine.

The pneumatic doors opened and the noise level rose as a busload of retirees passed through the lobby into the adjoining casino. Many looked A.J.'s age or older, but somehow Will couldn't picture his grandfather participating in that kind of organized activity. Since his return, A.J. had seemed at peace. Happy, even. But that was partly to do with Zoey's presence. Who knew what would happen when she left?

On the wall opposite Will was an oversize poster announcing the big Buck-Off scheduled to take place Labor Day weekend. A small, nostalgic flutter of anxiety passed through his belly before he glanced at his watch. He was impatient to return to the ranch. He wanted to take Zoey for a ride this afternoon. Just the two of them. The aspens were starting to turn color and Will wanted her to experience a tiny taste of autumn in the mountains before she returned to the city.

Unfortunately, he'd gotten a late start this morning because two guests had been determined to make Will understand how much they'd enjoyed their trip. "Best second honeymoon ever," the husband had said.

"Well, almost anything would beat our first," his wife had qualified. "He came down with food poisoning from his aunt's goose-liver pâté and we spent most of the time in the emergency room, but since then we've taken a lot of trips and this was by far the best."

"We're coming back for three weeks next year," the man promised.

Will had been pleased. He hadn't expected to care about this job. He'd planned to hide out in the barn most of the summer and let Anne handle the guests, but somewhere along the way, he'd gotten involved—and discovered that he liked the people who came to the ranch to experience a life radically different from their normal routine. Keeping them stimulated and entertained had become a challenge and, to his immense surprise, he'd discovered he was good at it.

"You're a born teacher," his grandfather had told him the other day after watching Will instruct several guests on the art and science of shoeing a horse. "Just like your mother."

Later, Will had asked A.J. to explain the comment.

"Your mother was a sweet gal who had plans to be a teacher until she fell in love with your daddy," Will's grandfather told him. "Kinda hard to go to school when you're on the road so much. And then you came along. But she was taking correspondence courses at the time of the accident. And she volunteered in your classroom quite a bit."

If Will had known that, he'd never given it any thought. Oddly, his entire focus had always been on his father. Why? he asked himself.

A.J. had provided the answer when he said, "John was larger than life. Loud. Demanding. Your mother was the steady one. You could count on her to get the job done in a quiet, more serious way. The way you do."

From his earliest memory, Will had wanted to be just like his father. His mother had receded into his mind as a fuzzy image. Perhaps her strength went unappreciated until he met Anne. No mother bear would defend her cub with greater zeal than Anne, who was willing to sacrifice her personal happiness to make the best life possible for her daughter. Never in a million years would she have gotten into a car with a drunk driver and risked not being a part of her child's life.

A shiver passed through his body. A shiver of understanding. Maybe the reason his mother had remained a blank spot in his memory was that Will resented her for leaving him. Mothers weren't supposed to die. Fathers did hurtful things sometimes, like bullying their sons or dying in an accident. But mothers were supposed to be there to ease the suffering.

He closed his eyes and rubbed a pain that had blossomed in the center of his forehead. He wished he could tell his mother he was sorry for ignoring her memory for so long.

"That's not the part of your head that's supposed to hurt," a voice said.

Will looked up. "The headache is from being kept waiting," he retorted. Rising, Will shook Walt Crain's hand. "How's it going, Doc? Have you got Saturday's lineup ready to go?"

Walt nodded toward the bar. "How 'bout I buy you a beer while we talk about it?"

"Sounds good to me."

Walt's eyebrow lifted. No doubt he was surprised that Will wasn't chomping at the bit to hear the results of his tests.

Will ushered him to the bar, where built-in video-poker games invited them to insert dollar bills into the slot provided. Will held up two fingers and gave the name of the beer he knew Walt favored. While they waited for the bartender to pour two drafts, Walt removed a folder from his calfskin briefcase. "I have the results of your CAT scan and MRI."

"Am I going to live?"

Walt chuckled. "Of course. You're not only remarkably tough, but you heal faster than anybody I've ever met. Still, if you're planning to ride this weekend, I'm going to require some extra—"

Will cut him off. "I'm not ridin', Doc. I've decided to retire."

Walt's eyes widened and he gave a low whistle. "Well, I'll be damned. You finally came to your senses." A grin spread across his florid face. "Must be a woman somewhere in this story."

Will had no reason to lie. "Her name is Anne, and she has a nine-year-old daughter. Zoey. I taught her to ride this summer."

Their beers arrived and Walt waited to lift his glass in a toast. "To the best news I've had all week. Congratulations, my friend."

Will made the obligatory clink. "Thank you."

"Have you set a date?"

Will took a healthy draught of the cold brew before answering. "Not exactly. First, I have to convince her to marry me."

Walt nodded as though he understood. "She wasn't wild about the idea of you spilling what's left of your brains on the arena floor, right?"

The image made Will shudder. "That was part of it, but there are other issues. Her job, for one. It's in New York. Where she is at the moment."

Walt gave him a pointed look. "Have you told her you're giving up bulls?"

"Not yet. I thought you deserved to hear it first." While Will didn't always agree with the man's opinion, he never doubted the M.D.'s integrity.

Walt obviously was touched by the gesture. "Well, I appreciate that, son, but you're not going to get her back by sitting here. Go tell her."

"I'm planning on it. Next week, when I take her daughter back home."

Walt reached out and flicked the crown of Will's head. "Did that last bull loosen a bolt in there? I didn't see it in the MRI, but those things aren't foolproof, you know."

Will rubbed the stinging spot. "What are you talking about?"

"Cowboys," Walt groaned, throwing up his hands. "The kind of courting you need to do is best done outta sight of the children. Groveling and begging will definitely be in order."

Before Will could muster a comeback, Walt pulled his cell phone from his briefcase and pushed a button. Will tried to follow the one-sided conversation, but since it mostly consisted of "yep," "nope" and "okay," he was thoroughly unprepared when Walt looked at him and said, "You're good to go. My jet will fly you to LaGuardia. From there, you take a taxi into town. After that, you're on your own."

Will gave his head a shake. "Since when do you have a private jet?"

Walt brightened like a little boy with a new toy. "I just bought it. My son-in-law is a pilot, so we can keep it in the family. Comes in handy when one of my superstar bull riders gets hurt and I happen to be golfing on the opposite side of the country."

He rose and urged Will to his feet. "Now get going. But, just so you know, this isn't a taxi service. The jet's coming straight back. I have to be in Albuquerque on Thursday. If she turns you down, it's a long walk back."

Will felt overwhelmed with gratitude. He didn't know what to say. He held out his hand. "Thanks, Doc. For everything."

Walt shook his hand then pulled him into a quick hug. "You were one of the best, Will. Don't ever doubt it. You had great heart, and you left your mark on the industry. What more can a man ask from a job?"

A job. Will repeated the word as he drove to the airstrip on the edge of town. Somewhere along the line, he'd lost sight of that simple fact. Bull riding had been his job. He'd made a good living from it. So good, in fact, he could afford to start a second career.

The job he was hoping for was a multifaceted position—husband, father and businessman. The first two depended on Anne.

ANNE PRESSED the send button on her keyboard and watched while the e-mail message disappear into cyberspace. She closed her eyes and took a deep breath to compose her jumbled thoughts. The long, grueling day had had a surreal edge to it. At times, Anne felt like Alice falling through a tunnel into a world where the future looked rosy, where every dream she had ever had about her place in business had come true.

Unfortunately, each tantalizing new aspect of the WHC reorganization proposal held less interest to her than the seed catalog that had somehow wound up in her mail.

She'd smiled and shook hands when prompted, like a marionette. "She's in shock," she'd heard Roger say time and again to explain her wooden responses.

Culture shock, she thought, picking up the colorful sales brochure that claimed to be "every gardener's friend." She could use that kind of friend, not the throng of people who'd come up to her after the press conference with fake smiles of congratulations.

Maybe she was suffering from reality shock. The reality that she didn't belong in this world anymore. She couldn't give this life the dedication she had in the past because its goals and objectives no longer mattered to her.

Success is relative, Anne thought. Doubling my tomato harvest would constitute success, wouldn't it? The basket of ripe, red fruit on the page made her mouth water.

Helping Zoey grow up into a generous, caring person would certainly qualify as a victory. And how could loving a man and being loved in return not be worth more than restricted use of the corporate jet?

Anne knew the answer. It had taken time for the truth to soak in. She wanted the life she'd come to adore in Nevada. The rustic old ranch house—there was still so much work to do on it. Her beautiful daughter—another work in progress. A.J.—with his wry wisdom and the history he had to share. And most of all—Will.

A single rap on the door made Anne sit up. Braced for the confrontation she knew was coming, she said, "Come in."

She closed her eyes for a moment to gather strength then folded her hands on her desk and took a steadying breath. "That was fast."

"Felt like forever to me."

Anne's mouth dropped open. Shock and joy pumped through her veins. She jumped to her feet so fast her chair went scuttling across the room and her head started to spin. "Will," she exclaimed. "Oh, my God, what are you doing here?"

He cleared the distance in three giant steps. His kiss was hard and needy, and might have lasted forever if he hadn't pulled back to tell her, "It takes heart to ride bulls. You've got to want it bad. But all I want is you, Anne. I have officially retired from bull riding."

Anne was too overwhelmed to speak. "Your dream—"

"Isn't worth squat without you. I'm moving to New York. I've decided to sell my land and use the money to go to college. I think I'd like to teach someday." He cradled her face in his hands. "It doesn't matter where we live, but we have to be together."

Tears clustered in her eyes and it was all she could do to say, "You're wrong, Will. It does matter where we live. We can't run the Silver Rose from New York."

"A.J. can run the Silver Rose," he said stubbornly then paused. "Did you say we?"

Anne nodded. "I love you, Will Cavanaugh. I want to be with you, but only if you'll marry me."

His face lit up. "You're asking me?"

"I looked it up in the male handbook. Modern men aren't afraid to let the woman do the asking. It shows they're sensitive and confident of their masculinity."

He threw back his head and laughed. "You are too much. And I love you." His expression grew serious. "I might not always say the right thing or do the right thing, but I will always love you, Anne. I always have."

Before Anne could reply, her office door flew open. Roger McFinney stormed in. "Anne, what the hell is going on?" he demanded, waving a page of printer paper. He stopped abruptly when he spotted Will. "Who the hell are you?"

Will wrapped an arm around Anne. "Will Cavanaugh. Anne's fiancé. You must be the jerk who kept her working night and day this summer."

Roger seemed to lose some of his bluster when faced with a no-nonsense bull rider in boots and a leather jacket. He took a step to the side and focused his attention on Anne. "I got your e-mail. Your resignation. Tell me you're not serious. You're not going to give up the opportunity of a lifetime to run off to some silly ranch and play cowgirl?"

Anne felt Will's low growl reverberate through her. She soothed him with a hand on his chest. "Yes, Roger, I meant every word. I appreciate the faith you've shown in me, but I can't accept the position of vice president. I've accepted a new job—chief cook and bottle washer at the Silver Rose."

Roger made a disparaging sound and shook his head. "Fine. It's your choice. You'll be bored out of your mind

within a year. In fact, what will you do all winter? Didn't
you tell me that place was a summer venue?''

She looked at Will. ''Gee, honey, if you're not going to
be riding bulls and I'm not going to have guests to look
after, what will we do this winter?''

The look he gave her could have melted chocolate at
ten paces. ''We'll think of something.''

Roger let out a loud huff and slammed the door on his
way out.

Anne looked after him and sighed. ''He's just upset because they made him CEO this morning and now he won't
have a proven flunky to pick up after him.''

Will kissed her temple. ''He's upset because he won't
be able to ride on your coattails anymore. He probably
won't last a month.''

He rested his backside against her desk and pulled her
into the space between his legs. His kiss reminded her of
everything they'd shared that glorious night, which with
luck, would soon be repeated.

As if sensing her distraction, he lifted his head and said,
''You aren't really worried about Gramps's business being
able to support us, are you? I talked to my accountant this
week, and he said all my investments have done extremely
well. I promise you, we won't go hungry. And Zoey's
health insurance won't be a problem.''

She cupped his jaw. ''I'm not worried about anything,
except telling Zoey. She's going to be so excited it might
set off an asthma attack, and I'm not sure A.J. and Joy can
handle that.''

''I called A.J. from the airport so he wouldn't worry
when I was late returning, but I asked him not to mention
this trip to Zoey in case…well, I wasn't sure what your
answer would be.''

''How is that possible? You know me better than I know
myself.''

She pressed herself against his wonderful body to see if he could read her mind. *Yep, exactly what I had in mind.*

He lifted his chin and eyed the door. Anne sighed. "I know. Roger probably has security on the way up. Let me pack and we'll head to my apartment."

Anne pictured her apartment. Her quiet, empty apartment. The idea of having Will to herself in complete privacy after a summer of living in a fishbowl held a definite allure. "You know, Will," she said, handing him a box she'd asked her secretary to pull from storage, "it could take us three or four days to pack. Maybe even a week." Her body almost hummed from the possibility. This was New York City. Takeout. Delivery. They wouldn't have to leave the bedroom, unless they wanted to. "Let's call Zoey now," Anne said impulsively. "She's a big girl. She can handle it."

Will blinked, as if trying to discern her underlying message. "Zoey has grown up a lot this summer," Will said. "And I'll tell you something else I found out about your daughter in the weeks since you've been gone. More than anything, Anne, she loves you and wants you to be happy."

Anne pressed her cheek to his chest. "Then this news will be good medicine, because I've never been happier."

He reached past her and turned the phone to face them. "Your call."

"No, Will, it's our call."

The look he gave her summed up his feelings as clearly as if they were written in stone. Their Silver Rose summer had opened a window to the past and a door to the future. While Will punched in the numbers, Anne looked at the two framed photos on her desk—Esther and Zoey. Anne closed her eyes and imagined her mother smiling down from heaven. Her mother who knew all about taking risks, but also knew that love was a sure thing when the right two people found each other. The rest was just logistics.

Anne hit the speaker button and pulled Will into a kiss while they waited for someone to pick up at the ranch. Will seemed tense, where a minute before he'd been relaxed and happy. "What's wrong?"

"You told Roger you were going to be chief cook and bottle washer. You didn't mean that part about cooking, did you?" His playful wink told her he was teasing. "I plan to keep you way too busy to cook."

"Silver Rose Guest Ranch. Zoey speaking."

"Hi, honey, it's me." Before Anne could say more, Zoey interrupted.

"Mommy, guess what Grandpa and I are doing? We're making a book from my journal and his postcards. We're gonna dedicate it to Grandma. Cool, huh?"

"That's wonderful, sweetie, I can't wait till Will and I get back home to see it."

"What? Back home? Will's...there? In New York?"

"Yes, he is. He came to ask me to marry him, but I asked him first."

A momentary pause was followed by a window-rattling shriek. "Grandpa, come quick. Mommy and Will are getting married."

Will and Anne looked at each other and made a face. "The girl's got a set of pipes on her," Will said.

He planted a quick kiss on Anne's lips—a kiss that promised more to come—then picked up the receiver. "Miss Z, take a deep breath. Nice and steady. As soon as you have your breathing under control, I'll tell you all about it. Are you ready?"

Anne blinked back tears as she listened to the man she loved tell her daughter that very soon they'd be a family. A family living at the Silver Rose.

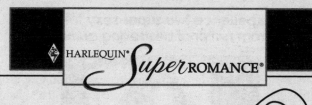
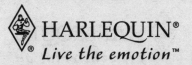

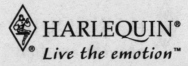

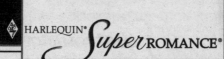

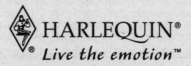

HARLEQUIN *Super*ROMANCE®

What if you discovered that all you ever wanted were the things you left behind?

GOING BACK

John Riley's Girl
by Inglath Cooper
(Superromance #1198)
On-sale April 2004

Olivia Ashford thought she had put her hometown and John Riley behind her. But an invitation to her fifteen-year high school reunion made her realize that she needs to go back to Summerville and lay some old ghosts to rest. After leaving John without a word so many years ago, would Olivia have the courage to face him again, if only to say goodbye?

Return to Little Hills by Janice Macdonald
(Superromance #1201) On-sale May 2004

Edie Robinson's relationship with her mother is a precarious one. Maude is feisty and independent, and not inclined to make life easy for her daughter even though Edie's come home to help out. Edie can't wait to leave the town she'd fled years ago. But slowly a new understanding between mother and daughter begins to develop. Then Edie meets widower Peter Darling who's specifically moved to Little Hills to give his four young daughters the security of a small-town childhood. Suddenly, Edie's seeing her home through new eyes.

Available wherever Harlequin Books are sold.

Visit us at www.eHarlequin.com

HSRGBCM

If you enjoyed what you just read,
then we've got an offer you can't resist!

Take 2 bestselling love stories FREE!

Plus get a FREE surprise gift!

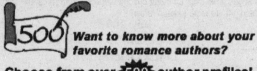

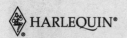

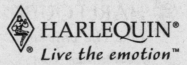